OPEN YOUR HEART

A Material Girls Novel

SOPHIA HENRY

Krasivo Creative

Open Your Heart
Copyright © 2018 by Sophia Henry
All rights reserved
Published by Krasivo Creative
ISBN: 978-1-949786-01-9

Cover design: Krasivo Creative
Cover photograph: Patronestaff via DepositPhotos.com
Editing: Rhonda Merwarth, Rhonda Edits & Kathy Bosman, Indie Editing Chick
Proofreading: Tandy Boese, Tandy Proofreads

Every one of us has the power to make the world
a better place. Look inside yourself.
Choose Respect. Choose Compassion. Choose Happiness. Choose Acceptance.
Choose Gratitude. Choose Kindness. Choose Love. Always Choose Love.

#BeKindLoveHard

CONNECT *with Sophia:*
www.sophiahenry.com

FACEBOOK
INSTAGRAM
BOOKBUB

PROLOGUE

Austin

SIX MONTHS EARLIER

"Jesus Christ!"

Pulling the wheel hard to the left, I swerve around a car protruding into the right lane.

Forget that I would've smashed into oncoming traffic if there had been any. Six in one hand, half-dozen in the other.

Once I regain my composure, I pull my pickup truck onto the shoulder and shift into park. My heart races; I'm wondering how long the mid-size SUV had been smashed between two trees—and how on earth it got there.

A steady stream of rain pelts my head as I rush to the vehicle. I hope whoever had been driving was all right—but from the looks of the wreck, it didn't bode well.

Holding my hand over my eyes to shield the shower, I peer into the driver's side window, squinting in the darkness. Then I lean back, wipe the rain away with my free hand, and look again.

Slumped over the wheel is a young woman with blood streaked from forehead to chin.

I jerk the door handle with urgency, knowing damn well it's not going to open.

The SUV looks like a fricking accordion in the front, smashed between two huge oak trees that must be at least a hundred years old. This neighborhood—one of Charlotte's oldest and wealthiest—has been around that long.

I run back to my truck, unlatch the tool case in the bed, and grab a rusty, old crowbar that hasn't seen the light of day in over ten years. Being prepared for disaster is one of the perks of inheriting my dad's truck after he died.

When I return to the SUV, I shove the narrow end into the crease between the window and the door frame, attempting to unlatch the lock.

If this doesn't work, I'll break the window. I don't want to do that, but the woman hasn't moved, so I know time is of the essence here. When the lock clicks, I tug at the door handle again. Thankfully, it opens with one swift pull. My fingers are so cold, I can barely curl them anymore.

I assess the driver to see if there's anything exceptionally traumatic that might clue me in that I shouldn't move her. And that's the trickiest part, since I'm no medical professional.

But the temperature has dropped significantly as the night closes in, and the freezing rain is already turning to ice, so I have to make a quick decision. If I don't help this girl now, she could be out here, unconscious and freezing, for hours. First response crews always get crazy busy during ice storms.

If I help her, I'm risking a major lawsuit if she's seriously injured. She could say it was from something I did.

Let her sue me. I can't walk away now and leave her here to freeze.

I lean over, reaching around to unlatch the seat belt, while making sure my body is there to brace hers if she falls forward when I unclip it. Pressing firmly, I release the latch.

My heart jumps when she releases a low, pained moan.

"It's okay, Hon—" I catch myself and add a 'Miss' in there to make the nickname seem slightly more respectful. "It's okay, Miss Honey. I'm not going to hurt you. I'll go slow," I tell her as I wrap my arms around her midsection and attempt to slide her from the vehicle slowly. There's slight resistance with her right hand which seems to be stuck between the seat and the console. Letting her body rest against mine while I reach over to her hand, I use the lightest touch possible to pull her wrist forward and up so it doesn't catch on anything. That's when I almost lose my dinner. Her hand is covered with blood. The index finger seems to be out of place, not necessarily hanging off, but it's turned sideways.

Fuck me. Why didn't I call an ambulance?

But there's no time to delay. Not with freezing rain soaking through my sweatshirt. I don't have anything to stop the blood, so I tuck it into her coat pocket to keep it contained. Once I've got her out, I switch my grip and heft her into my arms as if we were crossing the threshold. Making sure to steady myself first, I kick the door closed. Then I lean over, tucking her into my body, trying to shield her from as much of the steady shower of sleet as possible as I carry her to my truck.

After setting her on the seat in the passenger side and making sure her hand is still secure in her pocket, I hurry back to see if she has a purse in the car. Most women carry some kind of bag. With that, the medical staff will be able to check her ID and figure out who to call when I get her to the hospital.

As expected, she does have a purse. It's upside down on the passenger-side floor with almost all the contents splattered across the mat. Without paying attention to the items, I toss everything back in and bring it to my truck.

When I set the bag at her feet, her head rolls to the side, causing her hair to cover her face like a curtain. I can't help but want to get a better look at her. It doesn't matter, but there's this odd tug in my gut that makes me yearn to know her. To remember her face.

Blood has trickled onto the lapel of her immaculate cream-colored pea coat. I don't know anything about her, but I can tell by her clothing and pocketbook that she has money. And if she didn't *have* money she sure *spent* money.

I shake away the thought. Her face and finances are not my business. The only thing I care about right now is getting her to the hospital.

"Stay with me," I say, patting her knee as I pull onto the road.

WHEN I ARRIVE at the hospital, I secure the strap of Miss Honey's pocketbook over my shoulder, before gathering her in my arms and taking her in through the emergency entrance. They're probably going to ask me personal information—or at the very least—her name. My respectful term of endearment won't cut it. But I'm not about to go through her bag. I'll let the hospital staff deal with that.

"What happened?" a nurse asks, rushing toward me with a wheelchair. I place Miss Honey into it gently. Before I straighten up, I wipe the clumps of wet hair off her face and tuck it behind her ears, finally revealing her face. Her lips are full, but a pale blueish-purple—almost as pale as the skin over her sunken cheeks. I imagine they're a beautiful peachy-pink hue on a normal day.

Without her hair veiling her face, I can see that the blood, which had spilled onto her otherwise immaculate jacket, came from a nasty red slash across the bridge of her nose. But not even the ugly gash can mar the natural beauty of her face. Smooth, pale skin, high cheekbones, thick, meticulously groomed eyebrows.

A stream of blood has dried over her right cheek. I wish I would've assessed her injuries, or at least wiped her face, before I began driving. But it made more sense to get her help as soon as possible.

"Wreck over on Queens Road West. Car smashed between two trees on one of those curves. I found her unconscious behind the wheel." I sweep the rain-soaked hood from my head.

The nurse wastes no more time talking. "I'm taking her back," she says over her shoulder as she begins to wheel her away.

"Her right hand!" I call before she's out of sight.

"Excuse me?" She stops and turns around.

"Her right hand is messed up. I tucked it into her pocket because I didn't have anything to wrap it."

Though no sound comes out, I see her mouth form the word, *"Fuck."*

My heart pumps faster, adrenaline telling me I should stay, protect her, make sure she's okay. Why the hell am I this affected by a stranger? I swallow a lump in my throat.

"Can I go back with her?" I ask in desperation.

"Are you related?"

"No. I—I don't even know her name. I have her bag right here, but —" I ramble, pulling the strap off my shoulder and holding it out in front of me.

"We know her name."

Startled that the nurse knows who the girl is, I run a hand though my hair, sliding the falling locks back on top of my head. "You know her?"

"Yes. She's a surgeon here. I'm sorry, sir, but I need to get her help right now."

"Yeah." I nod, dropping my arm to the side. "Yes, of course. I'm sorry to keep you."

"Sir! I can take that bag," a woman calls to me from behind the desk. She's got the phone to her ear. When she speaks again, I know it's not me she's addressing. "Someone just brought Liz in. She was in an accident up the road. He said something about an injury to her right hand. Yes. Paige just brought her back. Can you let Dr. Crowder know?"

She hangs up the phone as I get to the desk. "Is she going to be okay?"

"I hope so. Thank you so much for bringing her in."

"She's a surgeon here?" I ask.

The woman looks around, as if she's worried to get caught answering my questions. "Yes, well, a surgical resident, but, I mean, even if she wasn't, we'd still know who she was. Her family's name is on this wing." She nods to the huge bronze plaque on the wall next to the automatic doors. "Not from around here, are you?"

Her rhetorical question almost makes me laugh, since I was born and raised in Charlotte, delivered at this very hospital, twenty-seven years ago.

The emergency room is in the Commons wing of the hospital.

Commons. Commons. I rack my brain in an attempt to remember which rich, white dude donated millions of dollars to have his name on the wing of the hospital.

Harris Commons.

Of course. The founder of *Commons*, the Charlotte-based department store chain. The stupid tagline from their annoying TV commercials pops into my head.

Commons—Affordable fashion for the common man.

Without wasting another second, I toss Miss Honey's purse on the desk. It lands with a thump, but I'm only slightly concerned if any of the valuable contents inside broke. I'm sure she can afford to replace anything I may have damaged in my haste.

Once I'm outside, I pull the hood of my black sweatshirt over my head again. It's soggy and wet, but I couldn't care less. I rub my hands together in the freezing rain. I've done my good deed for one of Charlotte's wealthiest families and now I'm literally washing my hands of them.

Chapter One

AUSTIN

*B*eing on stage is my favorite high. There's absolutely nothing better than playing in front of a crowd. The bigger the better. The more pumped they are, the more adrenaline gushes through my veins.

After three months of touring in North America, as the opening band for the uber-famous, indie rock band, Intermission, tonight, we're at The Underground in Charlotte, North Carolina. With roughly 750 people packing the place, it's one of the largest crowds we've played thus far. Not that we take any of the credit for that. But this is our final show with Intermission, and Charlotte is our hometown, so I'd like to think we had a positive effect on ticket sales.

Connection with the audience is an essential part of the experience for me. I want every single person in the crowd to walk away with at least three thoughts about my band, Drowned World:

Damn! They killed it.

What a phenomenal show.

Those guys are authentic and nice.

Yeah, I know musicians shouldn't give a fuck about being liked. But I do. Not because I need it for validation—I'm good in the self-confidence department, and I'd play my music no matter what anyone thinks of it.

My goal is to give our fans the ultimate experience. I want them to walk away thinking we were one of the best bands they've ever seen live. I want them to know they can talk to us after the show or hit us up on social media, and we're gonna interact and connect. We're not gonna be dicks. We honestly appreciate every single person.

The people who listen to our music and come to see our shows allow me to live my dream and pay my bills. Well, most of my bills. I still have to work another job. Hopefully that won't be for much longer.

Speaking of the people who come to our shows, there's a sexy brunette in the second row whom I haven't been able to keep my eyes off all night. It wasn't even her perfect rack that lured me in. Though her boobs look pretty fucking phenomenal propped up and on display in a plunging V-neck, black dress. Sure, I *noticed* her cleavage, but honestly, it was her eyes that hooked me.

I'm used to people staring. Women wanting. But usually those women want to fuck me. Not saying this girl doesn't, but her gaze doesn't seem sexual. It's intense and imploring—like she's trying to figure me out through my lyrics.

Maybe I'm romanticizing the connection. From her spot in the crowd, I've been able to see her the entire time, but it wasn't until the lights lit up the crowd for a good three seconds, illuminating the entire floor, that I caught the intensity in her gaze.

I'm probably making too much of it. Romanticizing is one of my favorite pastimes. It's where I do my best songwriting.

She's standing next to EmVee, a tattoo artist I've known for years, and looks eerily familiar. Yet, I swear I don't know her. Not like I expect to know everyone EmVee knows, but we run in the same circle and tend to know the same people.

When I launch into our final song, *Open Your Heart,* which got picked up by the major alternative-rock station on satellite radio a few months ago, and set us up on our first major North American tour, I make sure to catch my mystery girl's eyes. Maybe I'm singing for her.

No.

I know exactly who I'm singing for: Miss Honey, the nickname I gave the girl I wrote the song about. The girl I took to the hospital after I found her unconscious in her smashed SUV on the side of the road about six months ago. The girl I spent a total of thirty minutes of my life with who became the inspiration for the song that made our band blow up.

Fozzie and Tim, my band brothers, keep the beat of the song running. Before I launch into the last chorus, I stop to say, "We are Drowned World! Thank you for rocking with us tonight! Intermission is next!"

As expected, the crowd goes crazy when I mention the headliner. Taking that extra surge of energy, I jump back into the song for our big finish. I'm feeling the high when the crowd sings the last chorus with me. The enthusiasm fuels my entire body; adrenaline pushes me to do something I've only ever done one other time—and that was with Fozzie's permission. I cross the small stage and leap onto his bass drum, strumming my guitar with gusto as I rock out to the final notes. Just before the last chord, I jump off the drum—sending the crowd into a deafening chorus of cheers.

It's straight legend stuff. Go big or go home, right?

We want people to remember the show. You never know when it'll all be gone. The radio airplay. The packed venues. The screaming crowds. We're not arrogant, by any means, but we know we've got this moment to impress, and we're not throwing away our shot.

"Thank you so much, Charlotte! We'll be in the back after the show. Come say hi and ya know, maybe buy some merch."

I glance at the brunette in the second row one last time before following Fozzie and Tim offstage. She's still staring. And I'm still enthralled.

We head to the greenroom where we usually stay until Intermission finishes their set. Tonight will be a little different. We'll head back out in a few minutes and start signing early, while the crew sets up for the headliner. We want to make sure we get to everyone who wants to interact with us, especially for the hometown crowd. My mom, aunt, and cousin are out there, waiting to hug me.

After exchanging a few high-fives, fist bumps, and "Well done, boys!" with our crew, I accept the water bottle our tour manager hands me, pull out my phone, and start scrolling through social media. It's my usual routine right after we get off stage. The guys and our stage crew go back out and take down the equipment while I down a few bottles of water and relax for a minute. At the beginning of this most recent tour with Intermission, Fozzie suggested I take the time to chill out because he saw how much performing takes out of me—mentally and physically.

Honestly, it's one of the kindest things anyone's ever done for me. Don't get me wrong, I love performing. There's no bigger rush than being on stage and sharing our songs with the crowd live—the way they were meant to be heard. My body soaks up all the energy: the rush from the smiles, the heads bobbing, the hands in the air. But all of that is exhausting for me.

People assume I'm extroverted and outgoing because that's what I show them onstage and on social media. I love it, but it's a side of me that I've learned to play up, not the entire person I am.

Having a few minutes to myself, after the set, gives me what I need to calm down and recharge. I use the time to interact with people who might have tagged us on social media. Building relationships online has been a huge part of getting noticed and constructing our fan base. It's part of the grassroots marketing we've done since we started, building an audience with engagement. I try to like everything we're tagged in —if it's relevant. It's the easiest way to let our fans know that we see them and we appreciate them. Not everyone can get to a show, and online support can generate a huge buzz and get our music heard by more people.

Tonight, my motivation to get on social media is spurred by something else—or some*one* else. I can't get the beautiful brunette from the crowd out of my mind, and it's fucking with my head because even after three months of women in various cities throwing themselves at me night after night, the only person who stimulated my interest as much as this girl, in the last few years, was Miss Honey.

This is where being a hopeless romantic is a pain in my ass, because I'm not even obsessing over a real person. I'm obsessing over the person I created in my head. It makes for great songwriting material, but it's shit for my love life.

The tragic mind of a creative.

I don't screw around with groupies. I mean, I *have*, but I got that out of my system early in my music career when I was just a horny teenager sowing my oats. Back when I got excited by the mere thought that girls wanted to get with me. It's not my thing to have meaningless sex with a blur of faces. I need to feel a connection. Don't get me wrong, I can get off, but there's nothing better than looking into a woman's eyes when I'm fucking her and knowing there's a strong mental bond behind that.

Instead of stopping to read through all of the messages of people who've tagged me or the band, I immediately search for EmVee, wondering if she posted any pics or videos from the show, with the hope that she tagged the hottie.

"Boom!" I say out loud as I click on the most recent photo EmVee posted of herself, flanked by two other girls. The caption reads:

> Rocking out to Drowned World with my beautiful sisters! Love you @commonliz & @commonmaddie! #Underground #cltmusic

Sisters? These girls are sisters? I never would have guessed they were related at all. EmVee's covered in tats, with long, silver hair and a face painted with dramatic makeup. She probably has a YouTube channel where she gives makeup tips to goth girls. The girl on her left side is the stereotypical Southern belle. Big blond hair, wide, blue eyes, tanned, glowing skin on a Barbie body. I bet she knows how to use the correct forks and makes all the Chad's dicks jump.

The brunette almost seems plain standing next to the other two. That's not a slam. She's gorgeous, but in a completely different way. Her face looks natural, as if she's not wearing much makeup—if any— just the rosy cheeks of someone flushed from dancing. With loose, sable waves cascading over one shoulder and a bright smile, she's sultry as fuck in the most unassuming way. It triggers the librarian fantasy I've always had. Sexy, nerdy girls are my kink.

As I study the photo, I realize now that the neckline of her dress is actually quite modest. Her boobs seem to be spilling out because that's what happens to voluptuous girls who wear V-necks.

I wouldn't say I have a type, but I *am* partial to women who have some meat on their bones. There's nothing sexier than curves in all the right places. A round ass, big bouncing tits, and padding over her hips so I have something to grab onto when she's riding my...

"Jesus," I hiss. I'm getting a hard-on just thinking about her. I tip my water back and down what's left in one long pull.

"What'cha doing, Austin?" Tim asks from the doorway.

"Sexting your mom," I respond without missing a beat.

"She wishes," he says with a laugh. "You know she wants to grab your pretty hair and—"

"Oh my god! Stop!" I yell. I know I started it, but damn, Tim's always taking shit to the next level—the creepy level. I take a moment to scan the area, and notice our drummer isn't back yet. "Where's Fozzie?"

"Probably checking his bass drum for cracks."

Fuck." My stomach sinks. "I should have asked first."

"I don't think he cares, to be honest." Tim shrugs. "He's still out front talking to people. I'm heading out, too."

"I'll be there in a minute. Want to finish responding to a few messages."

"Tell mom I said hi!" he teases before ghosting.

Fucker.

But at least my boner's gone.

I do want to get back on the floor and start talking to people who are sure to be lined up at the merch table, buying T-shirts and CDs while waiting for us to come out. I won't let the exhaustion and my natural state of introversion take over until later.

One of my favorite parts of playing live is afterwards when we get to meet fans who came to see us—and the new people we convert who were here just to see the headliner. I'll never get bored with signing stuff and taking photos with fans. That powerful connection will make people talk about us.

But EmVee was kind enough to tag the picture with *@commonliz* directly over the brunette's rack, so I want to check the profile quickly. I need to know more about her.

Why does that social media handle sound familiar?

A quick thumb click takes me to her page—a page I vaguely recognize.

No way. No fucking way.

Liz Commons: Duke > Columbia > Surgical Resident. It's a beautiful day to save a life.

There's no fucking way Miss Honey and the girl in EmVee's photo are the same person.

Yet here I am, looking at the exact Instagram account that popped up when I'd entered "Liz Commons surgeon" into an internet search, to find out more about her the night I dropped her off at the hospital.

The girl in the profile photo, with mousy-brown hair and thick, black-framed glasses, looks nothing like the smokin' hot goddess from in the second row. Except those cheekbones—and the gorgeous peachy-pink tone I'd imagined her skin would have if it hadn't been purplish-blue last time I saw her.

The revelation is flipping my world upside down.

Maybe I shouldn't have brushed Miss Honey off so quickly. The girl I connected with tonight sure doesn't seem as boring as I'd imagined her to be when I checked out her profile six months ago.

Chapter Two

LIZ

"That was amazing, Em!" I tell my youngest sister after watching the opening band disappear around the wall behind the stage. Their phenomenal energy still has me buzzing.

"I'm glad you dug it," Emily says.

"Do you know both bands?" I ask.

As a tattoo artist, Emily connects with a ton of people in Charlotte's creative circle. She meets people from all over, but she's ingrained in the local community.

"Just the opening band. They're sweet guys. I've done a lot of Fozzie's tattoos. Ask to see the trampoline man. It's some of my best work." She says it with a wink, and I have no clue what that means.

The only time I get to see Em's work is when I scroll though her Instagram. She uses that as her portfolio. I don't know anyone she tattoos. Her art is amazing, though. It always has been, even when it's pencils to paper or acrylics to canvas.

"Sorry, but—which one was Fozzie?" I ask.

She mentioned Fozzie, Austin, and Tim multiple times tonight during drinks before the set, but I still don't know which guy plays which instrument.

Em smiles. "The drummer."

One of the things I love the most about her is that she's very chill. She accepts everyone. Well, almost everyone. She doesn't hold it against me that I don't know much about her life. We're almost seven years apart, which means we didn't really grow up together. We were never in high school or college at the same time. Growing up, I used to pretend she was my baby, even when our parents were around, but once she grew out of that cute newborn age, I grew out of babies. Emily is the eccentric, artistic, wild child who gives our parents regular headaches. Still.

She continues, "Austin is the lead singer who was eye-fucking you all night."

"Whatever. That's ridiculous." I brush off her comment. I mean, a part of me hoped his sexy gaze was for me, but I know I'm not the kind of girl hot musicians fall for, so I assumed he'd been staring at Emily, Maddie, or any number of random beautiful girls around us.

"Where did Maddie go?" I ask, craning my neck to search the crowded room.

Maddie is the middle child, the beautiful socialite with a huge personality. As Senior Vice President of Feminine Apparel and Cosmetics, she's the only one of us who works for Commons Department Store, the business our father started almost thirty years ago. (*Yes, that's her official title. Emily and I love to tease her about it.*)

Though, Em did work there for a few months after she graduated high school. In an effort to get her excited about working with the family, Daddy tried to incorporate her personal talents, asking her to design a clothing line. His vision was to have a section of the store geared toward younger, funkier patrons. For various reasons, that idea was never going to work out.

One: Emily didn't last long under Daddy's watchful eye and helpful advice. Two: She's opposed to the wealth and class differences corporate America creates in our country. Three: The appeal of the Commons Store leans more toward middle-aged soccer moms than Em's punk-rock goth vibe.

I have to give him credit for trying to get Emily involved, though. I know she thinks he tried to use her artistic eye as a pawn in his quest for more wealth. But I knew, deep down, he was trying to get her interested and involved in the family business by allowing her to use her talent and creativity. At least that's how I saw it.

"Oh, she's letting you call her Maddie? I have to call her Madeline when we're in public."

"She's still on that kick?" I roll my eyes. "It's so pretentious."

"Wow, Liz! Coming from you, that's saying something."

"Do you think I'm pretentious?" I ask.

Unlike Emily, I have this bad habit of caring what people think. I can't help it. It's the world I grew up in. As the oldest, I'd been groomed by my parents to swallow every spoonful of advice they dished out about how I'm supposed to be and how I should conduct myself. But I never thought of myself as pretentious. Then again, most people who are, probably don't think they are.

"You're Harris Commons' daughter and you're a surgeon. In many people's eyes, that's, like, the definition of pretentious." Emily winks at me. "I'm kidding, ya know. You're the most chill, down-to-earth surgeon I've ever met."

"Former surgeon," I mumble, looking down at the scar on my right ring finger. Reality flushes away the brief moment of happiness I'd found tonight losing myself in the first concert I'd attended since freshman year of college. The rush of adrenaline searing through my veins from watching the sultry, tattooed, lead singer quickly fades.

"Stop! You'll be chopping people up again in no time, Liz. Give your hand time to heal." She loops her arm in mine. "Come on! Let's go tell the guys how great they were."

Emily has no clue how bad my injury is. No one does.

Six months ago, I suffered a critical hand injury in a car accident. The antique diamond-and-sapphire ring my grandmother passed down to me on my sixteenth birthday got caught on something—I can't remember what—and tore the finger away from my hand. The injury, called ring avulsion, required multiple surgeries to repair severed tendons in my right hand. As bad as it was, it could have been much worse. In many cases ring avulsion results in amputation.

The injury took away my ability to operate—which brought the third year of my surgical residency to a grinding halt. Thankfully, my parents worked with my mentor and the head of the residency program at CHC—Carolina Hospital Center—to pull a ton of strings and push through a year-long fellowship in Surgical Critical Care. It will give me a year to rehab from my injury, with the ability to jump back into my residency when I get clearance to operate again. Had they not been able to do that, I would have been forced to quit the program altogether. Needless to say, a surgical residency is pretty intense and competitive, and there's no room for a surgeon who can't operate, no matter what the reason.

After months of intense physical therapy, I have this gut feeling that I'll never perform another surgery. Instead of coming clean and admitting it to my colleagues, I keep sleepwalking though the weeks, mouth plastered in a fake smile, pretending I'll be given the green light to operate soon. As each day passes, I fall deeper and deeper into a spiral.

What am I going to do if I can't perform surgery? All those years—all those dreams—wasted.

My sister leads me to the back of the venue where the bands have merchandise tables set up. While we stand in line, Emily bumps my shoulder with hers and nods toward the door. "Of course she'd find the most Chad-looking guy in here to talk to."

Turning my gaze in the direction Emily nodded, I groan internally at the sight. Maddie's talking to Jordan Fletcher, the head surgical resident in my program. My heart races and bile forms in my throat, building up so quickly I can barely swallow it back. A concert with my sisters was supposed to give me a break from the anxiety and anger swirling in my head, and through my blood, about the future of my career. Instead, I'm faced with the one person with the power to ruin my entire night. In trying to remove myself from all the crap piling up in my life, I've inadvertently shoveled more on top.

Jordan is the last person I expected to see here tonight. The Underground doesn't seem like the type of place where he'd hang out. Then again, I don't know much about his life outside of the hospital. He never accepts when any of us surgical residents ask him if he wants to grab a drink. We work ridiculous, exhausting hours, but there are times when we need to let off steam and talk with people who understand what we're going through. He rarely participates in any of our banter at the hospital either. If he speaks to us, his peers, at all, it's usually barking orders or a condescending remark about our performance. Evidently, the only people worth his time are the ones who can help him advance. If anyone could be called pretentious, it's him. Daddy would love him.

At first, I wonder how Maddie knows him, but as the social butterfly of our family, she'd earned the nickname Mayor Maddie years ago, so I shouldn't be surprised when she knows anyone.

Before I have a chance to tell Emily I don't want to go over there, she starts yelling.

"Madeline!" she calls out in the thickest redneck accent I've ever heard. "Madeline, when we gonna hit up that NASCAR race you been wantin' to go to? I ain't never been, but I reckon I'll go with you if you want to. I hear they throw chicken bones!"

When Maddie turns around, her brows are furrowed and her lips are spread in a thin line. It takes everything I have not to burst out laughing. She looks just like Mama when she's trying to let someone know how embarrassed she is, yet still keep her cool in front of other people.

"You're terrible," I say to Emily.

"After this we should go to the bar next door to do some shots. We'll get super trashed and barf in her car on the way home."

I think she's kidding, but just in case, I better shut it down. "As fun as that sounds—"

"I'm in," a male voice in front of us says.

"Austin!" Emily jumps into the arms of the man I recognize as the sexy singer of the opening band. With his dirty-blond hair and tattoos covering every inch of visible skin from neck down, he's hard to miss. "You guys fucking slayed!"

If his charisma on stage was enough to have me throbbing between my legs, standing a few feet away is practically orgasm-inducing. As he hugs Emily, his penetrating blue eyes catch mine from beneath the shadow of his black hoodie.

I lick my lips involuntarily, which makes his mouth quirk. A tingle zings though my system and I immediately cast my eyes downward.

The intensity of standing this close, and not having his hypnotizing performance as a reason to stare at him, is too much.

When Emily pulls away, he asks, "Who's this?"

"This is Liz, my oldest sister."

Oldest sister. Thanks, Em. Other terms that might have been equally embarrassing: Spinster. Cat lady. Nerd. Former medical professional. All true to varying degrees.

"Hug Fozzie. He said he has something to give you?" Austin shrugs.

"Awww yeah!" She practically tackles the tall, lanky, bleached-blond standing a bit behind Austin.

Crap. I guess it's my turn to say something. My hands shake as I try to think of something without Emily there as a buffer.

"It was a phenomenal show. You guys have really great, um, energy," I stammer, attempting to find the words to sound cool and hip, like I go to shows all the time. I don't know what else to say, but I'm not ready to walk away yet.

"Thank you," he says, as he swipes the hoodie from his head. "That means—"

"That last song really moved me. I almost cried," I gush without giving him a chance to finish speaking.

Our eyes lock for a moment before Austin drops his gaze to my chest. At first, I thought there was something behind our intense connection, but the appraisal makes my cheeks burn with embarrassment. He only wants one thing—and that thing is not my compliments on a silly song. That's what I get for romanticizing the situation instead of being my logical self.

"Can you, um, sign my ticket?" I reach into the pocket of my dress and pull out a limp piece of paper. I'm mortified when I realize it's damp from sweat. Before I can pull back, he plucks it out of my hand.

His smile falters for a split second as he holds the ticket, then he turns around and grabs a piece of paper from the table behind him. "How about I sign this for you? It's almost as good."

I'm so embarrassed, I want to crawl under their merchandise table, and I'm pretty sure Austin wants me to do the same. He's just too kind to say anything.

He finishes writing on the paper, but before he hands it over, he wraps his arms around me. The move surprises me, but I'm not upset by it. He's hugged almost every person that's come through the line, so I figure it's just what he does. The sense of warmth and safety I feel in his strong arms is unexplainable.

He starts to pull away, then pauses, his lips brushing my ear as he whispers, "You have the most gorgeous, intense eyes."

My heart speeds up and a shiver rushes through my body. Nothing about this man is as I expected him to be. It's a refreshing surprise. "Thank you."

He runs a hand through the long patch of hair on top of his head. It keeps flopping over the short sides. "You threw me off tonight."

Embarrassed, I try to take a step back. "Really? How—I'm sorry. I didn't—"

He shakes his head. "No sorries. It was brilliant. It felt like you could see into my soul. Haven't felt anything like that in a long time."

Good lord! What is this man doing to me? Everything he says sparks new flames in me.

When he releases me, Austin hands me the paper and says, "You gonna hang out for a minute? I'd like to talk more, but we have a few more people to meet." He nods behind me.

I glance over my shoulder, where the line stretches back to the bathrooms, which are located behind the stage, on the opposite end of the room.

"Oh, yeah. Of course." I lift my hand to slip the loose strands of hair behind my ears, but Austin's fingers get there before mine and he completes the task. A jolt of lust zings through my veins when his fingertips brush across my cheek and upper ear. His touch feels natural. Comfortable. Which makes me think the two drinks I've had tonight have already put me over the edge. I smile shyly while gazing at him through thick eyelashes.

I begin to walk away, dazed by the interaction.

"Hey!" Austin calls.

I turn around immediately, though he could be talking to someone else completely.

"Stay close."

"But—" He'll be back there all night with a line that long.

Austin must recognize my puzzled expression, because he says, "We don't sell merch or sign while Intermission is playing so I'll only be a few more minutes. We can catch their set together if that's cool?"

"Oh. Okay. Yeah." I nod like I understand anything about how this part of a show runs. I've never met a band before. I usually just listen to the music and leave.

My initial thought was to find Emily again, but now I'm unsure of exactly where I should go. It seems unnatural to hang out by myself near the merch table, so I step away from the line of people waiting to meet Austin and his bandmates, and lean against a railing.

I feel this odd, unexplainable connection to him. It's ridiculous to even think about. I'm sure a hundred girls in this venue would say they feel the same kind of connection. It's that innate charisma some performers have. But I can't get over the eerily familiar feeling when Austin reached out and tucked my hair behind my ear—almost intimate—like he'd done it before. Which is odd, because no one has ever done that—other than my mother when I was a kid.

"What's that?" Emily pops up behind me. She cranes her neck to get a better gaze at the paper I'm clutching. "You got a signed set list? Rock on, girl! I should take you to more shows." She pauses for a minute, then plucks the paper from my hands and holds it close to her face. "Is that a phone number?"

Startled at the question, I yank the paper back. Since asking Austin for his autograph was only an attempt to steer the conversation away from my awkwardness, I hadn't even looked to see what he'd written. "No. That's ridic—"

Yet there it is. A seven-digit number starting with 704—Charlotte's main area code.

"Austin gave you his digits. Damn, Liz! What the hell did you do? Offer to give him head after the show?"

"Emily! Geez." Heat rushes to my cheeks. I'm aware that it's her crude way of teasing, but she knows I don't appreciate jokes like that.

"I'm kidding."

"I know." I pause before folding the paper and tucking it into my dress pocket. "Hey Em!"

"Yeah?"

"Can we not tell Maddie about this?"

"No worries, babe. Your dirty little secret is safe with me."

And I knew it would be, because Maddie and Emily aren't close at all. I have no clue how Emily even got her to come out with us tonight. They are in very different social circles, as evidenced by the way Maddie ditched us as soon as the first set ended. She's not a brat, but she likes to feel comfortable when she's out. And she hasn't felt comfortable around Emily in years.

Hell, Em's circle isn't mine either. Then again, I don't really have one of those. I'd been busy for years, working my way through med school and the first three years of a five-year rotation in my surgical residency. Partying has never been a part of my life.

"How're you doing? Depression lifted now that you pulled the number of a hot rock god?" Em asks, throwing in a wink.

"It doesn't really work that way."

Her smile drops. "I know, Liz. I'm just trying to cheer you up. You've been in such a rough place since the accident."

Her comment surprises me; I didn't think Emily noticed anything about me or how I felt. I don't want to sound like I think my sister is an insensitive jerk so I keep my mouth shut. Sisters by blood, but not necessarily by choice. I could always picture Em hopping on a bus to New York or LA and never looking back. I know she loves us, but I also know how hard she's worked to distance herself from our family. I doubt any of her friends know anything about her background.

"Tonight definitely cheered me up." I press my shoulder against hers. "Thanks for asking me to hang out. I needed this."

"I know, Lou," she says, using the shortened form of Lizzie Lou, my childhood nickname. "Now let's go to the bar," Em says, taking my hand and tugging.

My feet stay firmly in place. "I can't."

"What does that mean?"

"Austin asked me to stay close." I glance at him quickly. He's beaming as a girl hands him something. Wrinkles crinkle at the sides of his eyes as a large open-mouth smile radiates from under his facial hair. His smile lights up the room.

"Are you a fucking black lab named Bella? You're not gonna sit and stay because a guy tells you to. Walk with me."

I never thought of it that way. I thought it was interest and lust. Is this a test of how much of a doormat I can be? Seeing how far he can push me? Do girls usually sit and stay at his command? Usually, I consider myself a strong, independent woman; now I feel like an idiot falling for the first person.

"I don't play relationship games, Em. If I like someone I let them know."

"It's not a game," she says sliding herself between two people at the bar. "It's self-respect and it shows you value yourself and your time. You're not the kind of girl who obeys a man's every command. What would you have said to John Stallings, MD, if he had told you to sit and stay?"

I laugh—which is exactly what I would have done to John. He didn't like being laughed at, which is funny because he always introduced himself as "John Stallings, MD" no matter what situation he was in—and that alone was enough to bust a gut. I guess he was extremely proud of his title. "I would have walked away to find you or Emily."

John Stallings, MD was my only long-term relationship. I'm not convinced our time together even qualifies as a relationship. We dated for two years while I was in med school and he was a resident at Columbia. Neither of us had time for each other, but he was the son of one of Mama's sorority sisters who was married to a hedge-fund manager—so, of course, we were the perfect match in our mothers' eyes.

But we all know perfect is an illusion. Perfect is subjective. Perfect changes from person to person. Imperfection is perfect.

Emily hands the bartender cash and grabs our drinks. She passes one to me. "Exactly. Don't change who you are for Austin. A hundred girls in here would drop to their knees and suck him off if he asked. Don't be that girl."

"I'm *not* that girl," I say without a shred of humor.

"I know you're not that girl. I just meant don't change who you are to be what you think someone else wants you to be. Be your strong self, Liz."

"I understand what you're saying, and I appreciate the reminder. There wasn't a power struggle. I know what those are, Em, believe me. This was regular old conversation. He said he wanted a chance to talk more," I say, looking over my shoulder as we retreat from the crowded bar. "And watch the next band with me."

"Well, look at you, you unassuming vixen! You just pulled the most elusive bachelor in the Charlotte music scene."

"Pulled what? What does that mean?"

"Caught him, lured him in, became the object of his attention," she explains. "Austin is, like, really introverted. He's friendly and cool, but he keeps to himself. Fozzie says he's a hopeless romantic, emphasis on the hopeless part."

"Why's that?"

"He's picky, I guess. He's not about sleeping around or screwing groupies in every city, ya know? Which isn't that odd for a normal human being, I suppose. Fozzie just likes that life."

My heart goes out to Emily. She and Fozzie have been friends for as long as I can remember. I'd always assumed they were a couple, but that's another example of all the things I don't know about Emily's life.

"I still have to check out the trampoline man you did for him," I say, changing the subject back to the tattoo she mentioned earlier. I don't want to hear about Austin's love life. Especially if it's just secondhand gossip.

Plus, it's none of my business since he's the equivalent of a celebrity crush, if anything.

"Oh yeah!" Emily's eyes light up.

As much as she tries to stay away from our family, she still has that spark of excitement when we ask about her work. No matter how cool or disconnected she tries to act, she wants validation. Who doesn't?

"Fozzie!" Emily grabs me by the arm and pushes through the line to the drummer of Drowned World. "Show Liz trampoline man!"

Fozzie grins for a photo with fans, then steps aside. He holds up his hand, palm facing me. Near the outer edge, underneath his pinky, is a tiny stick figure above an oval with four legs. When he bends his hand up and down ever so slightly, the crease makes it look like the figure is jumping on a tiny trampoline.

I burst out laughing. "Oh my gosh! That's great!" And it is. It's hilarious and clever. I'm almost jealous. I don't have any tattoos, but something like that wouldn't be so bad.

Suddenly I want a random tattoo that has zero meaning to me. What am I thinking?

"Told you it was my best work," Emily teases.

"I don't agree with that statement, but it's definitely clever."

"It's a metaphor for life," Fozzie says.

Emily and I both cock our heads and stare at him, silently asking him to explain.

"Life is just a bunch of ups and downs. One day you're so high you think you're flying, but even when you fall back down, you know it'll be okay. If you don't have a foundation you trust to help you bounce back up from the lows, you're gonna splat."

I stare at him for a moment, then I turn slowly to look at Emily. Her eyes are wide in awe. "I did not expect something like that to come out of your mouth," she says. Then she jumps into his arms and plants her lips on his.

It's rude to judge the intellect of a person I barely know, but I sure as heck didn't expect such a thoughtful answer, either. He's got a point. I've been high. This current low has me wondering if I even have a foundation.

Excusing myself, I cut through the line and almost bump into a petite, middle-aged woman wearing a black Drowned World T-shirt and skinny jeans. She's watching the band interact with fans, with a huge smile, which makes me wonder if she's waiting for kids to go through the line.

"Great show, wasn't it?" I ask.

"Oh absolutely! They were magnificent. I'll never get tired of seeing them live."

Oh, so maybe she's a fan. No wonder the happiness radiates from her. Silly of me to think age has anything to do with loving music.

"I believe that. This was my first time and I already want to see another show."

"You'll have plenty of opportunities. They've got big things coming up. I'm just so proud of them. They've worked so hard for this moment."

"How long have you been a fan?"

"I've been the lead singer's biggest fan for twenty-seven years." She smiles and leans closer as if informing me of a secret. "He's my son."

"Oh! Oh my gosh! That's awesome." I place a hand on her forearm. "I imagine you must be so proud."

"This is the dream he's worked for his entire life. There're no words to explain how happy I am for him."

The excitement she has for her son's career and accomplishments is beautiful. Though, it makes me feel a bit blue. I don't remember my parents ever getting that excited over anything I've ever done. Supportive, yes. But it's almost as if every time I reach the next level, it's expected, rather than something to celebrate. Even before the high wears off, there's the question, "What's next?"

"Sounds like you instilled some great work ethic in him," I say. My parents always love to hear people compliment their parenting, so I figure she probably likes it, too.

"The talent came from his father, but that drive to succeed is all his own. The only thing I tried to do was tell him it's okay to pursue his passion rather than settle for something he hated doing. Who am I to tell someone what type of life he should lead?"

Austin has the best mom ever. The only thing I've ever known is people telling me what kind of life I should lead. What kind of career I should have. What kind of people I should be friends with and date. I'm not saying I don't have free will, but I was raised with other people's expectations of how I should be.

I swallow back emotion. "That's brilliant parenting. More people should be that accepting."

"It's unconditional love, sweetheart. You'll understand someday." She pats my hand. "Excuse me, but my brother and nephew are about to leave and I'm going to see if I can scoot them in to see Austin right quick."

When she's far enough away, I release a breath. Okay, that was creepy—I had my hand on the poor woman's arm the entire conversation. Good thing it was quick. She's probably going to tell Austin about the creepy fan. As if I haven't been awkward enough around him.

He's just a human. A hot, popular, lusted-after, musician—but still a human. Time to get my head on straight. Because if Emily's observations are correct, and I *am* the object of his attention, I don't want to waste the opportunity. Our connection is too strong—even if it's purely physical.

"THANKS FOR WAITING," I hear at the same time I feel a warm hand on the small of my back. Austin leads me toward the bar. "What are you drinking?"

"Gin and tonic."

He nods, then leans over and orders a gin and tonic and Jack and Coke from the bartender, then turns his attention back to me.

"What do you do, Liz?" he asks as we wait for our drinks.

It's so casual, like regular conversation. Which is totally normal any other time, but it surprises me because he just stepped off the stage less than thirty minutes ago, before taking photos and signing autographs for a winding line of adoring fans. I expected questions about himself or the show.

"I'm in my residency. Surgical," I add. "To be a surgeon."

"That's rad."

"Well, I love it, but I don't know how rad it is." I pause, the word "rad" sticks in my throat. I've never used it before. "Playing music in front of hundreds of screaming fans seems a whole lot rad-der." I finish, feeling like an absolute idiot.

If Austin thinks I'm a complete tool, he doesn't show it. He takes our drinks off the bar and hands me one. "Guess we're both pretty phenomenal, eh, babe?"

"Thank you," I say accepting the drink. I'm not good at small talk or flirting. Or not turning into a complete tool around men who are ridiculously hot and out of my league.

"Oh my gosh! Austin! You were so awesome!" shrieks a tall, slim blonde in a black midriff top and low-slung jeans.

Suddenly he's flocked by a gaggle of giggling girls. I say girls, because I'm not even sure if they're out of high school yet. Then again, even college kids look super young to me and I'm not too far from their age. Sometimes I feel like I'm forty-five.

I take a step back, but Austin grabs my hand to keep me close.

"I appreciate that so much. We'll be at the merch table again after Intermission finishes up."

He tugs me toward the main floor where there's some empty space in the crowd, near the back, just as the lights go down. Intermission, the headlining band, takes the stage and immediately breaks into their first song, an insanely upbeat tune that gets me bouncing.

For as boring as most people assume I am, I've never been to a concert where the music didn't completely envelop my body and brain. With music, I lose all control. The world opens up. I feel out of body —the exact opposite of the reserved professional people know me as. I never feel as free as I do when I'm listening to live music and letting the beat take over.

I forgot how much I missed it. How much I need it to feel like myself. Playing an instrument has never been my forte—but man, do I enjoy listening. I've been so focused—and stressed out—by my studies and my career over the last few years, I forgot about the simplest things that bring me peace.

There's something about music that takes me out of my medical and academic mind. Or maybe it complements it? To get completely zoned in, I have a playlist of my favorite songs on when I'm in the operating room. Having familiar music playing in the background helps me keep my concentration.

Had. I *had* a playlist for surgery.

When Intermission launches into a cover of *Last Nite* by The Strokes, it zaps away the dismal thoughts, and brings me to my toes. Austin nods enthusiastically and grabs my hand, encouraging me to jump and bounce and spin and twist. He joins in and we dance and laugh together.

When the song ends and we finish clapping, Austin turns to me. "Damn, girl! You rock out."

I run my fingers through my hair to push away the strands sticking to my sweaty forehead. "It always feels good to dance it out, right?"

"I agree." Austin leans closer, grabs my hand and holds it at our sides. The contact makes me shiver. "You're nothing like you seemed at first."

"What does that mean?"

"I thought you'd be more reserved."

Reserved—another word for boring. Sometimes I wish I could be an extroverted, charismatic person that everyone wants to be around, but then I think: nope. I don't want to be that way because I wouldn't feel comfortable. I can only handle being in those situations for so long before I need solitude.

"I open up when I'm comfortable around people or in a situation. Dancing at a concert never bothered me. It's a release."

"So that means you feel comfortable around me?"

"Absolutely."

"I feel comfortable with you, too."

We spend the rest of the set holding hands and dancing together. Austin's smile and energy are infectious. I feel it from my head to my toes and swirling around in my stomach. When Intermission's set ends, we're elbowed and pushed by the stampede of people trying to leave the venue or get back to the merchandise tables. But we remain, our feet cemented to the floor.

"I gotta head back to the merch table," he says with a tone of reluctance.

"Oh, yeah! I get it. It was fun to watch the show with you. Thanks for dancing with me."

"You've got a beautiful vibe, Liz. Your energy is mesmerizing." He releases my hand and slides it onto my hip. He looks me in the eye and bites his bottom lip. Pure lust exudes from his pores. It's exhilarating and overwhelming in the best way.

"Don't look at me like that," I warn. "Not here. Not in public."

"Can I look at you like this in private?" He raises one eyebrow on his sexy face. "Later tonight?"

That nagging voice of reason tells me that making plans to hang out later is a ridiculous idea. I'm on the schedule for at least three procedures tomorrow, and that's not including anything else that might come up if I'm needed. I can't show up tired and spacey from a late night out.

"I'd love that," I say, ignoring my better judgment. Then again, my so-called better judgment has yet to steer me to anything remotely fun. Continuing the evening with Austin is worth a little bit of lethargy tomorrow.

"Awesome. I'm stoked!" he says with a huge grin. Then he motions to the merchandise table with a nod. "I really need to get over there. I'll find you in a bit, okay?"

"Yeah. Perfect."

As he walks away, he stops, turns around and winks at me. A zap of excitement rushes through my body like someone just shocked me with static electricity. I honestly can't remember being excited over a guy before.

WHILE AUSTIN'S WORKING, I hit the bathroom and find my sisters to say goodbye. Since we all came straight to the venue from work, we drove separately. No reason for either of them to know I'm hanging out with Austin tonight. Though, maybe I should at least tell Emily so someone knows where I am.

Emily and a few of her friends are hanging around to talk to the guys, in Drowned World, when they're finished, too, so I have people to wait with. The conversation swirls around me about people I don't know and places I've never been, but I'm barely listening because I'm watching Austin. His smile is genuine and he greets each person. A few times, I see his eyes get wide and I wonder what the person may have said, but he keeps smiling through it all. Never rolls his eyes or glances around as if bored or annoyed. He graciously accepts each and every interaction. It's not the kind of behavior I expected from a guy in a band at all. But we all have our assumptions—and they aren't always right.

After about an hour, the line has finally cleared. Austin catches my eye and holds up his index finger, while mouthing, "One minute."

I nod and watch him jog toward the back and behind the stage where the guys must have their stuff. It's another fifteen minutes by the time I feel his hand on my back and hear him say, "Ready to get out of here?" His voice is low, but commanding.

When I spin around, he's got his arm extended toward me, palm up.

A knot of excitement ties inside my stomach. "Yes." I slide my palm into his and follow close as he leads me toward the back of the room. There's no one to say goodbye to since my sisters left a few minutes ago, when we thought the band had said all their goodbyes. At least Emily knows who I'm with.

All I can think about is how it would feel to have Austin's lips on mine. Actually, all I can think about is laying naked next to him. The thought alone causes a barrage of mental insecurities to pop up. I haven't had a boyfriend in years—and I haven't had sex in that length of time either.

Suddenly, my mind races with the common insecurities a spontaneous hookup brings. What kind of underwear do I have on? Are my legs shaved? Thankfully, I wore a sexy black-lace bra-and-panty combo tonight and the laser hair removal I had done in my early twenties takes care of any shaving concerns.

I'm the epitome of an inexperienced dork, when a hot guy is about to take me home, and all I can think about is hair removal and underwear choices.

All I should be thinking about is Austin and what being with him represents.

Freedom. A night of no-strings-attached sex. A night that makes me forget that the career I worked so hard for is over before it even began. A night with someone who can make me forget who I thought I was and who I'll never be.

Chapter Three

AUSTIN

Liz's eyes widen and I see her gulp as she hovers next to my motorcycle.

"Come on." I pat the seat.

"I, um." She bites her bottom lip and looks around the empty parking lot. "I don't think I can get on that."

"I'll keep you safe, Liz, I promise. Just hold on to me. You can squeeze as hard as you want."

She looks scared shitless and I worry that I might have to call us a cab. I honestly have no problem doing that since it's drizzling, and riding in the rain isn't fun for anyone. Plus, an intense make-out session in the backseat, on the short drive to my place, would be amazing foreplay, but I'd rather get my bike home than leave it here overnight.

"Get on back; we'll go for a little spin right here in the parking lot so you can see how it feels."

She takes a small step toward me. I help her secure her helmet before she swings a leg over the bike. Once she's on, she wraps her arms around my waist tightly. I reach back and pat her outer thigh.

"I feel good between your legs, don't I?"

Her chest presses against my back when she laughs. Then her helmet knocks against mine.

"Sorry!" she yells.

"It's okay." I chuckle to myself and start the engine.

I know I said I was going to go for an easy spin around the parking lot, and I will, but I don't plan on stopping this bike until I'm in my driveway. If I told Liz, I'm pretty sure she never would have gotten on.

My house is less than ten minutes away, so she shouldn't hate me too much when I peel away without giving her proper notice.

Being on my bike is absolute freedom. Nothing caging me in, air flowing from all sides, the connection between the road and my mind. I have to concentrate and pay attention, yet my brain is constantly turning.

Why am I so attracted to Liz?

When I first saw her tonight, I could chalk it up to pure lust—the physical connection from our eye contact. The intoxicating feel of getting lost in the heat of the moment. A pull this intense doesn't happen to me often, so it's definitely a possibility.

Or is it because I found out that this girl is the girl I wrote a romanticized love song about? Are the emotions I get from singing the song distorting the way I see her?

Maybe it's because she's a bit shy and awkward? The way she stumbled over words to say to me after the show endeared her to me forever. I love introverted, yet badass, women. Reminds me of my mom—and myself—when I'm around my family and friends—those brilliant moments where I can put down my guard, shed the musician character, and just be Austin.

Or is it because her eyes penetrate into my soul? Every time she looks at me, there's more there—like she's searching for someone she already knows. Does she subconsciously remember me?

I push the why's out of my head and focus on the moment. No reason to think so much when it's simple. Right here. Right now. With Liz.

After parking my bike in the driveway at my place, I climb off and remove my helmet, then immediately turn around to help Liz dismount. I grab her by the waist and help her off, placing her on the ground gently. She braces herself on my chest, seemingly startled at my assistance. Her surprise makes me smile. Having her thighs squeeze my hips the entire ride has me riled up, ready to drop her onto my bed, hold her wrists above her head, and fuck her senseless. Which should be a challenge, since the girl is smart enough to be a surgeon.

As soon as she sets her helmet on the seat of my bike, I take her face in my hands, lean down, and brush her lips softly. She responds by pressing her mouth against mine with desperate hunger.

Oh, it's on.

The rain falls harder, but I barely notice. Grabbing her ass with both hands, I pull her pelvis toward mine and grind into her. She slides her hands into my wet hair and holds on, pulling tight. The slight pain as she tugs gets me hot as hell. I can't get enough of her taste or the feel of our tongues tangling with each other. I need more. I need to bury my face between her legs and work her clit until she's screaming my name.

When I try to retreat, she holds my bottom lip between her teeth. She's the epitome of sexy. And dangerous. She's the girl I shouldn't be lusting over. And yet, I'm lost in the thought of driving my cock into her over and over. The girl with the intense eyes—the ones that can read my soul.

At first, I was worried about what she saw, but she's here with me now, so it must've been positive.

When I let her go, Liz takes a slight step backward. Her foot slides on uneven pavement, and her ankle rolls. I wrap my arms around her to steady her. "Hey now!"

"Geez! I'm such a klutz." Her face turns pink with embarrassment. "That kiss was, ummm—" She rakes her fingers through her hair and swallows hard. "Intense."

"I know," I agree, my lips brushing her ear. "Now let's get inside, because I'm gonna fuck you so hard you won't be able walk when I'm done, and I don't feel like sleeping out here in the rain."

"Sounds good to me." We lock eyes. I implore hers to make sure she's down. I'm not into forcing chicks to do anything they don't want to do.

Her gaze doesn't waver. Not even a blink. That's how I know we're gonna have so much fun tonight.

Taking Liz's hand, I lead her across the gravel driveway to the walkway.

"Watch your step." I point to a spot where the concrete is uneven and broken. Her lips turn up in a small smile. When I look at the house, I notice multiple faces peering out the window, which means my roommates have people over. It doesn't bother me, but I hope Liz is okay with it. I mean, it's not like we're gonna stop to chat or anything. I'm taking her straight to my room. I couldn't care less if anyone hears us.

As soon as I open the door, every head swivels toward us. Smiles drop. Eyes widen. I don't pay attention, but Liz's grip tightens, so I rub her hand with my thumb as an unspoken gesture of reassurance.

"Austin!" someone calls.

"Hey!" I mumble, moving Liz so she's ahead of me as we go up the stairs.

"Great show, man!"

"Thanks. Appreciate it," I call over my shoulder. I don't want to seem ungrateful; I just want to get Liz out of the firing squad because it's bound to go from casual praise for the show to pointed questions about her.

At the top of the stairs, I place my hand on Liz's back and direct her to my bedroom. As we slip inside, the questions from below come fast and loud, like bullets from an assault rifle.

"What's up with the Becky?"

"What the fuck is he doing?"

"Who is she?"

"Fuck that. Who's got the herb?"

In all honesty, I'm not bothered by the comments, because once I've fallen for a woman, no one can sway me. But that doesn't mean I want to hear them. All I want to do right now is make this girl scream. Loud enough that everyone downstairs can hear it.

At least, I hope she screams. She's definitely more fun than I originally gave her credit for, but it still seems like she'd be reserved in bed.

No worries. I'm ready for the challenge.

I slam the door behind us and rush Liz immediately, taking her face in my hands and covering her mouth with my own. Her response is the same as before, crushing her body against mine, but this time she wraps her arms around me. I love that she wants to be closer. Every time our kiss deepens, her arms tighten around me. It's like she's trying to be one with me and it gets me hot as hell. Because becoming one with her is all I can think about, as well. Naked. For hours.

I move my hands to her legs, running my palms against her outer thighs to lift her skirt. Her breath hitches and she grinds her pelvis against the front of my jeans. Knowing how much she enjoys it makes my dick hard. I don't want to stop until I feel how excited she is.

I back her up until her legs hit the bed.

"I want you, Liz."

"I want you, too," she whispers. I wonder if it's because she's trying to be quiet so people downstairs don't hear us, or if she's just quiet in general. Her nervous smile melted me after the show. Seeing her whole, safe, and alive sent a buzz of excitement through me. Part of me wants to confess that I know her, but I don't want her to think it's because I'm one of these people that needs others to know when I've done something for them.

I would have stopped for anyone. Rich. Poor. Black. White. American. Russian. It wouldn't have mattered. But I can't shake the feeling that there had to be some universal reason for her showing up at my show tonight. She didn't know I took her to the hospital. EmVee didn't know. There has to be something to that.

There's a fucked-up Prince Charming part of me that wants to claim the girl I saved. I've never been the type to have a hero complex, but I guess that's because I've never been a hero. And technically, I don't even know that I saved her. An emergency crew could have been minutes away.

I can't explain the strong connection I felt the first time I saw her, but I'm feeling that same connection right now. The best way to test that connection is to look in her eyes while her pussy clenches around my cock.

I crouch down, grab Liz behind her knees, and flip her back onto the bed. The pure joy in her squeal tells me that she likes it. Her dress flips up to reveal creamy thighs and a tight stomach.

"God, you're so fucking sexy," I tell her.

Instead of going straight for the prize, I place my hands on each side of her, lean down and press my lips right above her belly button. Her back arches in anticipation which also lifts her tits to the sky. A reminder that I need to get this dress off her.

My cock strains against my jeans as I climb onto the bed, but I'm not ready to let it out yet. I need to know her body first. Need to see what makes her happy. See what gets her off. I want to taste her. Want to make sure she's completely satisfied, because once my cock comes out, I'm driving it straight inside her.

I move up to lay on my side, next to her. Before I have a chance to touch her, she sets her hands on my chest, curls into me, and presses her mouth against mine. She pulls back slightly and slides her tongue across my lips. Liz taking charge is a sexy surprise. I love that her first reaction is always to get closer. It's like she wants to mold herself against me. I can't get enough of that feeling. There's nothing better than when a woman wants to be with you.

Our eyes lock. And there it is. What started out as physical attraction, has morphed into something completely different. My body hums, fueled by an invisible connection between us. This isn't just sex, this is an energy exchange—thick, almost palpable—but absolutely unmistakable.

I've never felt anything like it.

Liz's lips curve into a sexy smile, then she grabs my hand and guides me to the promised land. She's so fucking wet, it makes me groan. "Fuck, Liz!"

Since I have permission, I slide her underwear down her legs, until they hit her calf. She uses one foot to push them the rest of the way down and fling them off. When I slip one finger in, she closes her eyes and takes a deep breath. Her chest bumps against mine before she lets out the breath, just as slowly as she inhaled. I've never been with a girl that took deep breaths. Maybe it's her way of gearing up for all the fast panting she's about to do.

Or not?

She keeps up the deep breathing as I finger-fuck her into oblivion. I do say oblivion, because I have never had a girl come so hard on my hand. I can usually tell when a someone is getting close by the way her breath hitches and her breathing increases. But Liz is completely different than anyone I've ever been with. She lifts her chest and hips on the inhale and releases on the exhale, as if her body is breathing in waves.

"Was that good?" I ask.

"Umm hmm," she moans, still writhing against my hand.

I think she's still orgasming. I don't know. Jesus, I feel like a fumbling novice. I need to know.

"Are you still coming?" I ask. Having to ask makes me feel like such an amateur, but this girl my judgmental friends labeled a "Becky" is surprising the fuck out of me.

"I'm riding it out. It still feels *really* good."

"Damn," I breathe out. Watching her roll her hips gets me harder by the second.

I love that rather than just lying there, she goes for it. First times with someone can be awkward, but Liz doesn't hold back and it's hot as hell. For someone who comes across quiet and shy, she's knows exactly what she wants and how to get it. That alone makes her a thousand times sexier than the majority of the girls I've been with. Liz is very aware of her body. She obviously knows what works for her and how to enhance it.

Suddenly, she opens her eyes and grins. "That was brilliant."

"Was that all from breathing?" I ask, curious about her goddess ways.

Her smile falters a bit, but doesn't disappear completely.

"It was amazing," I say quickly so she knows I enjoyed it and wasn't trying to make her feel self-conscious. "Watching you is hot."

"I work in medicine, so I research a lot of things." She stops, as if contemplating what to say next. I already know she's a surgeon, but I'm still hanging on every word.

She continues, "I'm very aware of my body. And of other people's bodies."

"Oh yeah?"

She nods. Her shy smile slides into a sexy smirk. "I'm extremely aware of your body right now."

Her fingers find the zipper of my jeans easily, and within seconds my pants are on the floor. Then she climbs on top of me and grabs the hem of her dress. I take a deep death as she slides the silky fabric up her body, slowly revealing every gorgeous curve. I knew she wasn't stick thin from holding her. It's a complete turn-on to see a girl who's fit and tight, yet not bony and hard. Her soft curves make my mouth water.

She slings her dress to the floor giving me full view of perfect, round breasts, contained by a sexy, black-lace bra. I reach out and place my hand on top of her heart. It races under my palm. Her energy pulses into me with every breath.

At first, I think she's going to climb on and start riding my dick, but she surprises me yet again by turning around. She takes the base of my cock in one hand, leans over, and licks the entire shaft before swirling her tongue around the tip lightly.

"Fuck," I groan, lifting my hips off the bed when she takes me into her mouth. As she works my cock, she lifts her hips, giving me full access to her pussy.

This reserved, professional woman wants to fucking sixty-nine.

I think I'm in love.

Without a second thought, I grab her hips and pull her onto my face. The rumble of her moan creates a phenomenal vibration against my dick.

Suddenly there's a knock on the door. Followed by someone calling out, "Austin!"

Liz removes her warm mouth from my dick.

"Don't worry about it, honey." I slap her thigh lightly to prod her on. "There's no way I'm answering that door."

Another pound. Then another. More yelling. Mother-fucking fuckers. I hate my friends.

Ignoring the knocking and yelling, I settle back into Liz's pussy, lapping and sucking and biting. I'm so completely into her—into this —that I don't want to think about anything else. I'm hoping she hasn't lost the mood. But how could she not when my idiot roommate is pounding on the door?

Yet, every time I think something about Liz, she flips it around on me.

So I can't say I'm totally surprised when she grinds her pussy against my face and gets back to work on my dick with more enthusiasm and gusto than before. She spits into her palm, then grabs onto the base and starts twisting her hand as she takes as much of me into her mouth as she can. It feels so good I could blow right now. I wouldn't—not the first time—but damn! This woman is talented.

When I'm sure I can't hold off any longer, I lift her up and toss her on the bed next to me. "Fuck, baby. Hold on. You're gonna make me come." Then I climb on top of her and say, "I want to be looking into your beautiful eyes when I explode in your pussy."

Her sultry smile says everything I need. I reach into the drawer next to my bed and pull out a condom. I want to be inside this girl so badly my hands are shaking as I roll it on. Without any more waiting or foreplay, I push into her with one swift thrust. Her eyes roll back and her lids close as pure ecstasy takes over. Her head presses into the pillow, chin in the air.

"Harder, Austin!"

Spurred on by her command and her nails digging into my back, I pull out slowly before slamming back in. She gasps with the impact, and her pussy clenches around my cock.

"Yes! Keep going!"

Normally, I'm not a jackhammer-sex kind of dude, but if that's what Liz wants, I'm going to do it. Whatever feels good for her. Her gasps turn into moans the more I thrust. Each reaction has me riding so high I'm about to come if I keep this up. Thrusting one more time, I stay deep inside, but lean down and grind my pelvis against her. Up and down, in circles, I know it feels good against her sensitive clit.

"Oh my god! Yes! Right there. Don't stop! Don't stop!"

I lower my head to kiss and bite the smooth skin of her neck. Her pulse beats against my lips—the blood pumping through her system bringing me to life. "Tell me when you're coming, baby. I'm going to explode with you."

"I'm—oh my god—I'm coming, Austin! Don't stop!"

She doesn't have to worry about that. There's no way would I stop when I know the sensation I'm creating is making her come undone.

"Austin! Austin! Austin!"

Liz's eyes flash open and that piercing gaze takes me to the next level. The sweet sound of her chanting my name, while staring into the depths of my soul, makes me come hard.

"Fuck!"

I've been on stage in front of hundreds of people staring at me, yelling and screaming their praise, but none of that compares to the high of staring into Liz's eyes while reaching the ultimate physical and mental connection.

What is this girl doing to me?

I lean over and press my lips against hers before collapsing on the bed next to her, breathing hard, wondering if my breath will ever resume to a normal pace when I'm around her.

"You okay?" she asks, reaching for my hand and intertwining her fingers with mine.

"Never better, baby," I answer. It's an honest, yet complicated answer.

While it's true that I've never felt better than I do right now, after having the most extraordinary orgasm of my life, I'm cautious, wondering if I should jump straight into the deep end and give this girl my heart. When I fall, I fall hard.

We lie together in silence, catching our breath amid the mild smell of sweat and sex.

"That was intense, Austin," Liz whispers.

Yeah, it was.

Pressing my eyes closed, I will myself not to speak. Because if I speak I'm either gonna say something so outlandish like, *"I love you"* or something completely asshole like, *"So you want me to take you home?"*

I don't want to go the asshole route, because even though *I* know it's based out of fear and self-sabotage, she won't understand, and it'll ruin any future we might be starting here.

Still, I feel like that's what I'm doing when I slide out of bed saying, "I'm gonna run to the bathroom. Be right back."

I dispose of the condom quickly and take a piss.

I've never had to deal with these feelings before. Usually, relation-ships happen the "normal" way, after the getting-to-know-you part and sexual buildup. It's never started with such a strong connection. Probably because I don't usually have strong connections with strangers. I don't really open up until I feel comfortable with someone.

Except she's not technically a stranger.

Fuck me and fuck feelings.

After washing my hands, I splash my face with water. It's never going to work between Liz and me. It's a connection I created and romanticized in my mind. Sure, the sex was mind-blowing and intense, but we have nothing in common. Pursuing a relationship with her would be an uphill battle I don't have the time or energy to fight right now. Not when I'm using every ounce of strength I have for making it in the music industry. We've never been this close and I'm not letting a stupid crush get in the way.

When I get back to my bedroom, Liz sits there with both feet on the floor, as if ready to make a run for it.

"Can I use your bathroom?" she asks, glancing at me, but not meeting my eyes.

"Absolutely. It's at the end of the hallway."

"Thanks," she says, getting up swiftly and sliding past me in the doorway.

Every reservation I had about pursuing her, every warning flag I raised in my head flies out the window when I see how dejected she looks—like a woman who already regrets sleeping with me.

I already screwed up by going to the bathroom instead of talking and cuddling first. Before she shuffles out of reach, I grab her hand and draw her toward me. She raises her eyes to mine tentatively.

"You are so completely amazing," I whisper before placing a soft kiss on her lips. "Hurry back."

The words make her eyes light up and her smile come alive again. Sometimes I'm such an awkward idiot I forget the little things—like compliments and how much I appreciate a woman sharing her body with me in the most intimate way possible.

When Liz returns, she climbs back into bed. I immediately open my arms, inviting her to snuggle in. She rests her head on my chest and places a hand over my heart. I kiss the top of her head.

"You gotta tell me about that orgasm, Liz."

"It was awesome. Amazing. Best I ever had?" The inflection at the end makes me realize that my questions sounded like I'm an egomaniac fishing for compliments.

"Well, I *know* that," I tease. "I meant how do you do it? I've never seen anyone slow-breathe through an orgasm. It's always a lot of fast, hyperventilating-type breaths."

"Oh." She laughs softly. The delighted vibrations send waves straight into my heart.

"I've read a lot of books and articles about how I can get the most out of the time with lovers. Though, the goal of sex isn't always to orgasm, it *is* a measurable representation of satisfaction. Once I learned that my orgasm is much more intense when I breathe slowly through it, I started practicing." She pauses and I feel her tense against me. "Not with a ton of men or anything. I practice by myself and take what I learn into my experiences."

"Wow." I don't have any other words. This woman researches sex and how to make it better. Her mind turns me on.

"There's so much talk about empowering women—which is absolutely brilliant—but the conversation doesn't move into the bedroom. I was raised to be a strong, independent woman. Why would I change who I am in one of the most important parts of a relationship? But it's not just about my own orgasm and satisfaction," she says quickly. "I research men, too. That's why I'm pretty good at giving head."

"Correction: you're fucking phenomenal at giving head." My mind wanders back to the way she worked my dick with enthusiasm and expertise. "How do you practice that by yourself?"

If I'm honest—I'm slightly intimidated by her intelligence while being exceptionally turned on at the same time.

"I'm sorry to break it to you, but I'm not a virgin," she deadpans.

I reach under her arm and tickle her gently. She laughs and shakes against me, sending her infectious vibes through me again. I love her laugh and her mind. She's blowing me away—literally and figuratively.

"You can practice on me whenever you want."

"I bet." She nestles back into me.

"I'm your slave, Liz. Whatever you want to do to me, go for it. I'll return the favor ten-fold."

"Noted," she says. "When did you start playing music?"

"Geez." I look up to the ceiling, trying to remember how old I was when Dad came home with my first guitar. "I think I was eight or nine when I started playing guitar. I messed around with piano before that, but only for fun. My parents always had instruments in the house. Neither of them played, but they really pushed creativity as an outlet for emotions. I think I wrote my first song at twelve or thirteen. A true story of betrayal and jealousy. Giving the girl I liked the soda from my lunch and having her turn around and give it to the guy she liked. The pain of heartbreak, ya know?"

"Ouch."

"Right?"

"In sixth grade, I thought I had my first boyfriend. We barely talked at school, but he always wanted to come over to my house. Nothing happened. We just watched TV or hung out. Then, one day, out of the blue, he asked if I could hook him up with Maddie. That happened a lot actually. Guys befriended me to get closer to Maddie. Personally, I don't see how breaking one sister's heart is a way to get on the other sister's good side, but she'd still date the guy if she liked him enough."

"That's really shitty."

"Yeah, but that's the competitive nature between sisters. Not like there was ever a competition. No one picked me over her." She says the last part in a whisper and I know that it's still a source of pain. For someone so confident in her career and self—she's still hurt by the juvenile shit idiot teenagers pulled.

"That's a good thing."

"What?"

"I don't know your sister, obviously, but I can tell you're completely different people. You don't want the guys who are attracted to Maddie. Those aren't your matches. Using you to get to her is a completely shit-bag thing to do, but be happy that you didn't get all wrapped up in that dude only to realize later that he wasn't the right fit in the first place."

Liz rests both hands on my chest and places her chin on top of them so we can look at each other as we talk. "I never looked at it that way."

"It's hard to see past the pain and hurt of a situation like that. You're way too smart and strong for those cowards anyway. You don't want a guy who has to go through your sister to get you. You need a guy who knows what he wants and goes for it." I reach out and run my thumb across her bottom lip. "One that lures you in with intense eye contact and asks you back to his house the same night you meet so you two can explore the obvious connection."

"Ohhh. Maybe a musician?"

"Absolutely. An okay-looking musician with lots of tattoos and a heart of gold."

She smiles. "Sounds like my kind of guy."

"I can hook you up with one."

"You know what you want and you go for it. I believe that about you. You seem very motivated. Goal-oriented."

"Did this turn into an interview?"

"No." She laughs. "I look for those qualities in people. You may not believe this, but it's hard to be with someone like me."

"What does 'someone like you' mean?"

"I work a lot. By the time I'm finished with my residency—" She pauses and I swear I see tears in her eyes. "These last few years have been some of the most intense I'll ever go through in my life. Some men are intimidated by what I do. Others can't handle the fact that I have very little free time to spend with them. They feel neglected and start resenting me. And then I second-guess my career and passion because some guy's feelings are hurt. I guess that's why I don't really pursue relationships right now. I'm sick of feeling bad about myself because I'm not meeting someone else's expectations for me."

Her words describe my life as a musician, trying to make it. My focus has been razor sharp recently. If it doesn't serve me or my career, it goes on the back burner—including relationships.

"Yeah, I completely understand. I've worked my ass off and been in band after band, trying to make a living out of this. Just when I think it all clicks—the people, the sound, our goals—something falls apart and

I start over again. I put every drop of sweat and blood into making this my full-time career. It's not easy. I work crazy hours. Sometimes I pick up and drive somewhere random for a weekend, to write. I need a lot of solitude. And now everything is blowing up. Two songs on the radio, millions of streams on YouTube, talking to record labels—" I stop, realizing that I sound like an insecure douchebag listing all my accomplishments like I'm trying to impress her. But I'm not; I know she understands the amount of time and work it takes to be successful. It's something we have in common.

"Go on," she says. Her eyes are bright and encouraging.

"Some people still think it's a hobby—that I can just drop it and move on. It's funny how many people say that and it's annoying, ya know? Maybe I didn't go to college, but I studied and practiced just as hard as anyone learning their craft. And I'm not in massive debt." I laugh. "My career is just as important to me as your career is to you."

"I understand, Austin. Believe me." Something in her eyes tells me to believe her. Trust her. "How long has Drowned World been together?"

"About three years. Fozzie and I started the band with another bass player, but he met a girl and wasn't interested in touring, so we brought Tim on. He's been with us about six months."

Just thinking about Tim and the issues that he's brought to the band makes my muscles tighten all over.

Either Liz can read my mind or she felt me tense up because she adjusts her body, tucking herself between my arm side, freeing up her hand to rub my chest soothingly. "Trouble with the new guy?"

Talking to her is almost like talking to a therapist. I'm free to say anything I want because she doesn't know any of these people.

"He's not as invested as Fozzie and I are. He's not even on the tracks that are on the radio. We recorded our EP with our old bassist. We're realizing that he's literally just with us for the free bar tab at gigs. None of the responsibility."

"Oh. That doesn't sound like a good situation."

"Yeah, it's—" I take a deep cleansing breath and release the bad vibes around talking about Tim. I want to focus on Liz. "Let's not talk about him. I'd rather do this." I shift to my side and wrap my arms around her, pulling her back to my chest. Then I nuzzle my face in her neck and kiss her below her earlobe. She responds with a soft "mmmm" sound which makes my heart race and my cock rise. Despite my body's reaction, I'm not ready for round two. I just want to hold her.

Miss Honey has completely surprised me. I knew she was intelligent—that part was obvious—but her down-to-earth vibe is what really gets me. She cares and listens. Huge shout-out to the universe for bringing her back to my life. There's a reason I found her on the side of the road and a reason she was here tonight. I believe in all that energy.

I still can't believe she's Harris Commons' daughter; then again, EmVee is one of the coolest chicks I know and she's his daughter, too. How did such an arrogant dick bag raise freaking amazing kids? Their mom must be a kick-ass lady.

Chapter Four

LIZ

I've never had someone spoon me all night. I didn't even know it was possible. In my experience, whoever I'm with usually rolls away, and we sleep with our backs to each other, hugging the edge of the mattress on our respective sides.

But Austin has been flush against my back all night. Even after I woke up and slid out to use the bathroom. When I climbed back into bed, he wrapped an arm and leg around me, snuggled his face into my neck, and we both fell back asleep. So it's no surprise when I woke up with his hand on my hip. If I'm completely honest, it's the kind of intimacy I've always longed for.

I've never had many boyfriends. Too busy. Too picky. Too cold.

So I've been told.

I don't think I'm cold, but that's what a few former beaus have told me. I guess I'm not as demonstrative as they'd have liked me to be. It bothered me at the time. In some ways it still does. I'm not the best at showing affection. I try to reign in my feelings and stay stoic most of the time. I had to learn that to be able to talk with my patients and their families. I care. Obviously, I care. But I can't let myself get too attached or I become useless. My head isn't where it needs to be.

I guess I took that into relationships as well. My focus isn't being extra cutesy for a guy. My focus was always studying, grades, intern-ships, and volunteering. Anything that took me to the next level to achieve my goals. Trusting another person too much, sometimes means they get the upper hand. They can use your weakness against you. And as a female in a male-dominated field, I can't let feelings get in the way of focus.

A relationship had never been a goal.

Maybe a relationship had never been a goal for me because I wasn't the one guys flocked to. Maddie and Emily never had a problem. I pretended it wasn't a big deal because I had bigger things to worry about, but deep down, I wondered why I never got pursued. Even when I was in relationships, with the "perfect" matches Mama steered me toward—I never felt a true connection with anyone.

Until Austin. His gaze during the show entranced me. The connec-tion was so thick it was almost visible. I can't explain why. It's like I knew him. Trusted him.

"Why are we awake?" Austin rasps. His eyes are still closed, his hair sticking up at every angle, which isn't too different from how it looked at the end of his set last night, so I have a feeling he doesn't care much about bedhead.

"I'm awake because I have to get to work. You should sleep."

"It's not even light out yet."

"My patients don't wait for the sun to rise," I say softly.

Austin rolls to his side, hooks his arms around my waist, and pulls me closer to him. "I imagine being responsible for so many people is exhausting—mentally and physically."

It's interesting that he mentioned the mental stress. He's right, it's just as mentally exhausting as it is physically, but most people don't acknowledge that aspect. "Yeah, it is. The hours are crazy. But my workload has changed recently, so it doesn't feel as overwhelming as it once did."

"Why is that?" His eyes are open now, seemingly interested. This isn't the morning-after conversation I expected to be having.

"I was in a car accident a few months ago and my hand was severely damaged." I flex my right hand as I speak, as if that will make it better. "For normal, everyday activities, it works just fine. Unfortunately, surgery isn't a normal activity and I'm unable to operate right now."

His entire body tenses. "Oh man. I'm sorry, Liz."

"It's okay," I tell him, touched by his concern.

"I don't believe that." He must notice the side-eye I'm throwing him, because he continues. "I'm sorry. I'm not trying to make you feel worse. I just mean, you can't possibly be okay with it. Not after all that school and training. Not being able to operate has to be killing you."

Tears spring to my eyes, but I blink them back. "Yeah. It sucks, but I was very lucky to have the opportunity to get into a fellowship while my hand heals."

Talking about the injury and healing out loud creates a lump of disappointment in my throat. Mostly because I won't be able to keep lying to people for much longer. Also because the way I got into my fellowship was total privilege bullshit. My mother and father both pulled every string they had in the hospital—which is a lot, considering they've given enough money to have their name on one of the wings.

"Did you always want to be a surgeon?"

"Yes and no. My parents had quite a bit of influence in my career."

"You're an adult now. You can choose your own path."

"Yes, I know, but, the expectations are—" I close my mouth and shake my head. He'd never understand the pressure I have from my family. Not just the pressure to become something—but to make them proud, and not tarnish the family name.

"We're not so different, Liz," Austin says. "Middle-class parents have expectations for their kids, too."

"I know. I didn't mean it that way."

"You think my mom loves that I barely graduated high school and I'm trying to make it as a musician? She's never tried to hinder my passion, but I'm sure she wanted me to choose something stable."

My mind wanders back to the brief conversation I had with his mom last night. It didn't sound like she ever wanted to push him toward a job he hated, just to be stable. But then again, I don't know their family dynamic. Or maybe Austin assumes something that his mom never really felt because that's what people who live a "non-traditional" life assume of their parents.

Case in point, Emily thinks Mama and Daddy hate her for the life she chose. It goes deeper than that. I truly think they would have accepted anything she wanted to pursue, but she chose to walk away from our family, which hurt and angered them. Because of that they're being even more judgmental than they probably would have been if she hadn't abandoned them.

"That's the difference," I say, rolling to my side to face him. His arm doesn't move, still resting across my waist. There's comfort in the way he keeps me close, which lulls me into believing this is a safe space to open up about anything.

I'm trying my hardest not to sound like I think I'm better than him because I'm not, but it's going to sound that way when I explain my family's expectations of me. "Your mom lets you live your own life. You didn't want to go to college—cool. You want to be a musician—she supports your decision to follow your passion even if it might not be the path she would have chosen for you."

"Yeah. She's pretty kick-ass."

I smile. *She seemed pretty kick-ass.*

"When I was—I don't know, ten?—I mentioned I wanted to be a doctor. Despite the countless other professions I'd mentioned in passing when I was a kid, that's the one my mother ran with. The next day I found a shiny new copy of the *Atlas of Human Anatomy,* wrapped with a red ribbon, on my bed with a note about the amazing Latin tutor she'd found for me."

"Ten?"

"Yes."

"Damn." He sweeps a hand across my skin, from hip to neck, where he stops to rub gently. It feels amazing on my stressed muscles.

"Yeah. After that, my future medical career was the only thing my parents talked about. They were enthusiastic about it. I loved the attention. Soon being a doctor wasn't just a random answer I gave when someone asked what I wanted to be when I grew up. It consumed my thoughts—and my life. It started with Latin lessons and online anatomy classes, on top of my regular schoolwork, continued into setting my class schedules according to classes that would be most relevant to the career. Then I had to observe at multiple medical practices and hospital departments to see which specialties and settings I liked best. By senior year of high school, I had interned with some of the top neurosurgeons, cardiologists, and oncologists in Charlotte. I had to choose from there."

Austin's face is pale, the eye that isn't hidden by the pillow is wide with surprise as I speak. It's a normal reaction, no matter who I tell. Even people who have overzealous parents, who want their kids to be as high-achieving as mine want me to be.

"You really had no choice."

I bite my lip. "I did. Just like you said. I could have told them I didn't want to be a doctor."

Austin laughs. "No. You couldn't."

"What does that mean?"

"I have a feeling you do things to please your parents. You would have never told them that you didn't want to be a doctor."

He's right. If the medical program had been too difficult for me, I probably would have told them, but other than that? Nope. I've never admitted that to anyone though. The Commons don't talk about "what ifs." We talk about accomplishments.

"That's true to an extent," I agree. "Technically, I did have a choice. I could have joined our family business. And while, I know my parents would've been happy with that choice, they had their hearts set on my becoming a surgeon. I was extremely aware of how much turning back would disappoint them. And I never wanted to disappoint my parents."

"Why?"

"Because they set me up with a beautiful life. And all the privilege. It would be like I was ungrateful for everything they gave me to be a step ahead of everyone else."

"But if that's not what's in your heart." He lifts his head and adjusts on the pillow so I can see his entire face.

I laugh hollowly. "My parents don't care about what's in my heart. Passion is just a seven-letter word. It's a hobby, not a career."

I glance at Austin, whose previously interested expression switches to a look of sadness.

"You think my father loves the stores? Heck no! He knew his older brother would take over my grandfather's company, so he had to create his own success. Constructing a business from the ground up gave him credibility and made him a powerful person in the community on his own—if you can call it that since he used a loan from my grandfather. It's the power. The influence. Not the actual business. I'm sure he can't wait until Maddie finally takes it over." I stop, realizing that I've said way too much. I've never said anything like that out loud about my father.

"Who's Maddie?"

"My other sister. There are three of us: Maddie, Em, and me."

Austin shakes his head as if trying to loosen thoughts. "Can we back up a minute? I don't know anything about you or your family. Your dad created Commons Department Stores? Not your grandfather? I thought that was your family's legacy, like how you guys got ri —"—he stops, changing his wording mid-sentence—"grew your wealth."

Being with Austin is so easy, it feels like we've known each other forever. I'm not used to having in-depth conversations with people who don't know my family. I forget that Austin isn't entrenched in Charlotte society. Then again, I probably wouldn't have gone off like I did if he were someone familiar with my family. I've never been able to talk this openly about it before. Things have a way of getting back to my father.

"No. My family's legacy is real estate. Commons Property Development."

"And Commons Department Stores?"

"Those are fairly recent, but obviously booming, and yes—they will be my father's legacy."

"Obviously," Austin repeats.

It's not angry or sarcastic, more like he's a bit overwhelmed. I'm not used to overwhelmed. I'm used to having to prove my family's worth against other families. It's not hard, but most men I've dated seemed to be in competition with me on whose family is wealthier or more powerful. Or else that's the reason they want to be with me—to enhance their status. As if we're back in the days of dowries and marriage to merge the most powerful families, to continue to conquer and rule.

I can't even imagine what Maddie would think if she knew I was lying naked next to Austin right now. I don't even know what I think.

What started as a fun, easy, one-night stand with a ridiculously sexy stranger, turned into a therapy session during a vulnerable time in my life. Not sure if the story of my first one-night stand gets any better than that.

I'm trying to ignore the pull to him that has me feeling like I'm going to cry on the ride home.

Two guitars rest on a stand in the far corner, the only items that give any indication of his personality. The rest of the room is plain. Not much color. Everything is worn—not dirty—worn, as if it's been used for years, but not antique. An oak dresser, matching nightstand. His bed is on the floor.

"What do your parents do?" I ask, changing the subject slightly. Though it seems like a weird question to be asking about his parent's jobs since we're both adults.

"My mom is the office manager at a small financial planning firm and my dad is dead."

"Oh! I'm sorry."

"Don't be sorry. You didn't kill him. He killed himself."

I don't know what to say. His bluntness isn't something I'm familiar with from other people. I'm usually the blunt one.

Thankfully, Austin continues, "My dad had an amazing mind. He also had bipolar disorder. Genius and madman."

"How long has he been gone?"

Austin glances at the ceiling as if it holds the answer. "Right around ten—no—fifteen years. Damn. Time flies."

"Indeed," I whisper.

Silence envelops the room, save for the distant chirping of birds waking up. Despite the heavy topic, it's not an uncomfortable quiet. I scoot closer and lay my cheek against Austin's chest, listening to the beat of his heart against my ear. He's completely calm, an interesting vibration after such an intense discussion. When I squeeze his torso, he tightens his arm around me.

"My father found peace," Austin says, breaking the silence. "We'd discussed his mental health as a family on multiple occasions. It's not like we were waiting for it to happen, but we weren't surprised when it did. Was it still absolutely devastating? Yes. But I know that he is at peace and his soul is free.

"I think that's part of what keeps me so focused on my music. There's always that thought in the back of my mind that I could get pulled down by that same kind of darkness. Music has been my outlet for as long as I can remember. If I don't create, I could go down the same road that he did."

"Are you bipolar?" I ask softly. Mental illness doesn't scare me, but knowing gives me the ability to understand him better and how to handle aspects of our relationship.

Relationship. Where did that thought come from?

"No. I mean, I don't think so. I've never been diagnosed. Mom has been pretty vigilant about keeping tabs on me. I've gone through bouts of situational depression, though I can't say I'm always depressed. It's usually due to something impacting my life. And I'm equipped with the tools to combat it."

"It's good that you have those tools. That's a huge part of the battle."

"I keep forgetting you're a medical professional. You probably know exactly what I'm talking about."

"Somewhat. It's not my specialty, but I'm fairly knowledgeable. I *am* a doctor, after all." I try to say it in a jovial way and hope Austin knows I'm kidding and not being obnoxious.

"Oh, I know. The big MD." His fingers dance across the skin under my arm and crawl up. I curl into him and laugh at the sensation. "You're ticklish, doctor? I would've thought you'd have tools to combat that."

"Oh, I do." I push myself up and out from under his arm, kneel over him, and attack his sides. He immediately brings his knees up to his chest to prevent me from getting to sensitive places, but I don't let up. "Tickle wars are known to combat situational depression after a one-night stand."

"Is there medical evidence supporting that claim?" Austin teases between laughing. "Can you point me to a journal article?"

"I'll write it," I tell him, finally halting the attack.

"I love your passion for life."

"Excuse me?" I'm completely taken aback. I'm hovering over the lowest point in my life right now. It takes every ounce of strength I have not to break down every day, wondering when the bottom will finally drop out.

"Your smile. Your energy. The way you dance. The way you fuck. I can tell you put everything you have into everything you do. I could see your light the first time I saw you. Your heart is even more beautiful than your face."

"I think that's a compliment."

"It is. I totally want to lick your heart."

"You're very strange."

"Thank you."

I laugh. "You can lick other things."

"What kind of things can I lick?" He lifts his hand to my face and caresses my cheek with the back of his fingers. "I need you to tell me. Out loud." He bites his bottom lip as he traces mine with his thumb.

The mirror effect. Those penetrating eyes. My heart hammers against my chest. Lust floods my core. It feels like he's about to pounce on me in five, four, three, two...

"My eyeball," I deadpan. Now is not the time to get all hot and heavy again. I really do have to get home and get ready for work.

"Who's the strange one now, Liz?"

"As my sister would say, I'm just trying to vibe on your level."

Austin laughs. "I don't even know your other sister, but I can tell that's an EmVee line."

"Yup."

Talking and laughing with Austin is so easy. The flow is there. I can say what I feel openly and honestly without having to think about forming the correct answers because I know he's not waiting to challenge me or pounce on something he can use as a weakness. I haven't had a conversation like this with a man. At least not in a relationship or with most of my colleagues.

If I really think about it, the only men I've spoken with, who didn't challenge me, were people who worked for our family. Erik, our landscaper, doesn't challenge me. He's a pretty chill guy. Then again, he's being paid by my parents, and the client is always right, so why would he challenge the people who help keep his business running?

Light rain pelts the window next to Austin's bed, reminding me again that I need to leave, even though I don't want to. "I should call my cab."

"I can give you a ride home."

The thought of getting back on Austin's motorcycle terrifies me. Not only because I'm scared of motorcycles, but also because it's raining and I've been extremely anxious about driving in the rain since my accident. It's a fear I need to let go of, but I haven't quite gotten there yet.

"I have a truck," Austin says, as if he can feel my apprehension. "I wouldn't ruin your sex hair by taking you home on my bike in the rain."

"What?" My hand flies to the back of my head, where the thick locks seem to be only slightly matted. Still, not being presentable in the presence of others isn't an option. "Can I use your bathroom?"

"Of course." Austin sits up, folds his pillow in half, then lays back down. "Wanna use my toothbrush, too?"

"Oh gosh, no! That's absolutely disgusting."

"I know. I'm *so* glad you didn't say yes."

"Has anyone ever said yes?"

"Yes."

I groan and roll off the bed. "I can't hear this right now."

"I didn't let him!" Austin calls behind me.

Without turning around, I slip out the door and tiptoe to the shared bathroom at the end of the hall. Doesn't seem like anyone else is up, but I don't want to take any chances. Especially after the reaction Austin got bringing me home last night. It was apparent that his friends did not approve of his choice. All that pounding on the door last night was an over-the-top way to let me know that I was not welcome. Which is fitting, I suppose, since my family and friends wouldn't approve of him either.

Everyone has their prejudices. It's not a one-way street. The animosity between classes runs both ways.

It makes me feel a bit uncomfortable to know that his friends hate me already.

Sure, I grew up wealthy, but I work with people from all walks of life. And I perform surgery on everyone. I don't discriminate.

Why am I even contemplating this? I'm going to walk out the door and never see this guy again—unless I go to another show. I'd definitely see them play again. Not only because I'd love to see Austin transform into that mesmerizing creature onstage, but also because I really felt the music.

Boys' bathrooms are gross in general, but I'm pretty sure Austin's could win some kind of award. I hover as I use the toilet, because I honestly don't want to touch the seat. Hair of all types and lengths surround my feet. Cut facial hair sticking to dried up toothpaste clumps sit in the sink. I don't even feel clean after washing my hands.

When I return, Austin opens one eye. "Why are we up this early again?"

"I have to be at the hospital by eight," I say as I grab my dress off the dresser. I don't even know how it got there. I'm pretty sure I threw it on the floor when I whipped it off. Maybe he moved it when he got up to use the bathroom. Which is sweet.

"I thought you said you couldn't perform surgery right now?" He leans over, grabs his black boxer briefs off the floor, then sits up. "The accident...your hand?"

"I can't, but I'm still responsible for all sorts of other procedures. I still make rounds and take care of critically ill patients. Operating is only one aspect of the job."

"Well, that's good, right? You're not completely out of the game."

I think about it for a moment. He's right. I am still in the game. I may not be able to operate, but everything I've learned up to this point can be used in treating patients and giving them the highest level of care.

"I like that way of thinking. I *am* still in the game. If I weren't, I'd be swept away quicker than all the hair on your bathroom floor."

"We're gross. I know." He stands up and pulls up his underwear, covering his perfect ass.

"Please don't take this the wrong way. I'm not trying to be judgy, but—how hard is it to sweep?"

"It's not!" Austin says. "It started as an experiment. I stopped cleaning, because I was the only one who did anything. That room is what happens when you wait for two other dudes to clean."

"I see how well that's working out for you guys."

"Uggh! I know!" He stands up. "Next time you come over you'll be able to eat on that floor."

Next time I come over? Does that mean he wants a next time? Or is it a line that accidentally slipped out? Insecurity and confusion have my heart skipping and my thoughts jumbled.

"Maybe you can eat me on that floor," I say in a rush of words that come out completely wrong.

Austin stares at me with wide eyes and a half-smile.

Oh. My. Gosh.

"That's not what I meant. I was trying to say *you* can eat off that floor, not *me*. Geez. I—I'm so sorry." The words rush out of my mouth without a pause.

Heat rushes to my cheeks. I cover my face with my hands, hoping that will make me invisible. The door is behind me. All I have to do is turn around and run out. At least he'll have a great story for how it all ended.

Within a second, he's in front of me, placing his hands over mine and moving them so he can see my face. "You are nothing like I expected you to be. So many surprises."

"Well, surgeon isn't a personality type. We all have our own quirks."

He laughs. "You're more than that. I haven't met anyone like you, Liz."

"Good. I like being an—"

Without letting me finish, Austin presses his lips on mine. He moves his hands to my hips and pulls me into him. I automatically grip his shoulders to stop my knees from buckling. Everything about him overwhelms me, yet calms me at the same time. His kiss is soft, yet aggressive. His body is rock-hard muscle, yet smooth and warm under my hands. He touches the parts of my heart no one has ever opened up before.

"I really like doing that," he says when he pulls away. His face is still so close, his lips brush mine as he speaks. "I really like everything about you, Liz."

"Even my awkwardness?" I ask, looking at him through thick lashes, clumped with last night's mascara.

"There's nothing awkward about you."

My phone is already opened to an app that will find me a ride within minutes. I hold it up. "How about the fact that I'm about to call a ride and slip out of here at 5 a.m.?"

"Well, *that* I actually expected. You probably don't want to be seen with me." He looks down, a rare flash of insecurity from a man who seems so self-assured.

"Exact opposite, *actually*. I do want to be seen with you." Austin lifts his eyes back to mine. "I want to parade you around the hospital and say, 'look at this phenomenal guy who likes me!'"

"You gonna make me wear a collar and leash?" Mischief flashes in his eyes and I wonder if that type of stuff is a kink for him. It's not one I want to explore.

"You're not a pet. You're completely different than the type of guy everyone expects me to be with."

He slides his hands through my hair and gazes into my eyes. A yellow ring circles his pupils, like a sunflower against the backdrop of a crystal-blue sky. "I want to be more than the bad boy you screw to show people you aren't what they think you are."

"Are you even a bad boy?" I ask, avoiding the other things his statement implies. That he wants to see me again. That this is more than a one-night stand. Despite the intense feelings, I'm not sure if I'm ready for more. While I have full confidence in my abilities to handle any situation that arises in the hospital, I don't trust my ability to handle the personal drama of losing my career and dating Austin simultaneously.

Neither is easy. Both have their own repercussions.

He releases me and takes a step back. "I don't think so, but you seem to think I am. Let me prove you wrong."

"Maybe some other time," I say as I press the screen to request my ride. It'll be here in two minutes. "I've gotta get downstairs."

"Can I call you?"

"You don't have my number."

Another step back. "Damn. That's cold."

With my hand still on the doorknob, I turn around. "Thank you, Austin. You made me feel more alive than I've felt in months. I really appreciate that."

"Happy I could help," he says, but he's not looking at me. "You have my number. Call me if you want to hang."

His words bring an immediate smile to my face and butterflies to my stomach. I can't remember the last time I felt true excitement about being with someone.

There's nothing wrong with stopping to enjoy the moment, but I can't let it get to my head. Two very different worlds. Very different goals.

He's not what I need right now. Not when I need to refocus and refigure my entire future.

Chapter Five

AUSTIN

"Why'd you bring the Becky home. You lose a bet?" Fozzie asks as I trudge down the stairs later that morning. I crashed so hard after Liz left, it's almost as if spending the night with her was a dream.

It seems really cliché to roll my eyes, but that's exactly what I do as I pass by and head straight to the kitchen. I open the cabinet to grab a coffee cup. Empty. Of course it is. Every cup or glass we have is all on the counter or on the table, or scattered all over the house, because the guys had people over last night. I'd dragged Liz past them without stopping to respond to any questions or dickhead comments. But I knew I'd have to face it.

My roommates are good guys, but they have annoyingly strong opinions of "Becky's and Chad's" which is what they call girls who only care about their appearance and keeping up with the latest trends and guys who are stereotypical frat-boy types. Otherwise known as basic people who look down on people who aren't like them. Classism at its finest. But, as long as there are such huge gaps in wealth, there will always be the haves and the have-nots.

When I was a kid, my mom made me watch some of the classic John Hughes films that she grew up on. I really connected with *The*

Breakfast Club and *Pretty in Pink*. They're different stories, but classism is the common link in those classic films from the 80's, and is still relevant today.

I feel like the place I work, The Usual Market, is the "poor kids" courtyard outside of the high school. But it's not necessarily about finances. It's about a different way of thinking and way of life. I hang out with a ton of creatives—artists, writers, musicians. Some of them have day jobs. Some of them make ends meet however they can. They don't care about a big house or expensive cars. Not saying none of them dream of a time when they don't live paycheck to paycheck, but they'd still keep the same mindset. Non-conformist.

"You're drooling," I say, swiping my fingers at my mouth and my chin. "Take care of that."

"You never answered my question."

"I saw a girl at the show I wanted. I brought her home. Simple as that." My chest tightens, as if warning me that I shouldn't be throwing shit like that into the universe when I know there's much more to my connection with Liz.

"Bull fucking shit." He chuckles. "I've known you for seven years and you've never brought home a girl like that."

"A girl like what?"

"Like she was spit out of a Brooks Brothers catalog."

"What does that even mean?" I ask with a laugh, forgetting to defend Liz for a second, because the random comment is funny as shit. But only partly true. Sure, Liz is perfectly put together, but that dress she had on last night was super sexy, light-years away from the bougie-casual Brooks Brothers attire.

My mind flashes back to the very first thing she did on my bed—flip around so we could go down on each other simultaneously—and that solidifies the fact that she's no model for an over-priced vanilla clothing line. She's got a wild side. I just need to figure out how to get her to let it out more often.

"She must've been good, bro, 'cuz you're licking your lips," Fozzie says, his voice shaking me out of my memory. "Ahhh! I get it now!"

"Huh?" I say wiping my mouth, unaware of my subconscious response. "Get what?"

"This isn't just random pussy. She must be your new muse."

"I wouldn't say new."

"Old flame?"

"She's the girl from the accident."

"Wait? What?" Fozzie stops grinding his weed and leans closer to me.

"Yeah. When I saw her in the crowd, she caught my eye, but not in the normal way. She looked familiar, but I couldn't place how. Then I saw her profile on IG and figured it out."

He swipes his hand across the table and sweeps the herb off the edge into the open palm of his other hand. "Fuuuuuuck! Does she know you wrote a song about her?"

"No! You want me to creep her out?"

"I can't believe it. That's random as fuck."

"Yeah, I know. And even more random—it's EmVee's sister."

"Oh. My. God. You're in love with like, the Queen of Beckys."

"I'm not in love."

It can't be love—it's just a crush and lust. A lusty crush and an intense connection that tricks my brain into feeling like love.

Jesus.

The only thing I can think about is the next time I can be with her —which we didn't even discuss. I don't even have her number, but I gave her mine. That means she has to make the next move. Unless I beg EmVee for her digits.

When I look up, Fozzie's staring at me. I hate him.

"It's not love! It's infatuation." I lean back and stretch out, resting my feet on the coffee table.

"You sound like a fucking girl." He lifts his eyes quickly as he sprinkles weed onto rolling paper.

"I refuse to accept your ignorant gender-stereotypical comment. Having feelings for someone doesn't make me any less of a man."

"Oh my God. Get a grip."

"Did you know Liz was EmVee's sister?"

"Nope. I don't know Em's family."

Fozzie and EmVee have been friends for years, so I'm slightly surprised he doesn't know her family. Then again, he's got this way of never getting too close to people, yet knowing everything about them. He must be soaking up every piece of information people put into the world when he doesn't seem to be paying attention.

"Did you know they're rich?"

"Yup." He lifts the paper up, rolling it in his fingers expertly.

"Why didn't you ever say anything?"

"One, it's never come up before. Two, it's not my place to say anything." Fozzie brings the joint to his mouth, licks the edge, then seals it. "And three, Em has been out of their house and off that money for years. So it's not an issue."

I shrug. "It's not an issue at all. I was just wondering."

"Have you heard from Nelson?" Fozzie changes the subject abruptly. Which isn't even odd. He never talks about his relationship with Em. I don't even know if I should call it a relationship. They're more than friends, but not together as a couple.

"Yeah. We've been figuring out the final details about the Mars tour."

After years of working our asses off trying to do everything for ourselves, Fozzie and I hired Nelson to manage the band. When *Open Your Heart* started getting a ton of satellite-radio play and YouTube streams, we realized we needed some help. Nelson is a good friend of ours and he's been in the music industry for years. He's got a ton of connections and a great business mind. He's taught us so much and helped us up our game.

"Being out with them is gonna be epic," he says during an inhale.

"Right?" I hold my fingers out for him to pass me the joint. Nelson worked his ass off getting us set up with Walk on Mars.

He hands it over immediately. "Shit is blowing up, homie. Did you see the Alt chart this week?"

I nod, unable to answer because I'm holding my inhale. "Number seven," I say in an exhale.

"Unreal."

"My mom keeps texting me every time she hears it. It's phenomenal." I return the joint to Fozzie. "Is Tim still here?"

"Yup. He was wasted so I let him crash in Q's room."

Tim was too wasted to get home? There's a huge surprise. I can't think of a time where he hasn't been wasted. Good thing our third roommate, Quinn, is rarely home. He practically lives at his girlfriend's place. But he still pays rent, so we don't care.

"Why the hell was he banging on my door last night?"

"'Cuz he was high out of his mind," Fozzie says. "He started talking about always wanting to be with a Becky and then he got on this kick about having a threesome with you and Liz. Marissa jumped in and said they should knock on your door to see if you guys would have an orgy."

"Fuck that."

"I figured you wouldn't share."

"Not Liz."

And not with them.

Orgies aren't even on my radar. That doesn't get me off.

Threesomes aren't my thing. Years ago, I had a few encounters with two women. I wasn't opposed to another guy in that situation; it just happens that my experiences were with two females. I barely trust Tim enough to have him in the band, so I'm not sure why he'd think I'd want to share a woman with him.

If I'm in a relationship, it's just me and my girl in bed. I have zero interest in sharing. I'm not gonna hate on what gets someone else off sexually—to each their own—but I want to concentrate on one person during sex. I want to put my all into her. Nothing feels better than the connection and intimacy with one person. Being with the right girl allows me the comfort to open my mind to explore and try new things.

"Hey! I'm sorry I jumped on your bass last night. I wasn't thinking. Just going with the energy."

"It's cool. We talked about it in New York."

"I know, but we didn't talk about it beforehand and you didn't have that bracket on it. I—"

"Dude," Fozzie interrupts me. "It's all good, man. I love when you get that energy. The crowd loves it. No harm to my drum. I've actually been thinking about a new setup where we can incorporate that more if you want. More brackets to make an industrial look around the drums. May have to wait for a headlining tour, though, 'cuz it'll be a bitch to take down between sets."

I nod.

"We really need to talk about Tim, though," Fozzie says. "How many times is that fucker not going to show up to soundcheck? He didn't set up his shit and was high as fuck when he got there last night."

When Fozzie uses the term "high as fuck"—he doesn't mean pot. We both know Tim does some harder shit. We just don't know what it is. We've already talked to him once about it and how we don't want that type of use in the band. He obviously doesn't give a shit about our concerns, but if he keeps it up, he's gonna get his ass kicked out.

"Jimmy knows all our songs and slays the bass. He's already been on tour with us and knows how to set everything up. We should talk to him about taking over for Tim."

I nod again. We have to figure it out soon, because going on tour with Walk on Mars means we'll be playing arenas. We can't even wrap our heads around that size crowd. The exposure is going to be ridiculous. Both Fozzie and I have been on edge, alternating between extreme excitement and extreme stress, ever since Nelson told us. Being heard by new listeners is the way to grow. That's how this becomes a career and not just a hobby. And that's the ultimate goal. I just hope we can get our shit together before then.

Chapter Six

LIZ

Hey! It's Liz! What are you up to?

A text at 9:55 p.m. probably seems like a booty call. If I'm honest, that *is* on my mind, but I haven't stopped thinking about Austin since I left his house two days ago. I wandered around work in a lust-struck daze. It wasn't so bad that I couldn't focus, but Austin occupied every second of non-medical thoughts I had today. Having someone completely take over my head hasn't happened to me in years. Not since freshman year when I had a crush on my English 101 TA. Maybe I've always had a thing for creative men who pour out their souls through words.

> **Austin:** Nothing much. Just waiting for you to text me because I didn't have your phone number.
> **Me:** Good thing I didn't keep you waiting long, eh?
> **Austin:** Word! Now I have your digits and I can bug the shit out of you.
> **Me:** You don't bug me.
> Austin: Yet. ;) What are you up to?
> **Me:** Lying in bed reading.

Austin: Ooohhhh! What are you wearing?

I glance down, convinced he wouldn't be impressed by my button-down pajama top. Sure, it's a silky fabric in the signature pink-and-white stripes of Victoria's Secret, but it doesn't scream sexy. I've worn the same kind of pajamas for years. Comfort over sex appeal. We're talking about sleep, after all.

Me: Nothing?
Austin: Is that a question or an answer?

I bite my lip, concealing a smile as my thumbs fly across the screen.

Me: It could be the answer. If you want to get laid.
Austin: Hell yes, Miss Honey! I haven't been able to get you out of my mind.

The nickname is new. He's never called me that before, but I remember hearing him sing it in the song I loved. Warmth floods my cheeks as I imagine being the girl he wrote about. I wonder who it is? Or was? Or if it's a real person at all.

Is this the life of dating a musician? Always wondering who the songs were written for or about? And if every time he sings that song, he's thinking about that girl. I'm not jealous—I know everyone has a past—but it's a bit unsettling to know that he uses the same nickname with me that he had for someone else.

Me: What time?
Austin: NOW

I'm already in bed, reading the results of a study in *The American Journal of Surgery* for an article I'm writing—or should be writing. No offense to N.E. Anton, et al., but reading the study, titled "Mental Skills Training Effectively Minimizes Operative Performance Deterioration Under Stressful Conditions" takes a backseat to being with Austin again.

Guilt and shame rip through me. The study is research for an article I was asked to write for a professional medical journal. Things that propel my career forward shouldn't take a backseat to sex. I should *want* to tell Austin I'm not available. I should *want* to finish this study more than I want to kiss him. Because this study impacts my life. My dream. My future.

But the connection Austin and I have is something I've never felt before. And maybe after all these years of putting education and my career first, I should let whatever this is between us happen instead of analyzing it to an early death.

It's not like anything in this article is going to help me right this minute. I can go back to it at any time. I flex my right hand, curling my fingers and extending them multiple times as I stare at the scar on my finger.

You'll be able to go back to it during all the free time you're going to have when you finally face the future with your injury.

The thought of being with Austin is much more alluring than thinking about the study or the future. Following the flutter in my stomach, I decide to disregard my duty. I set my iPad on the bedside table and pick up my phone again.

Me: What's your address?
Austin: I thought you were in bed?
Me: I am, but I can get dressed and head to your place.
Austin: Um, if you're already in bed, then I'm definitely coming over there. If that's cool?
Me: Absolutely.
Austin: I just got off work. I'm gonna order some food, then I'll be over. Text me your address. Can I grab you anything?
Me: No. I'm good. Thank you, though.

I text Austin my address.
He's coming over.
This is real.
My heart pounds, and a million things roll through my mind as I pull back the covers and head to the bathroom. I'm in pajamas. Should

I get dressed? Should I change into cuter pajamas or regular clothes? I'm not exactly sure how to proceed, but I definitely want to put on makeup. I can't let him see me not put together.

As I squeeze toothpaste onto my brush, I wonder why I'm doing this. It's late. I should text him and tell him I'm too tired. The reflection looking back at me as I brush has a hint of rose in her cheeks. A glint of sparkle in her eye. I barely recognize her. I haven't seen this sparkle since well before my accident.

I spit into the sink and rinse the bowl with a quick splash of water. Then I open up the drawer to the vanity and pull out my new NARS CC cream. It gives my skin a soft, dewy finish. I follow it up with my favorite blush from the same company—Orgasm. The name makes me smile. I've been wearing it for years, because it's a gorgeous peachy pink that complements my skin tone. Sweeping it over my cheeks makes me feel sexy and confident. I can't contain the smile that lifts my lips as I place it in the drawer and grab a mascara.

Once my face is complete, I run a brush and smoothing serum through my hair. It's not perfect, but it'll do. Before I leave my bedroom, I change into different pajamas, opting for a soft, hot-pink tank top and black shorts. Cute, comfy, casual—yet still sexy.

It feels good to be wanted. I can honestly say I've never had that before. Even with the few ex-boyfriends I've had. My relationships were about status—not passion. Who my parents wanted me to be with—or set me up with—since Mama loves to play matchmaker. Before Austin, I'd only had one orgasm in my life with someone else. He gave me two the first night we were together. I've never been with someone who paid attention to what I wanted. In any previous relationship, I would have chosen to lay in bed and read *The American Journal of Surgery* 100% of the time.

I can't help but wonder if I'm making the right decision. Do I like Austin for the right reasons? Is it the allure of a musician—the sexy bad boy? No. That can't be it. He's not a bad boy. He's a sweet, sensitive soul.

Is the possibility exciting because he's completely different than the men I'm used to? Probably, but why is that a reason *not* to pursue this? That may be the number one reason to continue. I'm not attracted to the guys in my social circle. Maybe stepping outside of my so-called comfort zone is a positive thing.

The attraction is there—and it's not just physical. I feel like I've known him my entire life. Which is ridiculous. I've never felt that way with anyone, not even people I have known my entire life—except for my sisters. With Austin it's excitement and butterflies and passion. I'm hanging on every text. Just thinking about being around him again gives me an instant injection of happiness.

I'm not sure how long it will take him to eat, but I know my minutes are limited before he gets here. I swirl around my house like a reverse tornado, picking up every piece of debris laying around.

I'm scrubbing the toilet when I hear the knock. It's go time. I fly out of the room without a thought about if I remembered to flush the bubbles out. Not that Austin should care, considering the state of his bathroom.

"Hey!" I say as I swing the door open. It's hard to feel sexy after scrubbing the toilet with bleach cleaner, but I push though, straightening my back and answering with confidence. "Sorry, I'm not dressed."

"You look absolutely amazing," Austin says, scanning me before our eyes meet and lock. Once that happens, I'm gone. He's got me under his spell.

"Thanks." Accepting compliments on my appearance isn't easy for me. I'm used to being complimented on my work ethic or compassion, but Austin doesn't know me in that regard so I guess him liking me for my physical appearance is acceptable. I'm not stick thin or conventionally beautiful like my sisters—who have been featured in brochures for Commons. Evidently photo-editing software can remove Emily's tattoos, but not my love handles. I'm toned, but I have curves. Big boobs, love handles. I like myself even if I'm not the skinny, blonde, tanned, the trophy-wife kind of beauty most men in my social circle seem to want. I have no ill will toward women like that; it's just not something I've ever aspired to be.

Austin follows me to the couch and sits down.

"Should we watch a movie?" I ask, grabbing the remote from the end table and turning on the TV.

"We can do whatever you want," he answers. Then reaches out and grabs me by the waist, pulling me onto his lap. A shriek escapes my lips, elated by his intimate playfulness.

"God! I've missed you." He buries his face in my neck and starts kissing me. The thought of him missing me fills me with instant happiness.

"It's only been two days." I tilt my neck, giving him better access.

"Two days felt like an eternity when I didn't know if I'd ever hear from you."

"Sorry I didn't leave my number. I—I don't know, I was confused."

"By me?"

"By the situation. I've never gone home with someone I just met. Or someone so—"

"So—what?" Austin asks, pausing his sensual assault on my neck.

"Hot. Sexy. In demand," I finish quickly. "I didn't think someone like you would be into me."

"I bet a lot of people like me want to be in you."

"Oh my gosh." I slap him lightly.

"You set me up, babe." He tightens this grip around me and brings his lips back to my neck, kissing the spot right behind my earlobe. "Truth be told, I wouldn't have waited much longer."

My entire body stiffens. "Oh." I can't help the disappointment in my voice. This really is just a booty call for him. We had sex the night we met and I texted him at ten o'clock tonight telling him I was in bed —naked. Why would he think anything different?

Oh my gosh! Am I one of those delusional girls pretending there's something more between Austin and I?

"If I didn't hear from you by tomorrow, I was gonna beg EmVee for your number." He chuckles softly. "I've got all this band shit going on that I should be worrying about. But my thoughts were consumed with wondering why you hadn't called me yet."

I lean back so I can see his face. "Really?"

His eyes are light, clear, gentle. "Um, yeah. I told you I had a crush on you. I haven't been able to get you out of my head. You're quite a distraction."

I'm a distraction? *He's* a distraction. A gorgeous, sexy, sweetheart of a distraction, but a distraction all the same. Another reminder of how similar we really are.

The reassurance that Austin has been thinking about me is a relief. I settle onto the couch next to him and drape my legs over his lap as the tension slowly releases.

"I'm going to tell you something about myself. Are you ready?" Austin asks.

I nod. Eagerly anticipating whatever he's about to reveal. I love his honesty and how easy it is for us to be open with each other.

"I like being in a relationship. And I know you said you weren't looking for that, you don't have time, and you don't want a needy dude—"

"Well, I didn't mean—" I start to protest.

Austin continues, "I really like you, Liz. I like your drive and your vibe. I feel really comfortable around you. I'm not saying we're in a relationship or anything; I just want to let you know that I'm not planning to mess around with anyone else. I feel too connected to you to not give this a real chance." As he speaks, he slides a hand up and down my thigh. It seems more like nervous energy rather than a sexual touch, but no matter his intention, it has my blood pumping. He finally looks at me. "I sound absolutely crazy, don't I?"

"No! It doesn't sound crazy. It's flattering and reassuring. I feel the same way, Austin. I want to give this a try. I'm glad to know that I'm not the only one who likes to have clear expectations of where we are and how we move forward. It's usually frowned upon in the world of dating."

"This is why we're a great match, Liz. Honesty and transparency. I'm not here to play games."

"Not even strip poker?" I ask.

"I didn't realize strip poker was on the table. I'm in if you are. But you better be good, because you're not wearing much."

"We both have the same amount of clothing on. Shirt, pants, underwear."

"Underwear?" Austin scoffs. "Speak for yourself." Then he unzips his jeans and shows me that he's completely commando—and getting excited.

"Guess you thought I was a sure thing."

"You're the one who answered the door in a tank top and hot pants."

"These are not hot pants!" I tug the hem of my black shorts. I mean, they're pretty short, but they cover everything.

"Should we just skip poker and get naked?" Austin asks.

I nod enthusiastically.

AUSTIN SLIDES his hand up and down my back, soothing me silently as we lay in my bed, basking in the afterglow of amazing sex. With my head on his chest, I'm lulled by the beat of his heart. It's like the world stops when we're together. My mind is calm instead of racing and thinking about all the things I have to do for work and other things I'm involved in. I'm completely content to be still in this moment with him. I haven't felt content to be calm in years. Maybe ever.

"So, Maddie's birthday is coming up and my parents are having a party for her in a few weeks. It's totally casual, nothing fancy. Everyone hangs out in the yard near the pool," I ramble. I don't want the fact that it's a couple weeks away to freak him out. He says he wants to spend time with me now, but we barely know each other. We may not even be seeing each other by the time the party comes around. "Would you want to go with me?"

"Yes," Austin says without hesitation.

The knots in my stomach uncoil. "Yeah?"

"Absolutely," he repeats before squeezing me to his side. "I want to spend every free second with you, Liz."

"I want that, too," I say honestly. It doesn't seem needy or suffocating. I know Austin has his own life. I know he's not really sitting by his phone waiting for me. But I like knowing that when we do have time, we'll spend it together. It gives me something to look forward to.

A rush of relief washes over me. Maybe we can make this work. Maybe we can learn to be with each other despite the barriers. "Barriers" being my family and all the superficial reasons they won't accept him at first. They'll hate his tattoos. They'll think he has no ambition

—because they won't know how hard he works. They'll judge him for not going to college. They'll lift their noses at the neighborhood where he grew up. Petty things that have nothing to do with a person's character. Once they get to know him and see how amazing and driven he is they'll see beyond the things they originally hated about him. They'll learn to accept him for who he is.

At least that's the happily-ever-after in the utopian world in my head. My family isn't as open. They tend to only mix with people they know and feel comfortable with. That's the drawback of parents who actually believe having money makes them better than other people. I wish they were different.

Instead of being honest about not wanting to pursue relationships with the people in my social circle, I've used my career as an excuse for not falling in love. Emily already crushed their dreams for her—but she completely broke away, and I don't want to do that. Maddie won't be breaking any molds anytime soon. She's been dating a narcissistic asshole for years because he's the son of one of Daddy's closest business partners. It's a match made in upper-class heaven.

When did I stop believing in love and start accepting arranged marriages?

Maybe Austin isn't the person they would have selected for me, but I'm hoping they can get past those judgments and see him for the amazing human he is.

Chapter Seven

AUSTIN

*W*hen Liz asked me to attend her sister's birthday party with her, I hid my trepidation and gave her a *yes* without hesitation. I wanted to give the relationship a real chance, rather than limit it with my insecurities. But I'd be a complete liar if I said I haven't been sick-to-my-stomach stressed-out, thinking about it over the last couple weeks.

Things with Liz and I have been absolutely awesome. She works a ton of hours at the hospital and I've been busy planning the tour, but we've been able to meet up for dinner and drinks and sleepovers. I love spending time with her. Every time we hang out, she surprises me with something quirky and nerdy—like her knowledge of music. I didn't expect her to introduce me to new artists, but I've created a huge playlist of bands that weren't even on my radar.

There's nothing pretentious about Liz as a human being. She's down-to-earth and silly. Smart, without being awkward or a know-it-all. She's kind to everyone she comes in contact with. And she has fifty million things going on, yet handles it with ease.

We've kept our relationship fairly low-key, getting to know each other before bringing other people into our bubble. Today will be the first time I meet her family and friends. I don't want the Commons' lifestyle; I don't care what they think about me—but it doesn't mean that I'm not sweating bullets as my cab gets closer and closer to the house. I know what everyone at this party will think of me before I even step on the property.

Eastover. Of course, the Commons live in Eastover, Charlotte's wealthiest neighborhood. And I'm talking old money—not new money. The people here aren't keeping up with the Joneses—they *are* the Joneses—the families who have run Charlotte for generations. They set the tone for all the wannabes living off credit cards.

A tightness builds in my chest, knowing I'll be on defense all night. I glance down at the artwork covering every inch of my arms. I don't regret a single piece—in theory. There are a few drunken designs I'll get covered someday, but in general, I love my ink and never think about a life without it. As widely accepted as tattoos are today—they aren't accepted by the wealthy, Southern boys' club. And that's the firing squad I'm throwing myself in front of today.

The car pulls up in front of a sprawling home with an immaculate yard. I don't know anything about architecture styles, but with the white-brick, multiple two-story columns, and a third-level wrought-iron balcony, it looks like someone picked it out of New Orleans's French Quarter and dropped it on a street in Charlotte.

"You want me to drive you up?" the driver asks, eyeing the two driveways. They're not necessarily circular, more U-shaped. I can tell that you go up one side to get to the house and down the other side to leave, but I don't want him to have to navigate the pristine Beemers and Benzes parked along the route.

"No, thanks. I'll walk," I say and slide out of the car.

As I trek up the driveway that seems to go on for miles, I envision playing a show on the balcony. How ridiculously awesome would it be to fill the front lawn with friends and family, maybe do some giveaways for our fans to be there?

When I reach the door, I press the doorbell and wait. Within a few seconds, an older woman in an immaculate cream-colored dress opens the door, greeting me with a radiant smile. That smile falters slightly as she examines me. "Can I help you?"

The similarities in her facial features tell me that this woman is

Liz's mom, which throws me off my game. I wasn't expecting the lady of the house to answer the door. I thought they'd have a maid or something.

"Yeah, hi! I'm here for Maddie's party. Liz invited me."

The woman's smile falters a bit, yet she keeps it together as she speaks. "She invited you?"

"Yeah. *Yes*," I correct myself, feeling like the lead character in that Sandra Bullock movie Mom made me watch with her a million times. The one where she's trying to become a proper lady for the Miss United States contest. "As her guest. We're"—I pause—"dating."

I'm not sure if that was the right thing to say because I don't know what—or if—Liz told her family about us. I can't imagine she was going to introduce me as a friend. A girl like her doesn't bring a friend like me to one of these parties.

Her eyes widen, yet that smile stays plastered. "Of course. Austin, right?" She takes a step back. "Please come in. I'll grab Elizabeth."

"Thank you." I step into the largest home I've ever entered in my life. The foyer alone is bigger than the entire living room at Mom's house. The collared shirt I borrowed from Nelson, which was already too tight because our frames are so different, now feels suffocating.

As my eyes dart from the spotless, white marble floors, under my feet, to the obscenely ornate glass chandelier, hanging above my head, my shoulders start to tighten. There aren't many situations where I feel uncomfortable, not because I'm some guru of awesomeness, but mainly because I try not to put myself in situations where I'd feel that way.

I definitely feel awkward here and I haven't even reached the party yet.

Finally, after what seems like hours, Liz appears radiant and delicious in a flowing, sleeveless sundress made of taupe gauze-like fabric. It hugs the upper half of her body, creating a deep V on her chest before wrapping around her tiny waist. The long skirt has a huge slit that shows off her gorgeous tanned legs with each step she takes toward me. My dick presses against my shorts.

How i the world did chump like me get this lucky?

"I'm so glad you're here!"

She falls into my arms and presses her mouth on mine. Her lips part immediately, allowing our tongues to tangle softly. I'll never get tired of being greeted like that.

When I let go, Liz backs up a bit. "You look absolutely stunning," I say.

Her cheeks flush which makes my heart soar, but then she casts her gaze to the floor, and a pang of sadness hits. It's unfortunate that my compliments make her feel awkward. She's beautiful, intelligent, and has the heart of a saint. How could her previous boyfriends not make her feel like a goddess every day? How could they say they loved her or wanted to be with her without ever truly appreciating her?

"Thank you."

"I thought it was a pool party," I say tentatively. I'm not trying to make her feel bad, but she's standing before me in a gorgeous dress and I'm in black board shorts and a black-and-white-striped, collared shirt.

"Are you wearing—" She scans my outfit. "You look great. I didn't even realize those were swim trunks."

Her approval puts me at ease. "Cool."

"I can't tell you how happy I am to have you here. I've known most of these people for years, yet I'm on edge around them. When Mama said you were here, a sense of calmness came over me. Thank you."

"I'm here for you, babe. I like being your calm. I appreciate that you trust me enough to let me be that for you."

"Ready?" she asks, squeezing my hand.

"Let's do this." I create a half circle with my arm and she loops hers through.

Liz guides me through the magnificent house, to the back door, which leads to a humongous, meticulously landscaped yard, complete with a massive in-ground pool. This yard could be a city park.

When Liz and I walk out together, arm-in-arm, every head turns. Don't get me wrong, I knew that would happen, because people always look when a new person enters a party. And it's hosted by the Commons, so it makes total sense that partygoers would turn to see who Liz enters with.

I also knew that there would be staring—and not in the good way like when people stare at me while I'm on stage. I honestly don't expect one single person here to recognize me from my band. They just know that I am an extremely tatted-up dude who doesn't seem to belong.

There's staring, then there are side-mouthed conversations while keeping their gazes on Liz and I. Maybe I'm overreacting, letting social anxiety get the best of me. I'm projecting my own insecurity onto them and I need to stop.

"Do you mind if we hit up Maddie first?" I say in Liz's ear. "I want to say Happy Birthday before this party gets crazy."

Liz laughs. "Of course!"

We cross the yard until we're standing near the pool in a group gathered around Maddie. All eyes are on the birthday girl as she tells a story, confirming the things Liz has already told me about her sister— the life of the party—the socialite. She's very comfortable in the spotlight.

"Austin! I'm so glad you made it!" Maddie stops her story to give me a hug. I wasn't expecting that kind of greeting since I've never met her before. I honestly didn't know what she thought about me. Maybe this party won't be as bad as I thought.

"Absolutely. Happy Birthday!" I say when she releases me.

"Who's this?" says a guy in a seersucker suit. No joke. That super-douchey light blue-and-white pinstripe pattern that only rich bros think is cool. I often wonder if guys who wear it do it as a joke—like, they know how lame it is, and that's why they do it. Nope.

"This is Austin! He's from that band Emily took us to see a few weeks back. Remember I told you about him?"

I hold my hand out to shake his, but he just stares at it. In my circle of friends, I'd be flattered at how hard he's studying the ink artwork that covers it, but this dude is inspecting it like I rubbed my palm with rat crap before extending it to him.

Instead of giving him another second of my time, I drop my hand and turn back to Maddie. "This is a beautiful party. Thanks so much for having me."

Maddie ignores her rude male friend and addresses me again. "Liz said that you're playing the Atlanta Music Fest. That's so exciting, Austin!"

Knowing that my girl has been talking to her family about me fills my heart with pride. Knowing that she's been telling her family about me shows me that she really is all in for our relationship. "Yeah, it's our first big festival. We're super-stoked about it."

"Austin's band has that song *Open Your Heart* on the radio. I know some of you guys have heard it."

"*Two* songs on the radio," Liz chimes in, glancing at me with a proud smile.

I appreciate her building me up, but insecurity nags at me. They've brought up all of my major musical accomplishments within the first minute just to get the people in this group interested in me. It feels icky, like when I'm talking to the suits from a record label.

Almost as if they have to prove that I deserve to be here. Just existing as a human being doesn't cut it for this party.

"We're very grateful for our recent success. The satellite-radio listeners rally hard core for us." Sweat rolls down my back, which makes me realize I'm not as at ease as I thought I was. I survey the yard, looking for the closest exit or safe spot. Oh look! There's a bar near the door out.

"Any money to be made in music, Austin? All I hear is how hard it is to make a living doing that. There's quite a few 'starving' artists in the industry, right?" seersucker suit asks. I still don't know his name, nor do I care.

"I guess it's like any industry—if you're good at it, work your ass off, and have a business plan, you can make it work."

"A business plan? You have a business plan?" he asks.

Fuck me for adding that part about a business plan just to get this douchebag to realize that I'm not stupid, despite my lack of a diploma from some overpriced university. I don't owe him any kind of explanation.

And fuck me twice for sweating while answering his question. Why do I let him get to me?

"Anyone in business for themselves should have some sort of plan, wouldn't you agree?"

"I do. I'd be interested to hear what you found from your competitive analysis and what kind of marketing strategies you derived to distinguish yourself from your competitors in the industry. Knowing that is important for success, wouldn't you agree?"

"Austin!" A familiar voice calls from behind me. Emily runs up and grabs my hand, pulling me away from the group—and Liz.

"Why do you have to be so rude, Trent?" Maddie says. "You're going to ruin my party treating guests like that."

"Don't you dare try to blame me, Madeline. You're the one who allowed someone like him to attend your precious party. If it's ruined, it's your fault," Seersucker Suit says in a sharp tone, loud enough for all to hear.

Wow. Way to embarrass the woman of the hour.

"How's your fellowship going, Liz?" I hear another person in the group ask as Emily whisks me farther away.

"I saved you!" Emily says once we're away from the group.

"I could've held my own, Em. I actually do have a business plan—and I understand it, too." Technically, I do have a business plan, thanks to the business class I was on my way to the night I found Liz in the accident. I'm not saying I follow the plan to a tee, but we have one.

"No, you couldn't," she says and quickly follows up with, "and I don't mean that as an insult to you. Even if you answered with something intelligent, Trent would keep coming at you until he slammed you. That's what he does when he feels challenged by someone he doesn't feel is on his level."

"I wasn't challenging—" I begin to protest.

"You know that. I know that. But we're talking about the poster child for white privilege. He wants to embarrass you to put you in your place," she says, using air quotes. "It's not all of them, believe me. Trent is just a special breed of douche."

I glance back at the group, where Liz listens and nods with a polite smile plastered on her lips. "Is Maddie dating him?"

"Unfortunately. And he treats everyone like that. He'll even challenge Daddy."

"Yikes."

"Yeah. I don't know how Maddie even puts up with him. He treats her like crap, too."

Conversations with Emily are as different as night and day than those with Liz. Em's mouth runs a mile a minute with zero filter.

"So what's the lure? Why stay with him? She seems like she has a bright personality."

"His father is the owner of Anderson Architecture, the company that designs all of Daddy's stores. It's an exclusive contract."

"Ahhhh! The exclusive contract," I joke. I guess that's a wealthy businessman's version of pissing on something to mark their territory.

"Come on, let's go get drinks. It'll make this party bearable."

A drink is exactly what I need to loosen up a bit. I follow Emily toward a bar set up near the entrance to the house.

"Two Jack and Cokes, please," she orders for us. "Oh, and Maria, can you put them in pint glasses, please?"

The bartender nods and grabs two glasses from under the bar. "Of course, Miss Emily."

"Did Hugo ever call to schedule his appointment? I'm stoked to do that portrait piece on him."

"He did," Maria says as she pours whiskey into one glass. "But he said you have a long wait list."

"Oh shit! Yeah, I do. I'll tell Syd to put him on my list of people who get called when a spot opens in my schedule—like if someone cancels or I decide to come in on a day off."

"Thank you so much. He's gonna love to hear that. The loss has hit him hard."

"I know." Emily reaches over the bar and places her hand over Maria's. "I've been thinking about both of you."

Maria finishes the drinks and hooks a lime to each rim.

"Hugo is Maria's husband," Emily explains as we walk away from the bar. "His mom passed away a few weeks ago after a long battle with breast cancer. He's devastated."

"That sucks."

"Yeah. I'm gonna do a portrait for him at like, one quarter of what I'd normally charge for a piece like that. They don't have the money, and I know it would help him so much in his healing."

"That's awesome, Em."

"Life is about being good to others, right? Not money."

I raise my glass to clink with hers. "Cheers to that."

It's ironic because we're standing in a massive backyard, drinking freely from an open bar, at a party put on to impress wealthy people.

"Though, I gotta admit, having money can help," Emily continues. "Hugo and Maria have been part of our family for years. She's part of the housekeeping team and he works with our landscaper, Erik. When Hugo's mom got sick, she didn't have insurance and they couldn't afford her treatments. Liz jumped into action. She found them an oncologist, started a non-profit, put together a silent auction fundraiser. I still can't believe she did all that with everything she had going on at the hospital. But that's Liz."

Nothing about that story surprises me. Liz is an overachiever with a heart of gold—and she never would have told me she did all that unless it came up somehow.

As I sip my drink, I glance over at Liz. She's moved to a different circle, this one filled with people in a much older age range than the other group. Her mother stands next to her, confident and regal. They look so much alike.

Something churns in the pit of my stomach. Is this Liz's future? Pool parties where no one swims and douchebags who actively try to put down everyone they speak with? Plastic smiles to pretend she cares about what the person she's speaking with has to say? Faking who she really is and what she wants out of life because her peers won't understand a person who wants to help others who can't afford quality care rather than be the premier surgeon in Charlotte?

Is this my future if we stay together? Heads turning because my body is covered in tattoos rather than seersucker suits? Liz ticking off my accomplishments to prove my career has value to people I don't give two shits about impressing? Sneaking off with Emily because having her as an ally makes being around these people tolerable?

The first pint of Jack and Coke goes down way too easily as I think about what a super-shitty boyfriend I'm being right now. I'm being just as judgmental as these people are.

"I'm surprised you're here," I say to Emily.

"Oh, I'm not staying long! I'm just making an appearance to down enough free drinks to piss off my parents. But it's Maddie's twenty-fifth and she made me feel guilty when I said I wasn't going to come."

"Are you two close?"

Emily snorts, which causes heads to turn our way. She raises her glass and curtsies. "No."

It's funny, because Emily and Maddie are very similar personality-wise. Emily is just the tatted goth version. But I have a feeling she'd think that assessment was an insult, so I keep my mouth shut.

"The dynamic has changed over the years." She pauses when a waiter appears next to us with two brand new pints of Jack and Coke. I set my empty glass on the tray and take the new drink. Looks like Maria has Emily completely hooked up. "Maddie and Liz are two years apart, so they used to be closer. They've grown apart recently, and Liz and I have gotten closer. I blame you for that."

"You're welcome," I say.

Emily pulls her long mane of silver hair over one shoulder. "It's nice to have a relationship with her. Liz has been out in medical-land for so long. She hasn't had much time for any of us. I get it, believe me."

"She works her ass off."

"Absolutely, but it was also her way of getting away from all this shit, ya know? I know she hates it. I can tell." She gestures around the yard, without a care in the world of who sees her. "I left the family with a bang. She left with a whisper."

She's paraphrasing *The Hollow Men*, one of my favorite poems by T.S. Eliot, and I'm glad she changed the word "whimper' to whisper, because Liz does not whimper. My girl is rock solid.

"So this isn't her thing?" I ask, looking at her over the rim of my glass.

"She can play the part. I bet it's like you when you're on stage. Is that your natural habitat? No, but you put on a realistic performance."

I nod. The similarities hadn't crossed my mind. Why is it so easy to see the things that will break people apart rather than the things that will bring us together?

"It just sucks because she's gonna be around people like this all the time. That's the field she chose. I hate to stereotype, because we both know not all people fit into any one mold, but damn, there are a lot of pretentious asses in her field. She just doesn't fit in."

"Hey!" Liz touches my arm.

"Hey!"

She looks between Emily and I as if watching a tennis game, even though we're both still. "Can I grab you for a minute; I want to introduce you to my dad."

My stomach tightens. Meeting Harris Commons is the absolute last thing I want to do tonight. I'd rather create a tattoo on my arm with cigarette burns.

"You're gonna introduce Austin as your boyfriend here? At Maddie's party?" Emily asks. "Don't you think that's a bit rude?"

Liz pulls her shoulders back. "Why would it be rude to introduce Austin here? I thought it would be rude to invite him and not introduce him at all."

"Because this is Daddy's favorite way to brag. Gathering his snobby friends, puffing up his chest as he moves about the grounds of his beautiful home, pretending to have a perfect life and family."

I scoff at the last example. Perfect family, my ass. They're one event away from a major blow up. What if my being here is that event? I don't know if I can take that stress.

"So what? I still want Austin to meet him."

"Austin, are you ready to be grilled?" She lowers her voice in an attempt to sound like her father. "What do you do? Oh, a musician? Looks like we have another creative. Not much money in a field like that, is there? You must have another job, yes? At The Usual Market, you say? Well, isn't that blue-collar. What do your parents do? Oh, well. How did you and Elizabeth meet? Did you know that she graduated at the very top of her class at Columbia? You know Columbia, right? It's one of the best medical schools in the country. Where did you go to university?"

"You can stop now," Liz says through clenched teeth.

"Plus," Emily continues. "Don't you think Austin already feels out of place? You couldn't give him the heads up as to how to dress for this?"

My hands fly to the hem of the borrowed polo. Liz said I looked fine.

"His outfit is completely acceptable," Liz says quietly, glaring at her sister.

"Yeah, for a normal human's pool party! Did you tell him that this is a garden party? And—even though we all hang out by the pool—no one actually swims?" Emily gestures toward the water where many are gathered around, but no one is actually in. No one here, except me, is wearing anything that would be deemed swimwear.

"Please stop," I say, trying to quell the anger building up between the sisters. Liz's bottom lip is quivering as if she's about to lose her shit. And I know that's not something she wants anyone to see. "Should I jump in and get this pool party rolling?"

"No!" Both girls cry in unison.

I had no intention of jumping in the pool. I just wanted to get the two sisters to stop arguing.

"Elizabeth! There you are." Mrs. Commons stops next to Liz. "Dr. Crowder and his wife just arrived. Come say hello."

Dr. Crowder's name rings familiar as Liz's mentor at the hospital. The fact that he was invited to Maddie's birthday party seems a little odd, but then again, maybe the families are longtime friends. I have no clue.

Liz hesitates, but her mother won't allow that. "Emily will be happy to keep Austin busy for a few more minutes, right?"

Her wording strikes a chord. When she says "a few more minutes" it seems like she's noticed that Liz and I haven't spent a lot of time together and that's the way she wants to keep it.

Emily smiles sweetly. "Of course, Mama."

"Cut it out," Mrs. Commons says in a clipped voice. "You and I have a few things to discuss later."

Emily rolls her eyes and lifts her drink to her lips. Without waiting for Liz to answer, Mrs. Commons whisks her away.

"Welcome to the family," Emily quips without a smile.

I'm trying not to be the needy guy who gets pissed that Liz and I have barely spent any time together at the party she invited me to, but it gets even more difficult with each passing minute. Thankfully, I have

Emily to talk to. This isn't an environment where I feel comfortable enough to strike up a conversation with any random person. Though Emily mentioned that Trent was a special kind of douche, I'm fairly certain there are more guys like him, who get off on trying to make people feel badly about their lives.

I'm not ashamed in the least, but I also don't feel like spending the entire evening on defense with people who will never understand my way of thinking. They don't want to. They can only see things from their own perspective.

Emily and I spend the entire evening shooting the shit about people we know and catching up on things going on in our respective careers. I'm not the only one with exciting things happening. Emily is one of the most requested tattoo artists in Charlotte. People come in from all over to be tattooed by her. Which is an amazing accomplishment for as young as she is. Speaks volumes about the quality of her work.

"This party is lame," I tell Emily. "I was in NYC, partying with the guys from Scared Bunny on my twenty-fifth."

"Oh, look at you, Mr. Big Stuff! Is the ickiness infiltrating your pores, making you feel the need to brag about who you know and where you've been?"

"Fuck off."

"I was kidding!"

"I know, but there was some truth in it and I'm pissed at myself."

"You need to cleanse your chakras."

I don't know what the hell she's talking about. I'm not a very new-age, spiritual guy. "Will more Jack Daniels do that?"

"Dude! You can't get sloppy drunk. My parents will hate you."

Our eyes meet and we both bust out laughing. There is no doubt in either of our minds that her parents hate me already.

It's never a good thing when I start keeping track of time based on how many drinks I've consumed rather than numbers on a clock. *How long have you been here? I don't know, about four Jack and Cokes?*

"You're so different than your family, Em. How the hell did you come from this?" I open my arms and spin around. Which is not the best decision for someone who's downed four pint glasses of Jack Daniels and Coke.

"I don't even know. We should get out of here. Wanna share a ride?"

"Yeah," I answer without thinking. "Drinks at The Market?"

"I'm down," she says. "Let me run in and get my bag."

Emily and I weave through groups of people who stare at us with every step we take. I don't see myself as that different, but I guess when people look at me, with almost every inch of visible skin from the neck down covered in tattoos, they get nervous. They see something they don't understand, so they condemn it.

When I swing open one of the French doors to allow Emily to enter the house first, Liz is there.

"Hey!" she says with a smile. Her eyes dart between Emily and me, causing her smile to falter. "Are you leaving?" Her voice rings in my ears like a song. The song I wrote about two people who would never work out because they come from completely different backgrounds has never rung as true as it has tonight.

"Does it matter?"

"Well, yeah. I mean, were you going to tell me? Say goodbye?"

"I wasn't sure where you were. You kinda ditched me."

"Ditched you? We were in the middle of a conversation and then you ran off with Emily."

"Remember the night we met, Liz? At my house when my friends were yelling things and being complete assholes? I didn't leave you alone to chat with them because I didn't want to put you in a situation that I knew would make you uncomfortable. You may think I have nerves of steel, but I don't. I came here tonight because I was excited that you wanted me to meet your family and friends. I thought that I meant something to you."

Liz's eyes are wide, as if surprised. "That's exactly why I invited you." She reaches out to touch my arm, but I back away.

"And yet, you dropped me right into an uncomfortable situation. You and Maddie had to come out, guns blazing, right? Bragging about my accomplishments just so your friends thought I had worth. Am I not good enough without a few songs on the radio, Liz?"

"You know that's not—"

Emily cuts Liz off. "Hey guys, let's, uh, take this somewhere else." Then she presses two palms into Liz's back and shoves her inside the house.

I glance over my shoulder, realizing that we've created a commotion. Most heads are turned toward us, staring and whispering. *Get it together, Austin. You're embarrassing Liz.*

When I look at my girl, her eyes are glassy, as if tears are seconds away from spilling over her cheeks. She's wringing her hands in front of her. "Can we please go somewhere to talk?"

I nod, forgetting Emily is even there, and follow Liz as she leads me through the house and up a massive, ornate, winding staircase. Every step reminds me of how much I don't belong here—and don't want to belong here.

Who needs a staircase like this? Who needs a house like this? The overly ornamental marble fireplace; gaudy mahogany everything; wrought-iron fixtures jutting out of the walls for no reason; gilded mirrors taller than my six-foot-three frame around every corner.

When we get to the top of the stairs, a painting of a woman and little girl catches my eye. There is no doubt the woman is Cookie Commons about twenty to twenty-five years younger. There's only one girl in the picture in a household of three girls, so I can only conclude that it's their firstborn.

"Is that—?" I point to the wall.

"Shut up." Liz dismisses me without even looking at the artwork I'm pointing to. I close my mouth. There's no need to point out that they have a custom oil painting of themselves on the wall of their home when we're in the middle of a scuffle.

Liz opens the door to the right of the painting. As soon as she turns on the light I'm flooded by her—or what used to be her. The familiar smell of amber and vanilla, Liz's signature scent, floods my senses and tells me she's been wearing the same perfume or body lotion since high school. The thought makes me smile. It's very much like her to find something she likes and stick with it, even as trends come and go. She's not swayed by the masses.

Built-in shelves, bursting with books, span an entire wall. A plush, purple cushion lines the bench of a beautiful bay window. I imagine Liz sitting there, reading, studying, looking out at the stars, wondering when her life would be her own. The queen bed has an ornate fabric headboard, with bronze nailhead trim around the top, and is draped with a purple comforter.

The walk to her room has given me the time I needed to calm down. If Emily hadn't interrupted us, I may have lashed out and said something I couldn't take back. I'm usually an easygoing drunk, but I allowed the alcohol to intensify an already anxious situation for me. Then I ran my mouth and projected my insecurity onto Liz. Never a good combination.

Liz sits on the bed and looks up at me. "I'm sorry."

"I am too," I say, taking a seat next to her. "I didn't mean to—I—" I grab my hair with both fists and take a deep breath. *Just spit it out, tough guy.* "I felt really insecure out there, Liz. And that's not your fault, it's mine, but—"

"It *is* my fault. I'm sorry I put you in that situation. I invited you because I'm proud of you—of us. I couldn't wait to introduce you to my family and friends." She lifts her eyes to mine, but drops them quickly. "But then we got here and I realized that this was not the right situation to bring you into. I should have introduced you to my parents alone, without others around. Not because I'm ashamed of you," she explains quickly, "but because I should have known how uncomfortable it would be. I should have known that my parents would be taken off-guard when they saw you and would try to compensate that by being rude to you. I'd like to believe my friends would be kind, but sometimes I give them too much credit."

"I get it."

"And then I got jealous because you were hanging out with Emily all night." She scratches a pull in the duvet, an imperfection I missed at first glance. When we look deeper into what we think is perfection, the flaws become visible, those unique imperfections that make us human.

"I wasn't trying to make you jealous at all. I understood that there were people you needed to talk to and at first it was cool because I had Emily there. But as the night went on, and I had more drinks, I admit,

I got upset. I was like 'Hey! I'll just be over here waiting for you to make me part of your life.'"

"It was never my intention to make you feel that way. I'm sorry. I—maybe that's why we'll never work, Austin. We're too different. You and Emily have so much more in common. She's—"

I grab her hands and squeeze them in mine. "I don't want to be with Emily. I want to be with you."

"Why?"

"Why?" I chuckle. "Because you're hot as hell."

She cocks her head and huffs. She doesn't believe me. Which is absolutely tragic.

"We complement each other," I continue. "We're both career-driven, compassionate, introverted, dorks."

My words bring a smile to Liz's lips. "You're the furthest thing from a dork."

"You're only saying that because you know me now. If you would've known teenage me, you'd totally agree."

"I guess I see you as this wild, bold, extroverted personality."

My head swivels right and left, looking for an imaginary bold, wild, extroverted person behind me. "Who? Me? Where the hell did you get that impression?"

"Every time I'm with you. You exude an easy confidence." She reaches up and flattens my collar.

Was my collar popped out there? Please tell me my collar was not popped while I was around all those Chads.

I grab her hand and squeeze it. "One more reason I like being with you. You see me as the person I hope to be someday."

"You already are that person."

"Sometimes I think so and then I think about a night like tonight, where I didn't feel confident at all. I let my insecurity get the best of me. Instead of being myself and proud of who I am, I ran away and hung out where it was comfortable."

"I get it. I've been really lost recently."

"I can tell."

"Really?"

"Don't get me wrong, babe. You're still confident, I just sense that you're low. Wanna talk about it?"

Liz closes her eyes, then she drops her head in her hands. "I—geez —I honestly don't think I'll ever be able operate again. I'm going to have to quit the surgical program and start over. And I can't deal with it right now."

Jesus. That was not what I expected to come out of her mouth.

I throw my arms around her, even though I'm completely taken aback. I knew Liz had been going to physical therapy to get her hand strong enough to operate after the accident, but I didn't realize her injury was that bad. I didn't realize she's been dealing with the weight of losing her entire career.

"I'm sorry, babe. What can I do?" I say as I squeeze her harder, trying to transfer my energy to her.

"I haven't told anyone, Austin. I'm scared. If I'm not a surgeon, what am I? What do I do from here?"

"What do you want to do?"

Liz is silent. And I realize it's probably an insensitive question. She's on the verge of losing her career, and I'm throwing back the question she's probably been stressing over since she realized her injury was career-ending. But I've found that it helps when someone else says it. It makes the brain recalibrate.

"If you couldn't be a surgeon, what would you do?"

"Ever since I was a kid, I wanted to help people. I wanted to be a teacher, a firefighter, a doctor. But sometimes I don't feel like I'm making a difference in the bigger picture with the path I chose. Doing that is almost impossible in this country."

My heart swells, because we're becoming closer than I ever imagined we would. Sure, I dreamed that we would have this kind of relationship, but I didn't expect it. "What do you mean?"

"Healthcare is big business in America," she says. "There's a lot of money in making people sick and keeping people sick."

"Go on."

Her body tenses, but she continues, "We live in a country of convenience. We live in a country that doesn't regulate food like they should. It makes people sick. It makes them obese. It causes disease. So who do they need? Doctors. And medication. Do you think the people who profit off our unhealthy society are really going to try to stop it? Nope. It's about a paycheck. It's actually about millions of paychecks. Imagine how many people would be out of jobs if we had a healthier country.

"Can you really say you're a doctor who cares about your patients if you aren't actively and loudly seeking regulations on what goes into food and looking for ways to make people healthier?"

"Dang. That doesn't sound like anything any doctor I've ever met would say."

She rubs the crown of her head with her fingers. "Yeah, I know."

"You're right, though." I use the tip of my forefinger to draw invisible stars on her palm. "Disease will never go away. Too much money to be made. Too many people with jobs in that field. I mean, back in the day, it was revered to find cures or vaccinations. Now it's like 'Shhh! We can't tell anyone about that.'"

She laughs humorlessly. "Right? If someone came up with a cure for cancer, think of how many people would lose their jobs."

"Not just in the healthcare industry either. What about all the charities that make money off sickness?" I add.

"I am aware." She tucks a lock of hair behind her ear.

"Say it, Liz."

"Say what?"

"You totally want to blast a charity right now. I can see it."

"As in any industry, there are charities that take advantage of people. I, personally, don't believe the president of a nonprofit should make hundreds of thousands of dollars per year. I question their motives. Are they in it for the cause or the paycheck? I'm not against someone wanting to make money. But if you want six and seven-figure salaries, you should be the president of a for-profit company."

"I get it, totally. And I love how passionate you are about it. About justice. About doing things for the right reasons. About not taking advantage of people. It's beautiful."

She looks toward the window, avoiding my eyes. "Strength is beautiful. People who know what they want to do. People who start a path and finish it." Almost instantly, the fire is gone. I've hit a nerve, and now I have to figure out the real reason so I can help her.

"Why are you so hard on yourself? It was an accident. It wasn't your fault."

"It *was* my fault. *I* was driving. *I* lost control. *I* crashed my car and ruined my hand. *I* destroyed my career."

"Okay, fine. If you want to get super-technical, yes, it was your fault in the sense of you were driving. But you didn't do it on purpose. You didn't think, 'Hey, I should fuck up my hand so I can't be a surgeon anymore.' It was an accident."

"You know what's sad, Austin?" she asks, then automatically continues, "Sometimes I feel relief because it gave me an out."

"An out?"

She shrugs. "I don't know. I mean, I've been so focused on surgery, but the more I saw people struggling to afford even basic care, the more I wanted to help *them*. Healthcare isn't just for the rich. For some reason we vilify people who can't afford care. It's sad. And it's not the attitude about people that I want to have, despite—" She closes her eyes and shakes her head.

It's almost as if a lightbulb pops up over my head.

At first, I questioned my attraction to Liz—the connection was palpable—but I didn't understand the energy that brought us together because I didn't really know her yet. But now I do. I see her beautiful heart—and I finally see her internal struggle.

This injury, and the loss of her career as a surgeon is hard on her, of course, but the deeper struggle is that she doesn't want to disappoint her parents. Not only that, but her fundamental feelings about healthcare go against her parents' values. She's having trouble breaking free from the people who gave her the means to her career.

I wrap my arms around her and bring her into my chest. "It's okay to admit that you want something different than what your parents want for you," I say before placing my lips on her head. "You'll never be happy until you take the path that's in your heart. The quicker you break free from the expectations of others, the quicker you'll feel good about the one you chose yourself."

Her body shakes against mine, silently sobbing and nodding. I rock her gently, letting her know that I'll hold her for as long as she needs. I'm here for her through whatever comes next.

After a minute, she leans back and I loosen my grip. She tucks a leg under her, then grabs my hands, placing them in her lap.

"Admitting is the first step." She sniffs.

"Absolutely. Now we can plan, right? How can you help people in the way you'd feel good about? You're already a doctor. Can't you just open an office or something?"

"I wish it were that easy." She lets go of one hand to wipe her cheek. "I still have to complete a residency. I've been in surgery for three years. Changing my specialty means I start over. Or at least from year two. I think the first would count toward a family-medicine residency. I'll have to check."

"Okay. So that's your plan?"

"Yeah. That's my plan," she says quietly.

"I'm sorry. I didn't mean to sound so flippant. I know it hurts, Liz. All those years—"

"Wasted," she finishes.

"No. Not wasted. You gained amazing experience. You'll be able to take that into helping patients in the future. What if someone needs care after surgery? You know what to do. Maybe one of those procedure things you know how to do."

She laughs, but I know it's *with* me, not *at* me. I have no clue what she's talking about when she starts going off about central lines and PV catheters and bronchoscopies. All that shit is a foreign language to me, but I love listening because she's passionate about her work.

Liz slides her palm across my cheek. "Thank you."

"I see you, Liz. I see your beautiful soul. I see the way you treat others and the love you have for your career. You're going to accomplish amazing things, no matter how it works out." She closes her eyes as I speak, so I lean over and kiss her eyelids. "It *will* work out."

When she opens her eyes, they're glassy with tears. "How did I get so lucky to find you, Austin?"

"The universe brought us together for a reason, babe. I really believe that. There are no coincidences. We never would have met if it weren't meant to be."

"Is it weird to feel this much for you so quickly? Because no one else has ever made me feel as special as you make me feel."

"You're asking the wrong guy. I'm so completely smitten with you it scares me."

"I'm sorry I put you in an awkward situation tonight, but I'm glad we can work through it. Thank you for forgiving me."

"You know how you can make it up to me?" I ask.

"How?"

I pat the bed and lift my eyebrows suggestively. She cocks her head in disbelief.

"Really? Here? Now?"

"I can't help it," I admit sheepishly. "I love your mind. And your heart. And the fact that we can talk about all this stuff like adults. It got me all excited." I watch Liz's gaze drop to my crotch, where my dick is practically busting out of my swim trunks, and smile. "Then my mind veered off into how sexy you are and how much you turn me on. I have a short attention span."

"I've never had sex in this bed," she says quietly.

Our eyes meet. Anticipation hangs thick in the air, making my heart beat faster. I raise my eyebrows.

Liz breaks the eye contact first, glancing at the door. "The party is still going. All those people are—"

"Outside." I drop to my knees in front of her and slide my hands up the outside of her thighs. "Not in here."

She bites her bottom lip and grabs the hem of her dress, pulling it up to reveal her long, tanned legs, which fall open easily. I can't keep the smile off my face when I realize she's not wearing any underwear. I slide my hands under her ass and pull her closer to my mouth.

She immediately responds with a moan, which makes me go all-in, full force. Though, I'd love to push into her and feel her tight pussy squeezing my cock, I want this to be about her—her pleasure, her release. We can do it all later, when we aren't in her parent's house.

"Just lie back and relax, baby. I got you."

AFTER WE'VE both had a few minutes to pull ourselves together, we join hands and head down the spiral staircase. I feel like king of the world. Or maybe the scoundrel who stole the king's girl. Either way, I'm on cloud nine.

The discomfort of the situation and the ability to talk through it gave me confidence in our relationship. I feel completely bonded to Liz. Nothing can get in the way. Nothing will tear us apart.

Except maybe the couple staring coldly at us from the bottom of the stairs. Though I haven't met him yet, I've seen Harris Commons on TV and in the local news enough to know who he is. He's one of the most influential people in Charlotte, seemingly involved in everything.

"Daddy!" Liz says with excitement. Maybe she doesn't see the look of absolute disgust in her parents' eyes as we descend the stairs. Or maybe I'm just being paranoid. "This is Austin."

Harris seems relatively fine, but Cookie is glaring at me. If looks could kill, I would have never been born.

"Nice to finally meet you, Austin," Harris says.

Well, that wasn't so bad.

"What were you doing upstairs? The party is outside," Harris asks.

"I needed a break from the party, so I was showing Austin around the house."

"We don't need people roaming around in places where no one is around. Last time that happened your grandmother's pearls went missing." Cookie glances at me.

Ahhh! There it is! The insulting insinuation that I'm a thief. I expected nothing less from the Commons family. *Thanks, Cookie.*

"Mom!" Liz snaps. She grabs my hand and squeezes it tightly.

"This is never going to work. End it now," Cookie says in a hushed tone. Instead of answering, Liz shakes her head and tugs me past her parents.

When I first met Liz, I assumed she had a kick-ass mom because I couldn't believe a guy like Harris Commons could raise human beings as awesome as her and her sisters. One night around her just proved that my initial assumption was completely wrong.

Cookie Commons is a complete and total bee-yotch.

Chapter Eight

LIZ

Because my schedule at the hospital has been absolutely crazy over the last few weeks, I had to cancel a few physical therapy appointments. I didn't think much of it because I know the therapy isn't doing any good, but then had a checkup with Dr. Sharma, the surgeon who operated on my hand, and he railed me for missing appointments. Then he ordered x-rays to see how I'm healing. I made sure to schedule an appointment as soon as I could. I've got to get my head on straight. The last thing I need is Dr. Sharma reporting to Dr. Crowder that I'm not doing what I need to do to rehab my hand.

When I arrive at Vikram Patel's office, I'm filled with anxiety. I know he and Dr. Sharma have already had a chance to go over my x-rays before today's appointment, and I feel like I'm about to be exposed as a fraud.

"When am I going to be able to do the good stuff?" I ask before Vik starts leading me through exercises that aren't doing me any good.

His warm, brown eyes flicker and a small smile creeps across his lips. "The good stuff?"

I press my lips together to hold back my own smile. I'm not interested in Vik, but it doesn't mean I'm immune to his charm.

Any woman in her right mind would be falling at Vik's feet. Which is probably why my parents strongly suggested Vik over Cindy, the sweet, portly, Paula Dean look-a-like who works in the same practice. He is exactly the type of man they want me to fall in love with. From his fashionably cut, perfectly gelled, dark hair, to his smooth, brown skin, right down to the five o' clock shadow dusting his upper lip and jawline, he's the complete package.

There's also the insignificant detail that before he moved to the States, he was a former Mr. India contestant. He didn't win that particular contest, but he quickly won the hearts of the ladies at the hospital. I'd heard about him long before I met him.

Too bad my parents don't understand cultural differences and the fact that no matter how many non-Indian chicks he dates to get it out of his system, he's going to marry an Indian girl someday. That's not me being stereotypical. Vik told me that himself.

Maybe they do understand and they don't care. Anything to get me away from Austin.

"Strengthening my grip? Keeping a steady hand during intricate procedures?"

Vik's long pause is enough to tell me what's coming next. When he speaks, his voice is low, "I spoke with Dr. Sharma about the x-rays you had last week. Everything is healing well, Liz, but as you knew, with an injury like this you may never have full use of your hand. At least not for things like operating."

Tears spring to my eyes even though he's not telling me anything I don't already know. It's been months and it's physically impossible for me to hold a scalpel strongly enough or still enough to make precision cuts.

Someone else knows my dirty secret. I can't prolong the inevitable anymore. I'll never be able to go back to surgery.

How will I face my peers? My family? My friends? Being a surgeon is who I am.

"I'm sorry, Liz." Vik places his hand over mine. "Look, that's the worst-case scenario. We can keep working on it." He's got a great bedside manner, so gentle when giving people bad news. I can't imagine him getting angry or raising his voice.

"It's okay," I say after a slight pause to compose myself. I'll never let any of my colleagues see me cry. There's no place for weakness, even in the face of soul-crushing news.

"Do you want to continue today?"

I shake my head. "No. It's not really necessary anymore is it?"

Vik sighs. "My next appointment isn't until two. Wanna grab a bite next door?"

It's almost noon, and I really should eat before I get back to the hospital. I have a few procedures today and patients to check in on. Once I get there I won't get a break.

"We can go to Grabbagreen," he says in a singsong voice as he records his notes from our session into his tablet. "I know you love that place."

Vik trying to cheer me up, by offering to go to my favorite cafe near his office, is seriously the cutest thing, though I long to be with Austin.

"Do you want to go somewhere else?" I ask, grabbing my pocket-book and slinging it over my shoulder.

Vik tosses his tablet onto his desk. After he stands, he takes a moment to brush over creases crinkling his khaki pants near the upper thigh. "No. I need all the green I can consume after the weekend I had." He holds the door open for me.

"Spill," I say glancing over my shoulder.

"You first," he counters.

"Dating a new guy. Avoiding my parents. Ya know, just another random Tuesday."

"Avoiding your parents?" Vik asks. "Why?"

"They took their most recent interference in my life a bit too far. Avoiding them is the way I choose to handle the issue. It's the best way." It's been over a month since Maddie's birthday party and I still haven't forgiven them for being so rude to Austin.

"Is it?" Vik asks.

"If you knew my parents, you wouldn't even ask me that."

Vik laughs. "I know enough about them to understand why you'd want to avoid them."

My jaw hits the floor. No one except Austin has ever had the balls to say anything like that to my face about my parents. People are scared that I'll go running back and tell them what was said. Which could literally ruin someone's life. My father can be a ruthless man.

"Despite that," Vik continues, "I still don't think avoidance is the way to handle anything. You should confront the issue."

"Easier said than done."

"Never said it would be easy."

"They don't approve of Austin, and they never will," I tell Vik as we walk down a set of stairs.

"Because he's a musician?" Vik asks.

"Because he's poor. Or rather, lower class." I use air quotes when I say 'lower class,' because that's my parent's phrase, not mine. They're the ones who put a huge weight on wealth. I don't see people as dollar signs.

"Ahhhhh." He nods knowingly. Which makes me wonder if his parents have ever thought that way about any of the girls he's dated.

When we get to Grabbagreen, we halt the conversation to order and gather our food.

Vik digs right back in when we settle at a table.

"I understand parental influence. I mean, you know my situation. I'm gonna marry an Indian girl. And that's not just because my parents expect me to. I want to, ya know? I love my culture and the traditions and as long as *I* get to pick the girl"—Vik laughs—"I'm happy with it."

I stab a big chunk of avocado in my southwest bowl.

Vik's smile disappears. "That's where the difference comes in. My people are my people, no matter what their financial status."

"And my parents don't care that Austin works as hard as anyone I've ever met. Maybe even harder. He's busting his ass and it's all coming together for him. Songs on the radio, music festivals, a huge tour coming up."

"That's awesome!"

"I know." I can't help smiling when I think of all Austin and his bandmates have done to get to this point. I'm proud of him. "But my parents just see: tattoos. Lower class. Starving artist. Drugs. Alcohol. Tour life. Groupies."

"Is that what your parents see or what you see?"

"What does that mean?"

"It sounds like you have reservations about him and your relation-ship. Deep down, do you see it as something long-lasting?"

"I—yea—I—" I stumble on the answer.

He continues, "Is it about a real relationship or is it about rebelling against your parents?"

"No," I say with absolute certainty. "It's real. I really like him. I like who he is and how I feel when I'm with him."

"How's that?"

"Like myself without filters. Saying what I really want to say and being who I am without having to worry about what other people think."

"Well then, I think you have your answer. Forget what other people think and live your life."

Chapter Nine

AUSTIN

The house I grew up in is only a few minutes away from the house I rent with friends. I've lived in the same neighborhood since I was a toddler. Modest houses and mature trees line the streets just minutes from center city—close enough to businesses and nightlife, yet far enough away that you can actually have a yard. When the textile mills began to close, the working-class neighborhood fell into poverty and disrepair. While growing up, it was pretty rough— shootings, muggings, drug deals, prostitutes—and some of that is still around, but it's much less frequent because of how much the area has changed.

About thirty years ago, artists, creatives, and entrepreneurs started moving in because rent was cheap and they had the freedom to do what they wanted. The revitalization that brought an eclectic, artsy, funky vibe to the neighborhood is the reason my parents chose the area when they moved to Charlotte from Chapel Hill after Dad graduated from college. He loved living in a place where he could paint a colorful mural on the side of our fence and have people stop to take pictures in front of it rather than tell him to wash it off or paint over it.

Pops of color and vibrancy began springing up with every creative endeavor and soon, our once-forgotten neighborhood became the trendy, new hot spot. And when you have a hip, fun area so close to Uptown (which is what Charlotteans call the downtown area), it draws large investors and more affluent residents—which changes the vibe of the neighborhood. There's always a double-sided coin that comes with dramatic change. It increases property values for long-time residents like Mom, who still owns one of the original mill-era homes. Increased home values and increased property taxes go hand in hand, and that puts more stress on her. Many of our neighbors have been pushed out because they couldn't afford the tax increase. Sky-high rent has made moving into the neighborhood—or staying in the neighborhood—almost impossible for those who started the revitalization and created the funky, eclectic oasis.

Multiple buyers and investors have approached her about selling—to the point that it's borderline harassment—but she refuses. She knows that, despite being able to sell her home for much more than she bought it for, she couldn't get enough for the house to buy or build another home in the neighborhood. And she doesn't want to leave the place she loves and supported while it was going through so much growth and change.

Someday I'm going to be able to afford to renovate this house. It's what Mom deserves. A fresh feel to the home she loves.

"Mom! You home?" I ask as I push open the door to the tiny brick ranch I grew up in. Memories flood my mind every single time. Wonderful memories. Heart-breaking memories.

My dad killed himself in the master bedroom.

If Mom were going to move, I would have expected it to happen after that. I thought living in the house would be too much pain for her to manage. So many amazing family memories with dad marred by the absolute worst. Mom doesn't see it that way. She sees the good. And she doesn't dwell on his death as a curse. She knows—we both know—that he's at peace.

Mental illness is a terrible disease. It's not like we didn't know how dad was feeling. He was open about his battle with bipolar disorder. I lived with the reality that something could happen at any time. I knew he was close to the edge on multiple occasions. I thought I could save him. Thought I could help. My dad knew we loved him. He knew we cared and that he meant something in this world. Our love was strong, but loving another person isn't enough; they have to love themselves.

Whatever demons Dad struggled with inside his head overpowered him. There was nothing anyone could do. We tried. We were there. We "saved" him multiple times. But you can't save someone who doesn't want to be saved. And, honestly, I don't know if you should. Why make someone suffer out of personal selfishness? I don't know. Suicide is hard to come to terms with for survivors. She thought she was enough—and she was—but she wasn't the magic cure for dad. No one could heal him. He wasn't ours to heal.

"In the kitchen!" Mom calls.

I make my way through the living room and into the kitchen where Mom stands at the sink, washing dishes. She always said a dishwasher was an unnecessary luxury. I understand now, because it's just her. I understood it when I lived at home, too, because I did all the dishes.

"Hi, Mom," I say as I lean over and kiss her cheek. Then I hip check her out of the way and take the soapy sponge out of her hand.

"I can do it, Austin, it's fine."

"I know you can. You can also take a seat and let me help you."

Mom holds her hands up before grabbing the dishtowel and wiping them dry.

"Thank you." She pulls out a chair from the kitchen table and collapses into it, seemingly more tired than usual. She reaches for a stack of mail and starts sorting it into piles. Loose strands of silver-streaked hair fall out of the bun on top of her head and frame her face. The bags under her eyes look darker than normal.

"You okay, Mom? You look tired."

"I'm always tired, sweet boy."

Mom has been at a local financial planning firm for over twenty-five years; she worked her way to office manager and stayed there for the last fifteen years.

"I know, but you look even more so than usual." I glance at her while I soap up a plate.

"Haven't been feeling well." She puts a palm to her forehead, but drops it quickly. "I think I'm coming down with something."

"Have you gone to the doctor?" I ask.

"Who goes to the doctor every time they get a cold? Haven't got time for that."

"But if it's been for a few days, you might be able to get on antibiotics or something."

Mom pushes back from the table and takes a pile of mail to the trash. When she walks back, she rubs my forearm. "I'm good. Thank you for your concern."

Then she grabs a dish towel and starts drying the dishes I've set in the other side of the sink.

"How's Franklin's leg?"

Mom has known Fozzie for years, but she always calls him Franklin, his given name. She must've seen our Instagram story when Fozzie cut his shin on the metal grate hanging off the back of a truck. While were unloading our equipment, he carried an amp around the back of a truck, not expecting a grate to be protruding. He'd run smack into it, causing a nasty slash. His shin was gushing blood. He missed sound-check for a trip to the emergency room. Thankfully our tour manager went with him so Tim and I could finish setting up. If Fozzie hadn't gotten back in time, we were somewhat prepared to do an acoustic set.

"He's fine. Had to get a few stitches, but he drank away the pain and played through."

Mom's dry sigh tells me she's not impressed. But no one's ever been impressed by Fozzie, outside of his drum skills.

"Where are you guys off to next?"

"We're booked for a couple festivals this summer, and we've got that tour with Walk on Mars in the fall. We're at a festival in Atlanta in a couple weeks. Wanna go?"

"To a music festival?" Mom asks. "At my age?"

"Who cares about your age, Mom? You're cooler than half the kids I know."

She laughs. "Doesn't sound like my kind of fun, my dear, but I appreciate the invite."

"Rocking out in the sun with a drink in your hand. It'll be like the days when you followed Widespread Panic."

"I was young and stupid when I followed the Spread. Getting

sunburned and dehydrated with people one third of my age now sounds like a prison sentence."

"Don't say I didn't invite you when you see all the videos and complain about how you wished you were there," I tease.

I know it's not Mom's thing anymore. But I do love the stories of when she and Dad traveled around to see bands. She kept all their ticket stubs for every show they went to. Even though I used to love going through that box when I was a kid, it means even more when I do it now. We have a few super fans, but I can't wait to be a band that fans travel the country to see.

"I'll try to contain my jealousy," Mom deadpans as she lifts a stack of dry plates onto a shelf in the cabinet above her head.

I grew up on all kinds of music. Mom and Dad let me listen to whatever I wanted, not just the music they liked or approved. In fact, they wanted me to listen to real music rather than watered-down kid's versions of songs or lame-ass Disney radio. They made sure to instill an appreciation for art and stressed the importance of self-expression and free speech. They made sure I knew that I was open to do whatever made me happy. I always appreciated that. Especially after hearing how Liz didn't have that choice. I can't even imagine if she would have told her parents she wanted to be in a band. Actually, I can. They probably would have made her train for Juilliard and join the symphony.

I never got into the jam bands my parents loved so much. I gravitated to emo, punk, and 90's alternative sounds. Though some of my fondest memories are when I watched my parents dance around the living room, high as hell. They never looked happier than when they were in each other's arms with their eyes locked.

When they would notice me watching—they always noticed me watching—Mom would hold out a hand and invite me to join. And we'd dance around the living room as a family. Free expression, arms and feet moving however we wanted with the rhythm of the music.

In moments like those, I learned how to love. I learned how to treat the person I loved. I learned what a marriage was supposed to be.

It would have been easy to focus on the negative. Dad's depression. His mental illness. The heartache that it caused Mom. But she always made sure I knew the bad times weren't who he was. It was the illness.

He loved us with everything he had. But he couldn't always love himself.

My racing mind overflows with memories to the point that I'm getting bummed out, so I reach over and push the button on the iPod mom has on the kitchen counter. The room floods with music, which makes both of us smile. We shake our hips and bounce around while we finish the dishes.

It's times like this that I remember how much I loved living in this house. I loved being around my parents. Sometimes I feel like I abandoned Mom when I moved out. But I had to. I couldn't stay after seeing Dad in the bathtub. I still can't go upstairs.

"How's Liz?" Mom reaches into the fridge and grabs me a beer.

"Good. Busy. She's working her ass off," I say, popping the top and taking a pull.

I follow her into the living room and collapse next to her on the worn, navy-blue sofa. I'll buy her a new one soon—before I even outfit my own place. I have a list of semi-extravagant purchases for Mom. Personally, I don't need much.

"Well, so are you, so that's good, right?" Mom bends her knees and curls her toes under my thigh. It's her signature move. She's always cold and loves tucking her toes under someone. She did it to Dad all the time.

Liz and I have been seeing each other for a few months now, and I've internally debated whether or not to tell Mom that Liz is the same girl I brought to the hospital last year. I know she'll be pissed if she remembers it was someone from the Commons family.

For some strange reason, my mom has always avoided Commons Department Stores. Granted, Mom is the lady who doesn't give places or products a second chance if they piss her off bad enough. I figured her hatred came from one of those situations. Maybe they didn't honor a coupon or something. It doesn't take much to bring out her feisty Italian side if she's in a mood.

She's also really into angels and universal connections and believing that people come into your life for a purpose. Her whole family believes in stuff like that. One of her cousins, in Staten Island, swears she can see ghosts and talk to the dead. Mom's all about that shit. She visits twice a year to see if Dad will speak to her. No luck yet.

"Remember when I told you about the connection I had with Liz the night I met her at the show? There was something about the way she looked at me—like she could see straight through to my soul." I pause. *Fuck it.* I've gotta come clean at some point. It's not like she's not going to find out. "I don't know how else to describe it. It's like we knew each other. But I had never met her. Or, so I thought."

Never have I ever been able to keep my mouth shut around my mom. She's my rock. My best friend. The person I share everything with. I trust her advice more than anyone I've ever met.

"Or so you thought?" Her toes wiggle under my leg, urging me to continue. Mom's eyes rarely light up, but me talking about a connection with a girl gets her all excited.

"Well, turns out she's the girl I found on the road during that ice storm. The one I took to the hospital."

That silly spark in mom's eyes extinguishes completely within a second. "The Commons girl?"

"Yeah," I admit. It suddenly feels like I'm under police surveillance. "I can't deny the connection, Mom. She was at my show that night for a reason, ya know? And it turns out she's this mind-blowing, amazing woman."

Mom thinks before she speaks. It's one of her best qualities, one that she passed down to me. I tend to stay calm and cool, until I sit down to write. I pour everything I'm feeling into journals. At the same time, once those lyrics become a song, my heart is on my sleeve for all to see—and stomp.

"You know I believe in those connections, Austin. And I believe in seeing where it goes."

"Here comes the 'but,'" I interject before she can continue.

"But—" She kicks the outside of my leg before burrowing her toes again. "You also need to be careful. She comes from a different world. Different values. Different moral compass. I want you to be happy, but I want you to be careful."

"I get it. It's like *Pretty in Pink* and I'm the girl."

"Oh my gosh, Austin!" Mom laughs. "I'm just saying—you have so much ahead of you."

"So does Liz, Mom. She's a surgeon."

Mom pauses. I think she wants to roll her eyes, but she's so much better than that. She's going to come at me the passive aggressive way. It's the annoying trait Mom has. One I'm glad she didn't pass on.

"I understand she has a life, as well. But you need to remember how hard you've worked to get where you are. You can't lose sight of your focus."

I know she's trying to be supportive of me and all the exciting things in my life, and reminding me how hard I've worked for everything that's coming together—but I can't help but think it's actually a passive aggressive dig at Liz. She doesn't think Liz had to work as hard because of her family. I beg to differ. I'd bet my right nut that she had to work her ass off to become a surgeon. The family she come from can give her the upper hand by sending her to the best schools money can buy, but it doesn't take the place of studying, clinical practice, and work ethic. I'm assuming not everyone—no matter what school they went to—has the talent to cut it as a surgeon.

"I know, Mom. I know more than anyone."

"Because you're my smart, passionate boy. I'm so proud of you. Always remember that."

I tap my temple with a finger. "It's ingrained."

"You have people who count on you. You keep that group together. You keep it running. You think Franklin could handle the business aspect?"

"Wow, Mom! You're beating Fozzie down today. What did he do?"

Mom must've seen something she didn't like. She follows our social media like a hawk. She rarely comments on any of the stupid shit we do when we're drunk and acting like fools. Honestly, she's the most nonjudgmental person. But Fozzie has always annoyed her and I don't know why. Mom being Mom, I guess. Just like her views about Liz and I getting involved. I know she's trying to save my heart from crashing and burning, but sometimes you have to let the birds fly.

"Is it noon?" I ask, scanning the walls for a clock that I know isn't hanging. The only time there had been a clock was on the front of our old VCR, and that was switched out for a DVD player years ago.

Mom retrieves her phone from her pocket—which I could have done—but I like making her feel like she's taking care of me. "It's five 'til."

"Fuuuck!" I jump off the couch. "Gotta get to work."

"Good thing it's two minutes away."

"Right?" Before I leave, I lean down and kiss her forehead. "I love you, Mom."

"I love you, too." Before I sail out the door, I turn around. "Will you promise to give Liz a chance?"

"Of course I will." Mom pauses. "Does this relationship run that deep for you Austin?"

"Yes. I mean, I don't know where it's going, but I want to continue it. I feel that strongly about us."

"There's only one thing I want for you in life and you know what it is."

"You want me to be happy."

"And if this girl is what does it, then I'll keep an open mind. I mean, Lord knows you've brought home worse."

That's keeping it real right there.

"Thank you." I blow her a kiss and shut the door behind me as I leave.

Mom isn't a liar, nor does she hold grudges against people for no reason. Sure, she has an unhealthy hatred for Commons Department Stores, but millions of people feel that way about Wally World, so how is her attitude any different?

Chapter Ten

LIZ

$\mathcal{E}$ver feel like a black cloud is following you? That's how I've felt since my last physical therapy appointment with Vik. The one where I realized that I can't continue pretending that I'll be able to operate again. I've been going through the motions for months, fooling people into thinking that I'll be ready to go once my fellowship is complete. Now all I feel is that sense of dread that comes with having to tell my mentor, Dr. Crowder. The quicker I come clean and stop wasting everyone's time, the quicker I can move on to healing—and figuring out a plan for what I'm going to do with my life.

"What are you doing here?" Jordan Fletcher asks when I enter the physician's lounge. Upon seeing him, all I want to do is turn around and walk out without a word. But I can't because I always have to play nice.

"I have an appointment with Dr. Crowder," I answer without looking at him. Instead, I head straight for the coffee machine and pour myself a cup. I arrived fifteen minutes early so I thought I'd stop in the lounge and say hello to anyone that was around. I regret the decision now.

"Were you at the Intermission show a few months back?" he asks.

Why is he making small talk? He never makes small talk.

"Yeah. I went with my sisters." I hope he doesn't ask me why I didn't say hello. Because there's no part of me that can create any kind of nice response to that question.

"I thought I saw you. I talked with Madeline a bit at the show, but it seemed like you were busy."

"Busy?" I ask, looking at him for the first time. "Yeah, I guess. It was a concert. I was there to see the bands."

I'll admit, Jordan has always intimidated me. He's the type of guy who will do anything and everything to get ahead. I don't understand that mentality even though I've been around it my entire life.

"You were talking to a guy from the first band. Full of tattoos. Messy hair." He rubs his head as if I don't know where hair is located. Maybe he's trying to be cute, but the demonstration only leaves his shaggy frat-boy coif a disheveled mess. If I were in a better mood, I might laugh, but not today.

"Austin. Yes. He's extremely talented. The band sounded great." I grab a paper cup off the counter and fill it with coffee.

"I saw you leave with him."

I pause. This isn't really territory I want to go into with Jordan, of all people.

He continues without waiting for me to speak, "Slumming it, don't you think?"

"Excuse me?" I ask. It annoys me, not only because he has the nerve to say it, but also because shallow thoughts like that crossed my mind when I first worried about what my family and friends would think about Austin.

"Not really your type, is he?"

I set my coffee cup on the counter before I throw it in his face. "I'm not sure how you think that is an appropriate conversation, but it's not."

"Sorry!" He holds his hands up as if telling me he's backing off. "Just making sure you're staying on top of your game, Liz."

"Don't worry about me, Jordan. I'm doing just fine."

He smirks. "You're doing just fine? Have you gotten a timeline for when you'll be able to operate yet?"

"Not yet," I admit, which is true but not the entire truth. It's not

Jordan's business. "My PT and I are working with Dr. Crowder on a plan to get back into rotation as soon as I finish my fellowship." It's a lie, but he doesn't need to know anything yet. I'll be the laughing stock soon enough.

"Oh, that's right! The fellowship that your parents used their power and influence to get you just so you could stay in the program. The one that knocked a deserving person, who actually applied, out of the running. How could I forget about your fellowship?"

In an effort to reel in my anger, I pause to count to five before speaking. Leave it to Jordan to dig straight into my internal insecurities. Other people may think what he does, but he's the only person who would ever say something like that to my face.

"My fellowship is none of your business," I say jabbing my finger toward his chest. "And you should probably tread lightly when talking to me because, as you stated, my parents *are* very influential in this hospital—and this city."

"Are you threatening me?"

Instead of an answer, I smile innocently, then grab my coffee cup and brush past him, elbowing him on my way toward the door.

I've never spoken up to Jordan before, and I never thought I would. But there's no way I'm letting this manipulative douchebag get the best of me. I've either come to terms with the fact that my career is ending or I'm trying to sabotage it myself.

Guess I'm about to find out.

I hurry down the hall to the office space where Dr. Crowder and I planned to meet before he heads into his next surgery today. When I arrive, he's relaxing behind the desk with his feet propped up and a magazine in his hands.

Thankfully, he's the only one in the lounge right now.

"Hey, Dr. Crowder!"

He looks up and smiles. "Liz! Come on in! Shut the door, please."

I nod and close the door behind me. "I assume you've talked to Dr. Sharma?" I ask, wringing my hands as if trying to twist the ability back into them.

"I have." He sits up, places his feet on the floor and stands. "I'm going to ask you a question and I need an honest answer."

I nod. I know what's coming. I know this is it.

The end.

"Do you believe you'll be able to perform surgical procedures within the next six months?" he asks in a gentle, but firm tone before reaching down to grab his coffee cup off the table.

I look him in the eye, because even though this is the hardest answer I've ever had to give in my life, I have to do it professionally. Dr. Crowder's respect and recommendation is essential to my future if I'm going to stay in the medical field.

"No," I say. It comes out in a squeak, so I clear my throat and continue. "I don't believe I will."

"I'm sorry, Liz." He steps closer to me and closes his eyes longer than a blink. "I'm truly sorry, because I know what happened with your hand is not your fault. You've been doing amazing work in your fellowship, but as you know, we created that opportunity to give you time to rehab. If you're not going to be able to operate when the fellowship ends, we have to look at the reality of your future in surgery."

I nod.

Keep it together, Elizabeth. Keep it together. I bite my bottom lip and lift my eyes to the ceiling quickly.

"You're the best surgeon I've mentored in years, Liz. I'm not just talking about skill and drive. You're always willing to step up. You figure things out on your own and work independently with little supervision needed. And patients absolutely love you. You have a way of easing their minds, making a scary experience a bit less stressful for them. That's a brilliant skill, one that can't be taught."

I nod.

Anyone in my position would beg to hear this kind of praise from Dr. Crowder. I know he's trying to make this easier on me, but it's making me feel worse. Being forced to walk away is already killing me —hearing someone I admire tell me how good he thinks I am is nailing spikes in my coffin.

"Everyone knows how talented you are. Everyone can see it."

"Not everyone," I say, thinking of Jordan.

"Absolutely everyone. Which is why you're seen as a threat to some." Dr. Crowder smiles.

I try to return it, but I can't. I physically cannot move the muscles to smile.

"I'm trying to help. I really am." He runs his fingers through his salt-and-pepper hair. To his credit, as a decent human being, he looks absolutely gutted, like he never wanted to have this conversation. "You have a bright future in medicine, Liz. Just because it's not surgery doesn't mean your career is over."

I nod. If I do anything else I'm going to break down right here in front of one of the most revered surgeons in Charlotte. Pathetic isn't a good look.

"I know how much this must hurt. But you're already very well-respected in this hospital, and that reputation will follow you into the next phase of your career. This isn't the end."

It *is* the end.

"Let's set up a time next week in my office to sit down and discuss options for your future, okay?"

At the risk of sounding completely paranoid, I wonder how long Dr. Crowder has been holding off on having this conversation? There's no doubt he's been getting pressure from the other surgeons. I've been dead weight for months and it's time to shed the excess baggage.

I understand completely. It still sucks.

I nod and paste a smile on my face. "Thank you, Dr. Crowder. I truly appreciate your kind words and encouragement."

"Harry. You can call me Harry." He extends his hand and I shake it firmly.

It's definitely the end.

"Thanks, Harry. I'll be in touch next week."

I exit the office feeling completely defeated. I knew this was coming, but instead of owning up to it and facing it head on, I kept faking to see how far I could put off the inevitable conversation because of my own damaged ego.

I wish I could be optimistic about the future. Finally admitting I can't perform surgery anymore frees me to move forward in the medical career that I want. I wish I could be as excited as I was when Austin and I discussed it, but I can't. I'm too consumed by the failure.

Chapter Eleven

AUSTIN

"*I* called you all to this fine establishment today," Nelson begins in a very regal voice, "to let you know that RGA Records wants to sign you." He lifts his beer in the air, silently asking the rest of us to clink our bottles.

"Holy shit!"

"Fuck yeah!"

Fozzie and Tim are over the moon, as anyone in our position would be. Being signed by a big-ass label is the dream. And then there's me—and I have doubts.

"Do we have time to think about it?" I ask.

All heads swivel toward the weirdo, which I expected.

I want to join in on the toast, because we should celebrate the fact that a label is interested. I just don't have it in my heart.

"Yeah, of course. I want you guys to weigh all of your options before you make a decision," Nelson says. I appreciate that he's a level-headed dude who gives us unbiased advice instead of trying to sway us one way or another.

I hate that my first reaction isn't happiness. I feel like a complete dick about it. But I can't ignore the sinking feeling in my gut that tells me signing with RGA isn't the best road for us.

It's no secret that Nelson has been sending our demo out and talking to various labels, since we all agreed on testing those waters just to see if there'd be any interest. We'd even flown to New York a few months ago to meet with RGA, but thought nothing came out of it.

"What're your thoughts, man?" Fozzie asks.

"Do you really want to sign? I mean, we said we'd take a look at our options, but we haven't really discussed everything that goes along with selling our souls."

Tim rolls his eyes, which makes me want to punch his stupid face because I don't even think he should have anything to do with this decision. Though, I will admit that using the term "selling our souls" may be a bit dramatic.

When I was younger, being signed by a major label was my number one goal. In my head, that was the epitome of "making it" as a musician. Until I realized, after research and talking to other artists and soul-searching for what I really want out of life—signing with a major label is not my goal anymore.

Everyone has a different path. And if the guys want to sign with RGA, maybe my path isn't with them. Which means starting over. Again.

"No, I'm with you," Fozzie agrees. "The game has changed. Signing might not be our best choice. We've got some things to work through as a band before we agree to anything."

I lean back in my chair and blink a few times. "I thought this was your ultimate dream?"

We've had the discussion numerous times in the past. He thinks being with a big label means more exposure and more opportunity, which eventually leads to fame and money. I don't agree with that. I think we could make more money by being with an indie label. Especially with how the music industry has changed over the last ten years. Plus, I don't want to sell my soul or be someone's puppet, and that's the feeling I get about signing a contract.

"It was—at one point. But I've been thinking about it more recently. Is it really my dream? Or is it some ego bullshit, ya know?" Fozzie looks around the dark bar, then back at me. "There's always been this voice in my head saying if a major label wants us, that means we're special. Look at how many bands get rejected. But if they pick us: Whoa!" I laugh when Fozzie wiggles spirit fingers in front of him. "But is that real or is it an illusion created by people struggling to keep their place in a changing industry?"

"Are you kidding me?"

"No. Look at how huge indies have become. Not in terms of corporate greed—but by doing right by the artists. Keeping creative control and making money. And look how many bands the big labels have screwed over? Nelson is a prime example." Fozzie tilts his beer toward our manager.

"Screwed me over *real* good," Nelson says before taking a drink.

"Screwed you how?" Tim asks, looking up from his phone.

Nelson picks up a cardboard coaster his beer was on, holds it between his middle finger and thumb and spins it. I know he hates telling the story, but it's completely relevant to our making a decision.

"I was in a band in the nineties. Put out some EPs, toured around the U.S., Europe. We were *huge* in Serbia," he says with a wink. "We signed with a big label who shall not be named. They sent us to L.A. for three months to record an album. And it released on September 10th, 2001."

"Sounds like the dream. So how'd they screw you?"

"Well, if you remember American history, September 11th, 2001, was a pretty shitty day for our country. The label cut all marketing and pulled the record."

Tim tosses his phone on the table and gives Nelson an evil eye. "Thousands of people died and you're pissed over a record label pulling your record and marketing?"

"No, dickbag, I'm not. I'm pissed that they took away our ability to bring in revenue and then sued us for the cost of making the record. We had to pay back the cost of the producers and the songwriters that helped us, even the studio we recorded at and the place we stayed in L.A. Everything," Nelson finishes.

"Oh." Tim huffs, slinking down in his chair. "Sorry, man."

"Contracts aren't written to benefit new artists. They're written to benefit the label. And if you don't realize what you're getting yourself into, you can be screwed big time," Nelson says.

"I read about this one band who got signed by a label of the dude who was their biggest competitor. The label never planned on releasing their music. They just wanted to shut the band up for years and years. So the other guy could become famous."

"I feel like you guys are all gloom and doom. These stories happen to the minority rather than the majority," Tim says.

"Do you ever research things? We hear shit like this all the time from guys we know and trust," Fozzie snaps.

"Gloom-and-doom stories aside, I, personally, don't want to give up the control or the freedom to make the music that we want. I don't want it overly produced or have our vision changed by suits because they think they know what's right," I say honestly.

I'm not trying to sound arrogant, or suggesting that people at large record labels don't know what they're doing. Obviously, they do. But if they want a certain sound or a certain look, a band has to conform, and I don't want to do that. I don't want our music changed to appease the masses. That's not what it's about for us. Personally, I'd rather sign with a small independent label.

"Yeah, I was thinking about that, too," Fozzie agrees.

"You guys know that Drowned World is my number one priority, but what about my other stuff? Will I be able to keep working on side projects?"

I'm constantly collaborating with others in the music scene on various projects. My latest is with a friend in DC; we've been recording our parts on our own and uploading it to a shared Dropbox account so we can mix it and bring it together.

I'm completely committed to my band and absolutely aware that other ventures will have to take a back seat, but if I have downtime, I need to make sure I'll still be able to work on projects with other artists. That's a huge deal-breaker for me.

"If Drowned World is your number one priority, why are you worried about side projects?" Tim sneers.

"Fuck you, man! At least Drowned World *is* a priority for me," I lash out at him. "I put all my time and energy into this band. Can you say the same?" My heart races and I can feel the anger heating my face. I didn't expect to have it out with Tim today, but here we are. I'm not about to sit here and let him question my commitment.

"What does that mean?"

"You're late all the time. You've skipped more sound checks then you've shown up at. You show up high, despite us having multiple conversations about how we don't want that shit in our band."

"*Your* band," Tim spits. "It's always *your* band. I'm part of this band, too!"

"Then maybe you should start acting like it," Fozzie says.

Tim has a nervous habit of bouncing his knee up and down quickly. Right now, the table is shaking so hard we all have to grab our beers to make sure they don't topple.

"I'm not signing a contract with you until I see changes," I tell him.

Tim's demeanor changes from anger to concern. "Am I on the chopping block? Do you want me out of the band?"

"Do you even want to be part of the band?" Fozzie asks. "It's a hell of a lot more work than showing up five minutes before a show."

"Yes," Tim says emphatically. "I want to be part of the band."

Fozzie and I exchange glances. We've talked about getting a new bassist on multiple occasions; we've just been too busy to really think about it. Maybe we're closer than we thought.

"We've got a few festivals coming up. Let's see what happens," I say, downing the rest of my beer and getting up from the table. "I've gotta get to work."

These are the things that keep me awake at night. Am I starting a major life event with someone who's not all in? Someone who sleeps through soundcheck and shows up minutes before shows, while Fozzie and I—and a few rad friends who lovingly act as our roadies—get everything set up.

I'm the one who's put my heart and soul into our success. I'm the one who paid for studio time to make our demo EP. I'm the one who booked all of our gigs—from regular appearances at local venues to mini tours where we'd take a month and travel to places within driving distance to be seen and get people excited about us.

This band is my baby, and there's a huge part of me that doesn't want my success tied to Tim.

We need to see some changes from Tim before we sign this contract—*if* we sign the contract.

Chapter Twelve

LIZ

*L*eaning back against the elaborate booth, I allow the waiter to drape a black napkin across my lap. The color matches my pencil skirt. Maddie got a white napkin because she's got a pair of white capris on.

It's the little pretentious things that I don't usually notice. Why does the color of the napkin matter when all I'm doing with it is wiping my dirty hands off?

Mama cares. Daddy cares. Hundreds of other people must care, because we're sitting in one of the busiest restaurants in Uptown Charlotte.

It's not the place I want to be right now. I'd rather be at my house, tucked in my king-sized bed with the duvet over my head, mourning my career alone like I did yesterday after leaving the hospital. Was it productive? Nope. But it was necessary.

Mama sets her menu on the table. "How's the planning coming along, Elizabeth?"

"Hmm?" I ask. So consumed in my own thoughts, I wasn't paying attention to her at all.

"The planning, for the auction? How's it coming?"

She's talking about the Silent Auction and dinner, an event I thought of three years ago when Hugo, one of the guys in the crew who landscapes my parent's yard, found out his mom had cancer. She didn't have insurance, and he and his wife, Maria, didn't have the means to pay the massive bills. I knew they were absolutely devastated, not only by the costs, and I had to do something to help.

Hugo and Maria's ordeal opened my eyes to how devastating it is for many families—even those with dual incomes, working at least forty hours a week—to pay for catastrophic medical expenses. Instead of using the event as a one-time fundraiser for a single family, I created a nonprofit to be able to help more families pay for medical care. The event was very well-received, thanks to the amazing event-planning company who took care of all the details. As someone who'd never planned a huge event before, I knew I had to hand it off. My parents and their friends really helped with the word of mouth. It's become one of the biggest events in, raising almost $500,000 over the last two years. We've been able to help multiple families with that money.

"Oh, good, I guess. I'm hands-off this year. Too much going on. Ariana and her crew are taking care of the details again."

"Are you getting that same band from last year?" Maddie asks. "They were so good. Trent loved them."

I make a mental note to make sure Ariana did not book the same band. If Trent loved them, I don't want them back.

"Or maybe Austin's band?" Maddie suggests.

"Well, that would be awkward, asking him out of the blue," Mama says. She lifts her water glass, then pauses and looks at me. "You *did* break it off with him, didn't you, Elizabeth?"

I scowl at Maddie, then shift my gaze to my own water to avoid eye contact with Mama. I've barely spoken to my parents since Maddie's birthday. On the rare occasions I have spoken with them, I didn't mention Austin at all. My personal life isn't open for anyone's opinion, despite what they might believe.

"I've been busy at the hospital, Mama. No time for much of anything."

"That didn't answer my question. I thought your father and I made it clear that you shouldn't be dating someone like him?"

Someone like him. Someone like your youngest daughter?

It takes all my might to bite my tongue. Instead I answer, "I've hung out with worse people in my life than an attractive, talented man who thinks I'm amazing, Mama."

"Of course he thinks you're amazing. I bet he says he loves you, too, doesn't he?" The mocking question slides out of her mouth, in a tone sweet as iced tea the server places in front of her.

The worst part about it isn't that she doesn't like Austin or she thinks he's with me for our money, it's the fact that Mama was the one who came from less money than Daddy. He was born into wealth, but she was born and raised regular, old middle class. It still makes me sad that she turned her back on her family when she got married. Slowly phased them out by the time I was in elementary school. She—of all people—has no right to question Austin's motives for wanting to be with me.

I allow the server to set our drinks down before I speak. "He's not what you think, Mama. He's very ambitious and interesting and deep."

"Deep," Mama repeats.

The only time she uses the word deep is when she's talking about the level of water in our pool. *Deep* isn't a trait my parents appreciate in others. They see it as a character flaw. Deep means introspective, maybe a dreamer. They have no use for dreamers. Logical, academic, business minds are the ones that impress them.

I can't do this right now. I thought going to lunch with Mama and Maddie would help me heal a little bit, but now I'm regretting my decision. In theory, these two people should be the ones I can open up to. They used to be the first people I turned to when I needed a shoulder to cry on.

The exact opposite is true today. Telling them my residency ended is a failure. Telling them I have to start over in another program is humiliating—not only for me—but for my family, as well. I can't say anything right now.

Part of me wants to call Emily; she wouldn't care at all. She'd be my cheerleader. She always has been if it's something that pisses my parents off.

I can't bear to be around anyone in my family right now.

I take a deep breath and pull my phone out of my pocketbook. At first, I open my texts and click on an old message, as if I'm reading something important that just came in. Then I pull up the number of the only person I want to talk to right now.

Austin.

Me: Hey! What are you up to?

Very casual. Easy. Keep it cool, Liz.

Me: Do you want to grab a drink?

Still casual. A little creepy that I double-messaged, instead of typing that in the first one. But hopefully he won't think anything of it. I set my phone down on the table next to my plate.

"Is that work?" Mama's voice is thick with disapproval when she speaks. She hates when anyone texts while engaging with people. She thinks it's the epitome of bad manners. "Do they need you?"

"Yeah. Things are crazy, as always."

Does she know that I talked to Dr. Crowder? It's not improbable since word travels fast and Mama seems to have ears all over the city.

"You know how rude it is to text at the table," Maddie says.

She becomes more and more like Mama every day, and that's not a compliment.

Me: Austin, I'm so sorry to bother you. I know you're hanging
out with your cousin, but I really need you. I'm sorry I didn't
call you yesterday. I had a meeting with Dr. Crowder and my
residency and fellowship are ending. I couldn't face anyone. I'm
devastated and lost and stuck at lunch with Mama and Maddie.
I can't even breathe without wanting to cry.
Me: You're the only person I want to be with right now.

A response text finally pops up.

Austin: Absolutely, babe. I'll be at your house in an hour.
Me: Thank you. See you soon.

"I HAVE TO GO IN," I say, shoving my phone in my purse. "I'm so sorry to rush out like this." I push back from the table and stand immediately, without waiting for any kind of response. "Thank you for lunch, Mama." I say even though I haven't ordered any food. Then I lean over and kiss her cheek. "Bye Maddie," I call over my shoulder as I rush toward the door of the restaurant.

Chapter Thirteen

AUSTIN

"Harris Commons' daughter?" Vinny asks, casting his line with ease. It lands inches away from mine.

"You couldn't have cast on the other side of the boat?" I ask dryly. I hate fishing. But I love hanging out with my cousin and we rarely get time together. Both of our jobs keep us out of town a lot. He's a traveling electrician and I've been touring.

"This is my side," he says with an unaffected shrug.

"It's my side, too."

"I'm older."

"This is why I stopped fishing with you."

"You stopped fishing with me because you suck at fishing."

Despite Vinny and I having been raised by native New Yorkers who moved to Charlotte before we were born—my cousin adopted a thick Southern accent. It's actually pretty comical when a dude who sounds like him introduces himself as Vinny. He's either a person who picks up accents easily and can't help it, or he amped up his Southern charm to impress girls.

Which goes to show that relationships and what people are looking for in a mate is subjective. I'm not trying to mess with girls who are impressed by his thick Southern accent. I prefer General American—

that sort of neutral, non-regional accent used by people in broadcasting.

After reeling in my line, I turn my back to Vinny and cast from the opposite side of the boat, knowing damn well I'm not going to catch a thing over here.

"Back to Harris Commons' daughter. How'd you get involved with her?"

"I was on my way to class a few months ago, the night we had that ice storm. Saw a car smashed between two trees while driving up Queens Road West on my way to class. I stopped to check on it and saw a girl slumped over the wheel."

"Did you make it to class?"

"What?" I glance at him over my shoulder. Not the question I expected.

"Did you make it to class or did you spend all your time saving the damsel in distress?"

"I made it to class...late."

I never cared much about school when I was in it. Going to college never crossed my mind. As I started learning more about the music industry and what I wanted out of my career, I decided to take a few classes. I'm not book-smart, but I can understand concepts that are interesting to me. And not getting screwed over by a management company or record label was very interesting to me. There are so many horror stories about mismanagement of money, having a basic understanding of accounting is essential. I have no problem with someone else handling the business aspects of our career, but needed to know enough so we weren't fleeced.

"You have to get over the hero complex, Austin," Vinny warns.

"What?"

"You're attracted to people who need saving."

"I'm not—" I begin.

"Don't even!"

"If you'd let me finish a goddamn sentence! I was saying that I'm not trying to save her. She doesn't need saving."

Vinny chuckles. "I thought you were denying your history."

No reason to deny anything. Vinny is right. I am attracted to broken people. People who need me. People who need *someone*. White-knight syndrome.

It's not just women, but friends. What can I say? I like the under-dog. I like making friends with the kid everyone is picking on and making sure he knows that I'm not going to be a bitch-ass bully just to impress the crowd. I'm gonna have his back. Maybe it was growing up with Vinny, the stereotypical alpha male, my entire life. Vinny's a dick —definitely had bully moments when we were kids. I'd take a bullet for him, but he can be a douche.

"So, you saw her car on the side of the road..." Vinny leads me back to the story.

"It had already started sleeting and there were accidents all over. I knew it would take hours for an emergency crew to get to her, so I took her to the hospital."

"If that was over a year ago, why am I just hearing about her now?"

"Well, we didn't actually meet that night. When I dropped her off, the nurse told me she was a surgeon at the hospital and in the Commons family. So I left. Then she came to that show we did with Intermission."

"The one I was at?"

"Yeah." I nod.

"Did she come to thank you or—?"

"No. She didn't know I brought her to the hospital. I never told anyone there my name or anything. Didn't post my heroic efforts on social media."

"Surprising, since you're an attention whore," Vinny jabs.

"I get my fix on stage."

"She randomly showed up at your show? And you recognized her—"

"No! Jesus, man! Let me finish the story! Have you always been this annoying?"

"Yes."

At least he admits it.

"I didn't recognize her at all. I fell for a gorgeous brunette in the second row."

"Here we go," Vinny says. I bet he's rolling his eyes.

"What?"

"You fell in love with a girl in the crowd that you'd never met or spoken to."

"There was a pull! I can't explain it, and even if I could, you wouldn't get it. We had this undeniable, intense connection."

"From the stage?" The disbelief in his voice is thick.

"Yes."

"Okay. What happened with the brunette and how does this all tie in to the girl you saved?"

"The brunette was her. It was Liz."

"Oh! Gotcha!"

"It was fate," I say, knowing he's about to rail me. He hates that I think in terms of fate and destiny and universal connections. And I hate that he can deny those things so easily. Life isn't always logical, neither is love.

"Your head is in the clouds, kid."

His condescending use of "kid" always annoys me since he's only two years older, and there's a very strong argument that I am more mature emotionally than he will ever be. Being introverted, introspective, and having feelings isn't a bad thing. It doesn't make me any less of a man.

"Why do you always discount me just because I see things differently?"

"I don't! Just listen for a second. She's a surgeon? From a prestigious family, right? You're the type of guy she's never met before. The sensitive soul. The dreamer. The romantic musician. Do you think that will last long?"

"Why wouldn't it?"

"You're gonna be pissed at anything I say..."

"When has that stopped you before?"

"You float through life, making ends meet however you can. And that's awesome, man! I know you aren't about material things. I love that about you. But do you think a woman like her sees you as a viable life partner or as someone fun for now? Women don't want a guy they have to take care of—that's why they have kids."

"You think I'm a gold digger?"

I'm offended and hurt to realize Vinny thinks of me that way. I've paid for my own shit—and helped my mom with bills—since I was old enough to work. Using Liz because of her money has never crossed my mind.

"Austin! No! I didn't mean it that way. I don't think that of you at all. I'm trying to show you some perspective. What do you think her family thinks about you?"

"I know what her family thinks about me. And I don't give a flying fuck."

"Maybe *you* don't, but she will. You think she's going it give it all up for you?"

"I'm not asking her to give anything up. This is a ridiculous conversation."

"You are two very different people from very different lifestyles. That's all I'm saying."

"Noted."

"Jesus. I'm not good with words like you are, Austin! Give me a break. I know you think I'm a caveman, cousin. If I've learned anything over the last five years, it's this: women want an equal. Strong women don't want someone they have to take care of, nor do they want someone to take care of them."

I raise my eyebrows. Not what I expected. "Okaaay."

"They want someone that matches their intellect and drive and has the same passion for life. But most of all, they want to be accepted for who they are, as they are. Not who you want them be. Or who you think you can change them into. There's enough pressure from the outside world. Just be her best friend. Love her. Grow with her."

Vinny has never spoken words at an introspective level like this before. I twist around and rake my fingers toward his face, pretending to unmask him. "Who are you and what did you do with my cousin?"

He bats my arm away. "Get off me before I throw you in the water."

"I'm just speechless. When did this happen? This hasn't always been your view."

"A pending divorce will do weird shit to your head, cuz. Makes you rethink what you once thought was the right way to be."

Vinny and his wife have been separated for about six months. In North Carolina you can't file for divorce until you've been separated for at least a year. Unfortunately, with our busy schedules, this is the first real conversation I've had with him since she left.

"You were a good husband," I tell him. Because I honestly thought he was from the interactions I saw.

"No, I wasn't. Not for Abby, at least. I would have been a good husband for someone else, but I wasn't right for her. She didn't need someone to take care of her. She needed a friend. Someone who liked her for who she was. Deep down, I didn't. I wanted her to be someone else, ya know?"

I've forgotten about fishing, and turned around to look at him. Vinny isn't normally a guy who talks about his feelings, so this is all surprising.

His gaze is locked on the water, but his voice seems miles away as he speaks. "She's kinda like you. Quiet, reserved, only opens up around people she feels comfortable with. I knew that when I married her. I loved that gentle shyness about her. I felt like I was her rock, her protector, but also the one who took her to do things she never would have done. But that's not what she wanted. She didn't want to do any of those things—or most of the things. She went along with it to make me happy. And I didn't see how much she hated it. She didn't hate *me* or our friends, but she constantly felt pressure to be someone she wasn't. I did that to her without even realizing it. We went on trips and had fun, but she was always unhappy because she was always anxious. I kept putting her in uncomfortable situations and she pretended to enjoy it."

"Jesus, Vinny. I'm sorry, man." I think about his situation for a moment. Vinny is a gregarious, extroverted, party guy. He's truly content when he's around other people—or fishing. Abby was absolutely an introvert. A lot of people mistake introverts for being unhappy or standoffish, but that's not always the case. Sometimes it's social anxiety. And when someone is uncomfortable in a social situation, they tend to be quiet.

"Now that you realize the issues, can the marriage be salvaged?"

"No. I mean, we don't want to salvage it. It's a completely amicable breakup. We both realize now that we're not a good fit. Neither of us are bad people, but we just don't work together. I'll always want that loud, outgoing girl who wants to go on adventures and have our friends over every weekend. And Abby will never want that. It's not a bad thing. I'm glad we realized it early—before kids."

"Why didn't you reach out? I would've been there for you, man. I didn't realize there was so much disconnect." My phone buzzes in my front pocket. I want to check it so badly to see if it's Liz, but I don't want Vinny to think I'm blowing him off.

"Yeah, we put on a good show around people." He adjusts the worn, camouflage baseball cap on his head.

My heart hurts for him. I don't think many people enter into a marriage thinking it'll end in divorce. It sounds like he's come to terms with the situation, which alleviates some of my concern.

"You're busy kicking ass, Austin. I'm not gonna burden you with my problems when you're on the road touring. That's not what you need to be thinking about."

Buzz. Buzz.

"Don't worry about burdening me. I'm always available to listen."

"Yeah, I know. That's one of those alpha-male things I can't get over yet."

"Fucking neanderthal," I joke.

Buzz. Buzz.

"Answer your fucking phone," Vinny commands. "Unless it's on some kind of alarm to jerk you off or something."

Without a second thought, I tug my phone out of my pocket and see a series of text messages from Liz.

Shit.

"Is that her?" Vinny asks.

"Yeah."

"Remember my story, Austin. Think about how different Abby and I were and what it did to us before you get in too deep with Liz."

In too deep? I'm already in love with her. How much deeper can it get?

"I appreciate your concern, Vinny, but Liz and I are nothing like you and Abby. We're both introverts."

"Is that all you got out of this?"

"Well, I didn't get any fish, if that's what you're asking."

Vinny ignores my attempt to lighten the mood. "I'm not saying you aren't good enough for her. I'm saying that just because you love each other, doesn't mean it will work. Sometimes love isn't enough when it comes to two completely different people."

"I have it under control," I tell him.

Despite my flippant response, Vinny's words sink to my core because I do think about the differences between how Liz and I live. I love everything about my life. I have a job that pays my bills and allows me the time and flexibility to make music and tour. I have a roof over my head and food in the fridge—usually. Even if I had the money to do it, I don't want a mega mansion in the wealthiest neighborhood in Charlotte. I don't want three BMWs in my circular driveway. I don't want to eat at places where one meal costs more than I spend on food in one month.

But that's the life Liz is used to. And even though she's never flaunted her wealth in front of me or made me feel bad about anything, I sometimes wonder if she'll truly be happy with someone who doesn't want to live an extravagant life.

"Can we head in soon?" I ask.

"Yup."

My fingers tap across the screen as I answer Liz's message.

Me: Absolutely, babe. I'll be at your house in an hour.
Liz: Thank you. See you soon.

I PUSH the thoughts out of my head. It's not that I'm brushing off Vinny's warning, but if I let myself stay in that place of questioning every single thing for too long, I'll screw everything up with my over-analyzing. I need to focus on one day at a time—and being in the moment. I'm not ready to throw in the towel just because Liz and I are different. We've already gotten through a few battles together and we came out stronger because of it.

WHEN I GET to Liz's house, she's on the couch waiting for me with red-rimmed eyes and Kleenex in her hand. Multiple tissues litter the floor around her feet. I've seen her frozen and unconscious, but nothing compares to the way my heart rips apart seeing her like this. Real grief. Real pain. I've had disappointments in my career: bands that didn't work out, songs I thought were phenomenal that never made a blip on the radio or any streaming service. The identity crisis she must be going through is beyond my comprehension.

All I can do is run to her side, sweep her into my arms and let her cry. She burrows into my chest, body shaking and trembling with every sob. I kiss the top of her head and keep my mouth on her hair, while holding her securely.

Knowing that she feels safe with me fills me with pride. I always want to be her shoulder to cry on. Always want to be here to console her and soothe her and come up with a plan for what's next. She needs the plan. She's not the person who will wander around lost forever.

Once her tumbling subsides, her body returns to calm, even breaths. She pulls back slightly and looks up at me.

"Thank you." She wipes her nose with the back of her hand. I grab a tissue from the box next to me and hand it to her. She laughs and sniffs simultaneously. "Thanks."

"Anytime."

"I'm really sorry that I bothered you while—"

"Nope." I rest my index finger on her lips. "No sorries. This is where I want to be. Right here with you. Always. Got it?"

She nods.

"I feel so stupid, Austin. I knew this was coming. In a way, I've been preparing myself, without really preparing."

"There's no reason to feel stupid, babe. It's a huge loss. You identified as a surgeon for years, so you're bound to grieve while you come to terms with it."

"How will I face people again, Austin? I still have to go back to the hospital and finish up care and documentation for the patients I've been working with. The other residents will think I couldn't cut it in the program. Everyone in my social circle will pity me and look at anything I do now as a complete failure. My parents will be so disappointed. A complete failure. The daughter they can't brag about anymore."

It hurts to know that Liz values those opinions more than she values what she thinks of herself. She's worried about judgment and the perception of who she is in the eyes of others.

"Forget that for a minute. I know it's hard to separate yourself from your career, but just take a step back. How do you feel? Deep down?"

"Shitty." She glares at me.

I sigh. "I know that. I meant, you've told me a few times that you didn't even know if being a surgeon was your ultimate dream. You said it was your parents' dream. Now that it's not an option anymore, how do you really feel?"

Liz is silent as she contemplates her answer.

"No! Don't think. How do you feel?"

"Relieved," she blurts.

"Why?" I press.

"Because now I have the freedom to do what I want. I don't have to fulfill anyone's expectations of me. My career path is really my own now." She pauses. "My career path is really my own now," she repeats, looking at me with a half-smile, as if it's just occurring to her.

"All right." I slap my hands together. "What's next and how can I help?"

"I really need to talk to Dr. Crowder to see what I need to do to switch modalities. I think Family Medicine is my best route to be involved in nonprofit work."

"Oh!" I say as I dig my phone out of my pocket. Her mentioning nonprofit work jogs my memory. Once I find the site I've bookmarked, I hold my phone out to her so she can see the screen. "I was looking for organizations for doctors who provide affordable healthcare to low-income communities and found this."

I glance up at Liz, who isn't looking at my discovery, but at me.

Tears fill her eyes and she's biting her bottom lip. Shit, maybe I'm pushing her too fast.

"We'll get through it, babe. I promise. I know how hard—"

"Thank you," she says before surging forward and planting her lips on mine. The force pushes me backward into the couch. I wrap my arms around her, absorbing her energy.

It feels so damn good to know the girl I love appreciates me.

Chapter Fourteen

LIZ

"*Oh my god! I'm so sick of yuppies trying to take over this place. Don't they know that this is not the spot for them?*"

"*They only come during the day. Then don't dare come around the scary freaks after dark.*"

"*The freaks come out at night?*"

"*Yeah. I love seeing the Chads flipping up their collars and running away in their casual—yet comfortable—boat shoes.*"

"*Right?*"

"*Becky's been sitting over there for the last half-hour. She looks lost. Hasn't even gone in yet. Keeps looking around like she's gonna get mugged.*"

"*That's not just a Becky. That's Austin's Becky.*"

"*Austin's Becky?*"

"*They've been together for months.*"

"*Wait! What? He's fucking her? She's so, so—*"

"*Becky?*" Someone laughs.

"*Plain,*" the girl finishes.

When Emily said she wanted to meet at The Usual Market for lunch, I agreed easily because I love the eclectic mix of people and funky vibe. Plus, it made sense for me to come to her since she's working all day and the tattoo shop is a few blocks away. Though I've only been here a few times, when Austin asked me to meet him for a drink after work, I never felt uncomfortable until the people a few tables away started talking about me loud enough for me to overhear. The black-and-white striped dress I picked up from Target at the beginning of the summer doesn't scream *"Look at all the money I have!"* So I'm unsure of how they even came to the conclusion that I'm a yuppie.

I know it's their own insecurity. I know they hate me for what they think I have because they don't have it. It annoys me that they chose to make someone feel bad about being here. Who decides where someone doesn't belong?

It's funny, because I wonder if any of them are like Emily. People who grew up in affluent—or at least middle-class families—but choose to insult people like me to prove they fit in. Money doesn't have anything to do with how you feel inside or who you identify with. I've felt like a loner my entire life, not because of a wealth divide, but because I'm quiet and reserved compared to the rest of my family. Wealth is not a measure of character.

We're on opposite sides of the high school gymnasium. Maybe someday, we'll move to the middle and start playing together.

"I seriously can't believe Austin would want her," the girl continues.

I take a deep breath and check the time on my phone, wondering why Emily is so late, without even texting. Chances are she's working on someone and hasn't even looked at the time, but I admit, my anxiety level creeps higher with every comment. Getting up and going inside means walking right by their table, and I don't want it to seem like they've gotten to me. Even though they have.

"She must have a magical pussy."

"Why are you analyzing my sex life?" Austin's voice rings out gruff, loud, angry.

His voice—and the ensuing commotion—makes me turn my head toward the people I've been trying to avoid looking at. Austin has the guy by the shirt collar.

"This place is for everyone. And you three can get out until you figure out what that means." He lets the guy go and points toward the street. "You too, sweetheart. Get your bitch-ass off this property."

"Jesus, Austin!"

"Is she really worth kicking out your friends?"

He crosses his arms over his chest. "The only friend of mine I see out here is that girl over there who's minding her fucking business while assholes talk shit about her. That's the kind of person I'll stick up for any day of the week."

The girl grabs her purse off the picnic table and lifts her middle finger as she walks away. The guy follows her without even a glance back at Austin. They left without putting up much of a fuss, which tells me that he's either got a lot of pull among his friend group or he never gets as mad as he just did.

When Austin looks at me I give him a small smile, then drop my eyes to my lap. I appreciate that he stood up for me, but I still feel like an idiot having to be saved by my boyfriend.

"You okay?" he asks. He's next to me now, the smell of bergamot and stale beer assaulting my senses. He always smells like beer when he gets home from work.

"Yeah." I meet his eyes.

"I don't feel the way they do, Liz." Austin sits next to me and places his hand on my leg.

"I know. It's okay." I brush off his words—but not his hand. His touch comforts me.

"I mean, you *do* have a magical pussy, but—" His fingers creep toward the sweet spot between my legs and I'm instantly happy I chose to wear this dress today.

"You think?" I ask.

Austin lowers his mouth to my ear. When he speaks it comes out as a hiss. "Absolutely."

Then his hand is underneath my skirt, his fingers slipping into my underwear. "All I can think about is fucking you with my tongue while your pussy grinds down on my face."

"Again?" I ask with a sharp intake of breath as his fingers work me.

"Every day, Miss Honey." He adds his thumb, rubbing hard, fast circles against my clit—the way he knows makes me get off.

"I could get used to that." My breath starts to match his rhythm, though I'm trying to hold onto my control. Am I really going to let him get me off in public? "What are you doing here? I thought you were off today?"

"Are you trying to distract me?" Austin grins.

I place my palms flat on the top of the picnic table, hoping for the strength to stay upright, rather than melt into him. My pulse speeds up. I look around the area, worried people may be watching, but it's empty except for us. "You're going to make me come. I don't know how I feel about that."

"You don't?" he asks. "Does it feel good?"

"Yes."

He leans closer to me, giving his fingers better access to hook into me. "It is exciting?"

"Yes," I whisper.

"Do you want me to stop?"

Instead of worrying about who might be looking at us, I turn my face to his, which is inches from mine. His bright blue eyes shine with a sharpness I've never seen. A crooked smile lifts his lips as if he's daring me to protest.

"No."

Austin seizes my mouth, kissing me with a desperation that sends me over the edge. I grab his head with both hands and keep our mouths molded together as I come hard. When his lips twist into a grin, I remove my mouth from his.

"Holy shit, that was sexy," Austin says, his breath fast and warm against my cheeks. "I'll never get enough of you, babe."

"Are you kidding me?" Emily's voice rings through the air thick and humid and filled with the scent of sex.

"Hey Em!" I squeak, embarrassed because I know she saw what just happened. If she's this close to us, there's no way she couldn't have.

"Did you guys just do what I think you did?"

"What? Kiss?" Austin asks innocently. The smirk on his face is anything but innocent. He looks absolutely thrilled with himself. "Yeah, we kissed. Kissing your sister is my favorite thing in the world to do. She's absolutely phenomenal."

"Enough of that." I stop him. "What are you doing here?"

"You let a guy finger-fuck you under the table and you don't even know where he works? Real classy, Liz," Emily teases.

I know it's sarcasm. And yet, it still sends flames of embarrassment to my cheeks. Emily says whatever she feels like. She's not hindered by any societal pressures of what's appropriate to talk about in public.

"He was supposed to have today off. I didn't realize he would be here."

"Liz knows that my real job is a musician. A musician whose band just got offered a contract with RGA."

"What?" Emily and I say in unison.

Austin smiles, but it doesn't reach his eyes so there must be more to the story. "We literally just got the offer a few days ago."

"Dude! I knew it. That's so rad!" Emily lifts her hand for a high five, then retracts it immediately. "You should probably wash your hand, dude."

"Yup," he says, lowering the arm he'd raised. I laugh.

"I mean, it's not signed yet," Austin continues. "We haven't worked out all the details, so if you could keep it on the down low, that'd be awesome."

"Yeah, man! Your secret is safe with me," Emily assures him. That's one of the things I love about her; she really does keep her mouth shut. Probably because she's had to keep her life secret for so long. I can tell by the way people treat her that they do not know her background. I wonder if it would change things.

"Can we talk later?" he whispers.

"Of course." I pull away, take his face in my hands, and plant my lips on his. I know he has reservations about signing a contract for various reasons. He must still be contemplating the pros and cons. Either way, I want to show my support. "I'm so proud of you."

Em drops her messenger bag on the picnic table. "Why the fuck didn't Fozzie text me?" Her thumbs tap her keyboard furiously.

"I don't know. Probably because we're still in shock. When Nelson said he had some big news, we thought it was something with the upcoming tour. We had no clue it was a label offering us a contract."

"It's the universe, man." Emily looks up from her phone. "All the good shit you put into the world is coming to you."

Austin nods. "Still a lot to work out. We'll see."

"Shit, Lizzy, I just saw your text. Sorry, I'm an asshole. I took a walk-in at the shop. Didn't realize it would take me as long as it did. Did you eat?"

"No, not yet. I don't even know what they have here," I admit. I feel like an idiot that I sat here for thirty minutes, so paralyzed by the people who were talking about me, that I didn't even go inside. Even though I've been here with Austin multiple times, I've never eaten at the deli.

"I'll grab you a menu," Austin says. "I gotta get back in there anyway. I'll take my break in a few and have lunch with you guys, is that cool?"

"I don't know. Is that cool, Liz? Or did you want time to gush about how much you love Austin without him here?"

"Shut up," I hiss, though I can't contain my smile. I don't love him, do I? I like him. A lot. The more I see him, the more I want to see him. Even after a few months together, I still can't get him out of my head. Every second with him makes me feel better and better about myself and my future.

"Oh shit. Sisters lunch, yeah. No. Don't worry. I was just—fuck! I didn't mean to intrude."

"I like your intrusions," I say without thinking about the double entendre.

But Emily doesn't miss it. "I can confirm that from where I was standing."

I drop my face into my hands.

"Give her a break, Em," Austin says. "She stepped out of her comfort zone to have lunch with you here."

His comment doesn't come across as angry or rude, but it still stings. I'm comfortable anywhere. I just wasn't comfortable with people talking shit about me while I was a few tables away.

Austin plants a kiss on my hair and goes back inside.

Em puts her hand on my head. "Lighten up, Liz! I'm kidding! Sorry I embarrassed you."

I lift my head. "It's okay. I'm not embarrassed by what you said. I'm embarrassed at how much I like him."

"Why would you be embarrassed about that?" Emily lowers herself onto the bench across from me and pulls her knees up to sit criss-cross applesauce. Her long, pale legs are covered in even more art than last time I saw her. She could have had the tattoos for years, but I feel like I notice something new every time I'm with her. Tattoos aren't my form of self-expression, but I absolutely appreciate how gorgeous they are and the talent of the artists.

I lift my gaze from her legs to her eyes. "He's—"

"Infatuated with you?"

"What? No. It's only been a few months." I dismiss her assumption.

"Who cares. Love doesn't have a timeline and that man fucking loves you."

"Have you talked to him?" I feel like we are sitting at a table in a middle-school cafeteria.

"No. I can see it. I've known Austin for a long time." Emily smiles as she pulls out a pack of cigarettes from her bag, then holds it up. "Do you mind?"

"Yes, but I know that won't stop you." Emily has heard enough of my lectures. I'm not one to waste more breath on a battle I have no control over.

"You're what? Twenty-seven? Twenty-eight?" she asks, holding the cancer stick in her mouth and lighting it. She takes a drag, then grabs it between two delicate fingers before she exhales. "And you can't even tell when a guy is head over heels for you. That makes me sad, Liz."

"He doesn't love me. We just started dat—whatever this is."

"You're so smart, yet so dumb."

Her words hit me hard, because of the truth behind them. She's right, I'm book-smart, and empathetic, but I really suck at relationships. But that's because I never had someone who treated me like Austin treats me.

I can't stop the smile on my face and the butterflies in my stomach when I think about him. I've never wanted to spend less hours at work, or put off a project that would advance my career just to hang out with another human. Until now. I want to spend every minute with him. He's ambitious and hardworking and empathetic and encouraging. He sees the best in me—which has nothing to do with wealth or a prestigious career. He sees what's inside my heart. And the sex is out of this world—which seems so insignificant compared to everything else, but for me, it's a huge part of a successful relationship.

And that's when it hits me. It *is* love. I absolutely love Austin. The feelings I have for him are powerful and real. The person he brings out in me is the person I've always wanted to be.

There's nothing I want more than his happiness and success and being on that journey with him. Isn't that part of love? Wanting to do everything possible to enhance the other person's happiness. Growing together, yet allowing each person to do their own thing? I don't know. I've never been in love, but I've always wanted that to be the way.

Mutual respect and enthusiasm for the other person's career has never been a part of my life. My boyfriends were either competing with me or pushing me to work harder. And maybe that's what some people need from their partner, but not me. I don't want to live life in a competition.

Honestly, I've been trying to enjoy the relationship day by day, rather than rush into thoughts about the future. But when I do look forward, I can't see my life without him. Not for one second.

WHEN AUSTIN COMES over for dinner later that night, I'm excited to hear all about the contract. I can't help but feel like I've been a huge black cloud over him recently. He's been helping me cope with the fallout of my injury when he should be excited and focused on all the amazing things happening.

"Tell me more about the record contract. That's exciting, right?" I ask.

"Yes. And no. On one hand, it's awesome that RGA is interested, but on the other hand—there are a million reasons to say no."

"Such as?"

"The biggest thing is Tim." He hesitates. "I honestly don't want to sign something this big with him. I don't trust him."

"Have you talked to him?"

Austin laughs. "Yup. We had a bit of a blowup when Nelson brought us all together. Basically, we told him that he had to get his shit together or we'd find a new bass player. We'll see how that goes."

I reach across the table and place my hand on his. "I'm sorry. I know that has to be hard to face, especially right now. Before the festival this summer and the tour coming up."

"Thanks, Liz." He smiles. "It had to be done, though. We've been letting him slide for too long. We'll see how he responds."

"Is Tim the only reservation you have about signing?" I ask.

"No. I don't want to lose creative control. I don't want to give up any control really," Austin admits. "And I know we'll have to. But I really don't think a big label is right for us."

"What does Fozzie think? Is he on the same page?"

"Yes. And no." Austin rubs his face in his hands. "He agrees with me, but at the same time, I think we were both dazzled by the fact that a label liked us and our music enough to want to sign us. It used to be the goal, ya know? What if we turn it down and regret it?" He spears a piece of broccoli. "The industry has changed so much. I'd rather be able to release the music we want. Keep money in our pockets. We don't need the label's money. We can figure it out. That's why we both work side jobs and save money. I'd rather keep working at The Market and doing mini tours to build our audience. We draw great crowds. We have a large following on social media. I think this tour coming up with Walk on Mars is gonna blow us up, Liz."

"I agree," I tell him. "Sounds like you already know what you want. No big label."

"It's not just my decision."

"I know, but it sounds like Fozzie feels the same way. He's a smart guy, too."

"Really?" he asks, squinting at me.

I think back to Fozzie's insightful explanation of his trampoline-man tattoo and nod. "Yeah."

"You don't work weekends anymore, right?" Austin asks.

"No. I'm off the call schedule and I only have a few more patients left. I can check on them during the week."

"Do you want to come to Atlanta?"

"For the festival?" I ask. I've never been to a music festival. I don't even know what to expect, but it sounds really fun.

"Yeah." He nods.

"I'd love to!" I jump from the chair and plant myself in his lap. Then I throw my arms around him. He squeezes me tightly.

"This is going to be huge for us, Liz," Austin whispers in my ear. "Nothing could be better than having you by my side the entire time."

My heart swells. I'm so excited for Austin. It's time to stop dwelling on my own problems and be there to support him in the biggest moment of his career.

Chapter Fifteen

AUSTIN

*L*iz curls up next to me, tucking her arms around me and throwing her legs over my lap. We're in the back row of the van, on the way to Atlanta, to play our first big music festival. There's a tense excitement in the air, and I'm so glad I invited her. She calms me, gives me focus, and keeps me from overanalyzing all the shit I have going on in my head that I don't need to think about right now. All I can do is take it one day at a time, and here we are.

We absolutely cannot sign a contract with him. We gave Tim a chance to prove that he cares about the band as much as we do, and he didn't show up for either rehearsal we had for this festival set. After this weekend, we'll get everything squared away. We have a few days before we go on tour with Walk on Mars. We should have kicked him out before we hit the road today, but how the hell were we going to find another bass player in such a short time?

Liz pulls her hair away from her neck, giving me a view of her soft, smooth collarbone and full breasts practically bursting out of her skimpy sundress. My dick presses against my jeans. Everything about her gets me hard. I want to reach under her skirt and play with her pussy while the guys goof off. They'll never know. Even if they do, they don't care. They know how I feel about Liz. Not only is she my muse, she's the person keeping me going as we navigate these exciting, but stressful times.

It makes me crazy knowing that she wears loose, flowy dresses for me. My shy, proper, straight-laced doctor knows that I want access to her at all times. She loves fulfilling every fantasy. She loves that there's no weirdness. It's all respect and open minds and mind-blowing orgasms.

I slide my fingers up the inside of her thigh, teasing her by rubbing through her panties. She arches into me, which spurs me on.

"You've got to be quiet, Miss Honey," I whisper. "Unless you want the guys to hear you."

Her forehead rubs against my chest, her way of giving me permission without speaking. I slip a finger inside her, turned on at how wet she is already. I work her with one finger before adding a second, excited at her involuntary reaction to squeeze me tightly. I love how she tries to contain herself. It must be killing her, because she's normally really loud.

When my thumb starts to rub on the outside of her underwear, her pussy tightens around my fingers. She knows she'll be coming soon. My cock swells under her legs. She writhes against my fingers, silently asking for more. I'm moving fast now, tapping her G-spot while rubbing fast circles with my thumb. I know she's gonna explode. I can't wait to feel her all over my hand.

I'm working furiously, not giving a fuck that it's obvious to anyone who looks back here what I'm doing. But I want Liz to come hard. She needs it. She needs to know that this is the sexy, part of life. It's normal to want each other. It's normal to get off. Maybe not in a van with six other guys, but hey, fantasy is fantasy.

Her teeth dig into my shoulder, and I know she's coming. She's riding my hand, grinding and squeezing. I want her mouth on my cock so fucking badly, but that's out of the question. Later, I'll make sure we're alone somewhere.

If finger-fucking her here, in the van, where we're slightly concealed, gets me this hard, I can only imagine what it'll be like when I'm doing this to her as we stand in the crowd, watching a concert.

Thankfully, our set isn't until tomorrow, so we have all day to relax and get our bearings in Atlanta today.

"We should get back to the van before the guys tonight so we can take this seat again."

"When are we going to the hotel?" Liz asks, words coming out as pants between breaths.

"We don't have a hotel. We sleep in the van at festivals."

Liz practically dries up on the spot; her pussy feels like my mouth after smoking weed. *Shit.*

"You sleep in the van?"

"Yeah. Hotels are expensive. We don't really have that budget yet."

"Okaaaay," she says. "But you asked me to come this weekend. Don't you think you should have said something?"

Yes, I should've.

"Yeah—I'm—Jesus, Liz. I'm sorry. I've been running around, trying to get everything ready for this, and I honestly didn't even think about it."

I expect her wrath. Hell, I deserve her wrath. The fact that it didn't even cross my mind to suggest to Liz that she might want to get a hotel makes me feel like a complete asshole. And I wasn't even trying to be. I really did forget.

"It's okay." She curls her fingers over my shoulders. "I know you've been really stressed."

"I really am sorry, baby. Jesus! I'm such an idiot."

She places a hand on my cheek and smiles. "I'm not mad at you, Austin. I'm proud of everything you've done to get here. This moment right here." She looks into my eyes. "You've worked your ass off. I haven't known you long, but I can see that."

There's nothing better she could have said in that moment. Nothing.

"Thank you, babe. That means the world to me." I squeeze her into my side and place my lips on the top of her head, breathing in the botanical scent of her hair and the positivity she emits.

How many girls would have railed me? Absolutely *railed* me for not telling her that we didn't have a hotel. Liz is used to having everything planned out, yet she can still put her expectations aside and see the situation from my point of view. The point of view of a guy doing everything I possibly can to make this band a success. She can forgive my oversight. I've never met a kinder woman.

When I release her, she digs into her purse and retrieves her phone.

"What are you doing?" I ask.

"Checking out hotels." Her fingers dance across her screen. "Oooh, the Marriott has a room available."

"I bet that costs a mint tonight. They up the prices for festivals."

"It's no big deal," she says absently.

"It's just a place to sleep and put your stuff."

Liz looks up from her phone. "And shower." She winks.

While I appreciate her dirty mind, I don't think she's getting my point. "Well, a motel on the outskirts of the city serves the same purpose. And it's probably one third the price."

"I'm sure it is, but I'd rather stay at the Marriott."

"Why? What does it matter? You're not even gonna be there for most of the time."

"Because I like to be comfortable and close. And honestly— because I can."

My mouth had been open, poised to strike, but I can't do it. Instead, I shake my head and smile. "Exactly."

"I don't have to defend myself to you."

"Never said you did."

"I can tell by your look."

"What can you tell by my look?"

"That you think I'm a spoiled, wasteful, rich bitch." She glances out the window, avoiding my eyes.

As much as I hate to admit it, the thought passed through my head. And it pisses me off that it was there, no matter how fleeting. I'm an asshole for putting that stereotype on Liz, when I know she's so much more than that.

"I don't feel that way about you at all, Liz. I'm sorry if it came across that way."

"I'm used to it." She shrugs.

"Maybe you are—" I run my hand through her hair and lock eyes with her. "But I never want to be the person who makes you feel that way."

By the way her expression changes from hurt to surprise, I can tell she's not expecting my words. She thinks I'm gonna call her out, treat her like shit like so many people before me. But I know she's a good person. She doesn't flaunt her wealth, she's just used to having it—and using it. She's trying to help in the way she knows how.

"Thank you."

I close my fist in her, pulling gently, holding her in place. Her breath hitches every time I do it, which is always my clue that she loves it. Sweat runs down my back, fueled by the intimate stance with Liz and the scorching Atlanta sun streaming through the window.

"I think it's silly to pay hundreds of dollars for a place to sleep—but that doesn't say anything about how I think of you as a person. I see your generosity. I know you just want us to be comfortable. Hell, someday I hope I don't have to think about how much a hotel room costs."

"It'll happen," Liz assures me, nudging my nose with hers. "And you'll still care, because not being wasteful is instilled in you. We'll spend our money wisely."

"We?" I ask.

"Yeah, we. Future us."

"I love when you talk like that."

Her acknowledgment of a future is exciting and scary simultaneously. I love that Liz sees a future with me. But whenever I think too far ahead, it seems to come crashing down around me. All I want to focus on is right now. It's all I can control.

Liz slides her hand onto my neck and massages the back. I melt into her touch, pulling our bodies even closer.

I can't help the slow moan that escapes as she kneads my neck. It's an erogenous zone. And Liz knows every time she touches me there, it gets me all worked up. It's like a secret weapon she uses to get me to chill out. She thinks she's tricky, and I let her. Because I love her hands on me.

"Too bad we don't have a room," I whisper in her ear. "I want to fuck you so badly right now."

She pulls away slightly and looks me in the eye. "Are you trying to pick a fight?"

My lips turn up in a smile, because I know she's kidding.

"I like when you get all feisty, babe. Makes you savage in bed."

"Whatever." Liz rolls her eyes.

But I'm not letting it go that easily. "You start scratching my back and biting my shoulder. You ask me to slam into you harder."

I can tell my words affect her by the way her breathing increases. She shivers and presses her body against mine. Heat pools in my torso and spreads straight to my dick. That same heat must be getting to Liz, too, because her cheeks flush a beautiful rosy pink. Which means I'm not gonna stop.

"I love the feeling of you grinding and writhing against my cock. It's so fucking sexy."

Suddenly, Liz's lips crash onto mine almost as if she can't help it. Magnets pulled together involuntarily. She moans into my mouth when I press my cock against her. I'm so ready to be inside my girl, I don't know if I'll be able to wait for a hotel room.

"Please let me fuck you?" I ask, breathing heavy onto her lips. "Right here."

"You'd like that, wouldn't you?"

I laugh. "It sounds much cooler than it would really be, right?" I glance down, though I can't even see the bench under our bodies. "This thing is too hard and small and covered in piss and—"

"Oh my god! Stop!" Liz sits up slightly.

I laugh again and hug her to me. "Sorry I mentioned that after we drove all the way here, sitting on it."

"I feel the need to Lysol my butt."

"Oh girl!" I nuzzle my face into her neck. "I'll take care of your ass. Don't you worry."

"You suck."

"Actually, you do. And you're damn good at it."

My comment makes her dip her head, hiding her face in my chest.

I don't understand how she can be so good at sex, yet so shy about it at the same time. As if she doesn't realize she's a fucking goddess. I consider it my personal mission to make her aware. Over and over again.

Chapter Sixteen

LIZ

*H*ow Austin makes me feel about myself is one of my favorite things about him. He has this knack for seeing the best part in people and telling them. I've seen him do it with his bandmates.

I haven't known many people who genuinely want to make others feel good about themselves without asking for something in return. Everyone's looking for personal gain. Nothing comes without a price.

I'm used to the competition—the rat race. Even in relationships. What can I get from the other person? How will a relationship benefit me? How can this person get me to where I want to be?

It's sad really.

It's also sad that, as much as I want to have sex with him right now, I'd be far more concerned with the cleanliness of this bench than the pleasure he gives me.

"Can I please book us a hotel room?" I ask. "I promise it won't be fancy."

Austin sighs. "I will agree if you let me pick the hotel."

I pause, unsure of how to respond. I know he'd never put is in a bad situation on purpose, but I'm still worried about the kind of place he'll pick.

Austin calls me on my hesitation immediately.

"Compromise, Liz. It's the key to successful relationships."

"You're right." I nod and hand him my phone. "You pick the place. But I also get to pick up the tab for rooms for the guys."

A look of surprise crosses Austin's face. "You'd do that?"

"Of course." I smile and brush my palm over his cheek and beard. "How mean would it be to stay in a hotel room and let the guys sweat to death in that van?"

Austin shrugs. "They've done it before." His lips slide into a smile.

I smack his bicep lightly. "You're a jerk."

"I prefer diva. The lead singer is always a diva." He winks at me.

My level-headed, sexy, scruffy boyfriend is the furthest thing from a diva.

He pulls me onto his lap, wrapping his arms around me as he scrolls the hotel options I've pulled up on my phone. Then he kisses the top of my head, an action that always makes me melt.

"You are the kindest, most generous person I've ever met, Miss Honey."

"It's no big deal," I say, nestling into him, resting my cheek on the soft, worn T-shirt covering his hard chest. "Three hotel rooms at whatever place you pick will cost less than one room at any place I would've picked."

"It's not about the money, Liz. It's about your heart."

I tilt my head back so I can see his face. "I have the means. Why wouldn't I?"

"Not everyone thinks that way."

"I've never thought any other way."

"I believe that, babe."

"But I've always had the means, so—"

"I bet we can both think of instances where someone who was more than able to didn't help out, yes?"

"Well, sure, but—"

"Liz?" Austin interrupts.

"Yeah?"

"Just take the compliment."

He's not angry or exasperated. He's genuinely trying to get me to see myself as he sees me.

"Thank you, Austin."

"Better. Now let me find us a hotel so I can fuck you before I have to walk around Atlanta with the most uncomfortable hard-on ever."

I bury my face in his chest again and laugh softly, inhaling the scent of sweat and detergent.

"I've been trying to ignore your conversation, but if I hear y'all start having sex, I'm getting it on video," Tim says, glancing over his shoulder at us.

"We're not having sex," Austin replies. He returns his gaze to the phone screen.

"A sex tape gone viral might be the injection we need to take this shit to the next level," Tim says. He actually sounds as if he's contemplating it.

I glance at Austin, who dismisses it with a grimace and shake of his head. A wave of relief calms me. As much as I love Austin, the thought of being in a viral sex tape makes me want to puke. That'd be a great thing to have to defend and dismiss at every stage of my career.

As much as I love Austin.

It's the first time I've admitted it to myself, though the feelings have been building for months—with every touch, every kiss, every conversation. Austin has burrowed himself into my heart, helping me overcome the devastation of the end of my surgical career, and helping me see the excitement of the next chapter in my life.

Pushing back the excitement of my personal revelation, I snuggle even closer to Austin and start scanning the hotel app with him. Once we start looking, we realize quickly that many of Atlanta's hotels are completely booked. We finally settle on a place outside of the city that seems to meet my cleanliness standards, as well as Austin's price point.

"Hey dickbags! My fucking amazing girlfriend got us rooms for this weekend. Let's go put our shit down before we head to the festival."

His announcement is met with:

"Sweet!"

"You rock, Liz! Thanks!"

"Sugar mama comes through."

Austin scowls and immediately lurches forward toward Tim. "If I ever hear you say anything like that again, you'll be sleeping in another band's van."

I gasp, startled at his threat. Then I place my hands on his shoulders and pull him back. "Austin, please don't."

"Jesus," Fozzie whispers.

"I was joking," Tim says.

"It's an unacceptable joke." Austin's jaw is hard, unyielding. I know his reaction encompasses more than just the current situation.

"Get a grip, Austin."

Leaning close to his ear, I whisper, "Please let it go. You're all excited and stressed about this festival. Tempers are high. I knew he was kidding."

The truth is, I don't think Tim is kidding at all, but it doesn't matter. What matters is not allowing the band to get into a fight about something so stupid a day before they're about to play their first big festival.

Never mind that the "something so stupid" is me.

AS THE VAN pulls into the hotel parking lot, I hold back a groan. Wealthy or not, I don't know one person that isn't creeped out by hotels with room doors on the outside. I don't know why. Maybe it feels like a lack of security. Anyone can walk right up—hitchhikers, prostitutes.

Suddenly, I'm ripped out of my thoughts because all eyes in the van are focused on me. Even Jimmy, who's driving, is looking at me in the rearview mirror.

"Don't worry, Liz. We'll keep you safe from hitchhikers and prostitutes," Fozzie says, breaking a moment of awkward silence.

I close my eyes and cover my face with one hand when I realize I voiced my concerns out loud.

"You're on your own with Austin, though. No one can tame him," he adds.

Interesting phrasing.

"I don't want to tame him," I answer, placing my hand on Austin's thigh and squeezing. "I like him wild."

I swear I hear his chest puff out, despite the laughter from the other guys.

It's true, though. There's not one thing I would change about him.

ONCE WE CHECK into the hotel and get rooms sorted, Austin and I hurry to ours. There's a king-sized bed, waiting for us to consummate, and yet, I can't help but wonder...

"You want to have sex in the van, don't you?" I ask, setting my phone on the dresser next to the TV.

Austin's face lights up, a sheepish grin turning his lips upward. "I've always wanted to fuck in there. It's a weird bucket list thing before we make it big and move to a tour bus."

I shake my head in disbelief, not at his fantasy, but at the words that are about to come out of my mouth. "Should we sneak out there tonight and do it?"

His eyes widen and that grin slides into a full kid-at-Christmas glow. "You'd do that for me?"

I nod without hesitation. "How can I say no when something so easy is bucket-list for you? I mean, that's a big-time fantasy." My heart speeds up as I realize just how much I'd do for this man.

"You're so fucking awesome."

His compliment both delights and confuses me. I've never had anyone think of me that way—and no one like a hot, brooding musician.

At the same time, I'm trying to wrap my mind around how unsanitary and uncomfortable it's going to be.

Boys are gross.

But the idea must make Austin happy, because he plants a quick kiss on my lips before skipping to the door. "You get settled and ready for bed. I'll be right back."

"Okay..."

"Gotta get pretty for my girl." He winks before disappearing through the door.

The room is brighter and cleaner than I imagined when we pulled up. Still, I immediately roll down the comforter until it's a fluffy log on the floor at the foot of the bed. Not going to touch that thing.

With Austin gone, it's my chance to freshen up from the sexy, sweaty bus ride. I've never had this kind of reaction to anyone before. That's not to say previous partners didn't get me aroused, but it's constant with Austin. All it takes is hearing his voice or seeing his face —hell, even an innocent text saying hello—and my body reacts. It's a bit embarrassing when I'm in public and he's not around.

Screw those guys who said I was cold. Maybe it was them. Maybe they didn't get me hot and bothered. I can't make my body react if it isn't stimulated.

As I unzip my Kate Spade weekender bag, I glance at Austin's grubby duffel. Sliding my finger across an especially worn area that looks like it'll rip at any moment, I make a mental note to get him a new one when we get home. He'll need a better bag for all the upcoming travel. I smile, proud, as I think about all of the hard work that has gone into getting where they are right now, and thrilled at the amazing opportunities they have lined up.

Because my head has been so scattered recently, I decide a mental note isn't going to do. I stand up and cross the room, grabbing my phone from the dresser. After a few quick searches, I decide on a beautiful sturdy Tumi bag and place the order immediately. It's basic black, nothing extravagant or flashy, as I know he wouldn't like that, but it's definitely something that will last through the upcoming travel.

I dig my toiletry case out of my bag and wander into the bathroom. I hadn't planned on taking a shower, but sweat still rolls down my back and I realize, it's a must. It was so hot out today and all we were doing was walking around Atlanta. I can't even imagine what it will be like standing outside tomorrow with the sun beating down. Austin's set is at 3:30 p.m.—when the sun is at its peak.

Leaning over the tub, I reach over and turn the water on, keeping my hand under the stream until it reaches the perfect temperature. After placing my shampoo, conditioner, and body gel on the edge of the tub, I whip my sundress to the floor and slide out of my underwear, before stepping into the shower. The cool water pelting my skin feels amazing.

As I work the shampoo into my hair, I start singing my favorite song of Austin's. I can't get over how much emotion it evokes from me, and I can't explain why.

"Hey, babe. I'm feeling dirty. Mind if I join you?"

"Holy crap!" I jump, almost knocking my head on the tiled wall. "Geez, Austin, you scared me!" My heart pounds against my chest, not just from the scare, but because this gorgeous man just climbed into the shower. I've never showered with anyone before.

He places his hands on my waist and steps closer, and I have to mentally remind myself to keep breathing. Shampoo slides down my temple, but I'm frozen to wipe it away.

"The most beautiful girl I've ever laid eyes on is naked, wet, and singing my song. I can tell you with complete honesty that I have never been this turned on."

Heat zings through my body, causing me to shudder. Austin feels it, because he tightens his grip on my waist. Then he brings his face to mine and kisses me softly. So softly. The flutter of his lips so gentle it's as if air whispers over my lips. A hint of passion, desire...

Love.

AFTER OUR SHOWER, I step out of the bathroom and scan the room, tapping my index finger against my lips.

"What has you perplexed, babe?" Austin asks, wrapping his arms around me from behind and placing a kiss on my neck.

"I have no clue what I'm going to wear tomorrow."

"Nothing?" he whispers, then slides his tongue over my ear. His teeth settle on my lobe, biting softly.

I press my backside into him and grind against his pelvis. The action is met with a low moan and I almost think he's going to devour me.

"Fuuuuck."

"Will you have any of those long, black tank tops at merch?"

"I can't answer merch questions right now, babe. I want to be inside you so bad."

"Focus," I say, turning my head slightly to meet his eyes.

"I am so completely focused I can't think of anything else." He moves his hands to the top of the towel secured above my breasts.

"I thought we were doing this in the van?"

The towel drops to the floor.

"Throw some clothes on. I need to fuck you right now," Austin growls, then slaps my bare bottom.

I jump and look at him with wide eyes.

"You like that."

It's a statement, not a question, because he knows the answer without me having to say it.

"I've got tanks in the van," he says as he slides a pair of silver basketball shorts up his legs.

"Oh good!" I grab a tank top and oversized boxer shorts out of my bag. "Can I buy one to wear tomorrow?"

Austin looks at me like I have three heads.

"What? Is it completely dorky for me to wear a band tank? Is that frowned upon?"

"No. I can't wait to see you rocking our stuff. But you're not going to pay for it."

"Why wouldn't I pay for it?" I ask, stepping into my shorts.

"You're my girl," he says as if that's all the answer necessary.

"So?" I ask. "I should still pay for a tank top. You paid for it. You have to recoup the money."

"You're not paying."

"Austin."

"Why you always gotta argue?"

"Because I like to be a pain in your ass."

"Oh girl, I'd *love* to be the pain in *your* ass," Austin says with a wide smile. He takes two steps toward me and we're nose to nose.

"I don't know how I feel about that comment."

He licks his lips. "I love when your cheeks get red because of something I suggest, because I know that no one has ever even suggested it before." He reaches between us and tweaks one of my nipples. "And I know that you're entertaining the idea in that beautiful brain of yours."

I bow my head, but he immediately places his fingers under my chin and lifts my face to his.

"You never have to be embarrassed with me, Liz. I would never do anything you didn't want. I respect you completely. I'm literally a slave at your feet."

His words are everything any girl wants to hear. Things every girl wants to believe. And all I can think of is how much I want to believe him, but then a stupid flash of insecurity peeks through and I wonder what he sees in me.

"Stop thinking," Austin commands. "Because I don't like whatever is going through your head. It's not true. You're the most phenomenal human I've met in my entire life. I don't care if you don't believe me right now. One day you will. And I'll spend every second until that day proving it to you."

Tears spring to my eyes.

"Nope." He licks the outside of my eye, where a drop has slid out. "Too high up for you to be wet." As he speaks, his fingers slide under one leg of my boxers and slip into me. "That's where I want you wet, babe."

I know I'm not disappointing him. Everything he does turns me on. Especially after his heartfelt declaration.

"Where were we?" he asks. His fingers work me without relent. My breathing gets heavy, deep, fast.

"I was paying you for a tank top," I manage to say, as I try to ignore his deft fingers; getting back to solid ground will help hold my emotions at bay.

"How about I give it to you to wear in exchange for—" Two fingers curl, pumping at my G-spot, faster and harder until I'm bucking onto his chest and squeezing his hand between my thighs.

"Austin!"

"Yeah, babe," he whispers, holding me as I collapse onto him. "Come for me, babe. I love when you come all over my hand. You're so fucking sexy."

He removes his fingers from inside me, twirls me around so my back is against his chest, and reaches around, hitting me with a three-finger assault on my clit, rubbing hard and fast in a circular motion. He knows exactly how to get me off. I try to breathe through it to enhance the orgasm and make it last, but I can't. My breath comes out in short, fast pants. The only thing holding me up is Austin's free arm around my waist.

"Oh! Oh god! Oh god!" When the orgasm hits, I arch against his chest and scream, "Austin!"

"Yes, Liz, yes! Fuck yes! I love when you say my name when you come." He knows I'm in the zone, but he won't let up, plunging his fingers into me again, his deft digits piston on my G-spot, helping me ride it out. Finally, the wave relents and I slump against him.

He kisses my neck as he removes his fingers. "I will never get enough of watching you come, Liz."

His hard, thick cock presses against my back, making my pussy throb.

"I will never get enough of letting you watch me come," I tease, still trying to catch my breath.

Austin laughs, then spins me around and wraps his arms around me. He rests his chin on my head, while I bury my face in his neck and inhale the scent of my amber, vanilla body wash on him.

"You ready to go get that tank top out of the van?"

"Do I get to ride your dick while we're out there?"

"Of course."

"Will you let me pay for the tank top?"

"You will be wearing a tank top with my band's name and logo all day long at our first major festival. That's called advertising. Giving you a free tank top in exchange for advertising is an intelligent business decision, wouldn't you agree?"

Shoot. He's got me.

"Yes. I agree with the statement."

"I knew you'd see it my way." He kisses me quickly. "But Liz—you're my girlfriend. You're gonna get free band shit. You gotta get over it."

"Fine!" I laugh. "Now that I know I'm a walking advertisement, I'm completely on board."

"Good. Now put some clothes on, woman! It's time to fuck in the van."

Once we're both wearing enough to walk around outside without being too risqué, Austin leads me down the sidewalk and around a corner. The van is parked in the back of the lot between two huge semi-trucks. Guess he's not as much of a voyeur as I thought.

Or maybe he did it for me, thinking I'd be more comfortable tucked away. It's comforting, but the thought of someone seeing us in the van is actually turning me on. Like when he fingered me at The Market. I never thought public sex acts would be such a turn-on. It's like he's peeling away my straight-laced layers one by one.

"You hid the van away?" I ask.

"Didn't want any hitchhikers or prostitutes walking in on us." He winks. The reference to my outburst earlier makes me giggle.

Austin opens the door and takes a step back so I can climb in. The scent of Lysol wipes fills the air—and I realize that's why he left the room earlier. He was out here cleaning the seat. My heart swells.

As I climb to the back, he smacks my butt and I lurch forward. "Geez!"

"I want to bite your ass so badly, Liz. It's perfect. Smooth, round, firm."

"Oh my gosh! Stop!"

"I want to do other things to it, too, but I won't scare you with all that tonight."

It's the second reference he's made to anal tonight. It's not a thought I've ever entertained before. Ever. But with Austin, in the right environment with the right preparation, it doesn't seem like it'd be so bad. If that's what he likes, I trust him enough to try.

"It doesn't scare me, Austin. I feel completely comfortable and safe with you," I say, looking at him as I collapse onto the bench on the last row.

"That's the best thing you've ever said to me. You'll always be safe with me, Liz. Body and soul."

No one has ever spoken to me like Austin does. He hits me in the heart and the brain. He's stability and strength in a way that I've never experienced before. Stability has always been the guy who went to a prestigious school, and has a good job and who can provide. More of a business transaction than a heart connection.

I reach out and pull him onto me, but I'm cramped in the back with my knees, and he falls directly on top of them rather than between, accidentally spearing him in the gut.

"Oh my gosh, Austin, I'm so sorry! Are you okay?" I ask, opening my legs so his body slides between them.

"Yup," he responds through teeth clenched in pain.

"Thank you for sanitizing the seat," I say in an effort to make up for the knees to the stomach. One hand slides through his hair, comforting him.

"How did you know?"

"It smells like what I imagine a red-light district bedroom smells like between clients."

Austin busts out laughing. "What in the world, Liz?"

"What?"

He shakes his head, the smile still painted on his face. "You crack me up."

He places a hand on the back of the seat, and uses it to shift a bit and lift himself toward my face. I know he's trying not to put his full body weight on me, which makes for a very awkward position for him.

"Maybe you should straddle me?" he suggests.

"Oh! Yeah! Good idea."

Figuring out logistics of fucking in the van is taking the sexy spontaneity out of our tryst.

After he lifts himself up and leans back on his calves, I scoot up enough to allow him to sit down, before throwing one leg over to straddle his lap. When I wiggle my butt, getting comfortable on his legs, I feel him hard and ready underneath me. Evidently the comical way we've gone about getting situated hasn't hindered his excitement.

"Fuck, that feels good."

I look into his eyes and lift my hands to his face, stroking his beard on both sides from temple to chin. I love how soft it is and I know he loves when I do it. He closes his eyes and I see the tension in his shoulders release. Knowing that he's completely relaxed makes me happy. I lean down and place my lips on his. The touch is soft at first.

Then I move my hands to his hair and grab hold, pulling at the roots as I intensify the kiss.

Austin doesn't hold back. He grabs my hips, digging his fingers into my flesh. Our tongues tangle with greater need the longer the kiss goes on. When I pull away, he catches my bottom lip in his teeth.

"You're really turned on by this, aren't you?" I ask softly.

"I'm fulfilling my groupie-van-sex fantasy with my hot girlfriend. What's not to like about that?"

His words make me laugh, but I want to play the groupie role, so I reach down, grab the hem of my tank top, and pull it over my head. Austin watches with hooded lids as I arch toward him, presenting my breasts to his face. He leans closer and licks one of my nipples. The touch makes me shiver.

"That's it, baby," I whisper seductively. "Make me your dirty whore."

Austin bursts out laughing for the second time in minutes. He hides his face between my breasts, though I can still feel him shaking.

"What?" I ask.

He removes his face from the valley between my boobs. "I wasn't prepared. I've never heard you say anything like that. I don't think I've ever even heard you swear before."

I shrug. "I've never had a reason to talk like that."

"Never?"

"If any guy I dated wanted a whore, he'd pay for one."

Austin flinches, which makes me want to take back my words immediately. I grab his face with both hands and say, "I didn't mean it that way. I just meant that none of those guys ever asked me to play that role. They didn't think I had 'bad girl' in me."

"That's hard to believe. You have such a dirty, sexy mind."

"They didn't know that. I never really felt comfortable enough to show that side of me. I don't know." I lean back, releasing his cheeks, and tuck my hair behind my ears. "All they saw was a book nerd. The girl who was always studying. I told you I haven't had many boyfriends, Austin. Some of them—" I glance out the side window. "A couple of them called me cold."

"Cold?" Austin asks.

I turn back to him, but don't lift my eyes, focusing instead on the intricate lines of his neck tattoo. "Cold. Ice Queen. Emotionally unavailable."

In my peripheral vision I see a look of understanding cross his face. He leans toward my exposed breasts and presses a kiss onto my chest, right over my heart.

"Forget them. You're not cold. You're guarded. You don't share yourself with men easily because they have to prove their worth before you give your heart away. But make no mistake, Elizabeth Commons. I've never known someone with a more beautiful soul. Warmth and love radiate from you. I felt that the first time I saw you—even when your lips were blue and you were shaking."

"Are we back to the groupie fantasy thing?" I ask, confused at his words. "Because I was burning up the first night we met. All that dancing and all those people cramped together."

Austin pauses, then shakes his head and laughs, "Yeah. No, I know. I was in another world for a second."

Tears prick at my eyes, but I refuse to let them fall. He's either mixing me up with another girl, or I really did give off a cold vibe that first time we met at The Underground. What had I done wrong? I thought it had been a wonderful night. I was open and free.

He's right about me. It does take me awhile to open up. Which is why I've never said I love you to any man. Not even a guy I dated for two years. Because I didn't love him. And I'm not going to throw those words around. They mean something to me.

And to think, I almost said it to Austin.

"You thought I was cold that night, didn't you? Stand-offish? Bitchy?" I fold my arms across my chest, trying to hide my exposed breasts. It's not going to work, because they're pretty large, but it makes me feel better to be somewhat covered.

"Fuck no! Liz! I just told you the first time I met you I was completely taken with you. I—Jesus, Liz, I couldn't take my eyes off you. And—there was so much more."

"What does that mean?"

"Can I tell you a story?" he asks. "About the song *Open Your Heart?*"

"Please," I say, intrigued because of how much the song resonates with me.

"I was late for class driving through a crazy-ass ice storm, when I saw a vehicle on the side of the road, smashed between two trees. I pulled over immediately and ran to the driver's side to make sure the person inside was okay. But she wasn't. She was slumped over the steering wheel, blood coming from who knows where."

I listen intently, keeping my eyes on Austin as he speaks.

"I ran back to my truck, grabbed a crowbar, and pried open the door, then I lifted the girl out gently and carried her to my truck. I didn't call nine-one-one. I should have, I know." He brushes hair away from my face and lets his fingers slide through until he reaches my shoulder. "It was pretty stupid of me to move her, but I had no clue how long she'd been there and the hospital was just up the road, so I took the chance."

"It wasn't until I brought her into the hospital that I saw her face. She was the most beautiful girl I'd ever seen, despite her blue lips." He smiles.

My mind—and my pulse—are both going a million miles a minute as his words come back to me.

The most beautiful girl he'd ever seen—despite her blue lips.

"...Warmth and love radiate from you. I felt that the first time I saw you—even when your lips were blue and you were shaking."

"When I told the nurse what happened, she immediately took the girl back to triage. As I stood there, another employee informed me of who the girl was."

I'm hanging on every word, my heart pumping faster with each piece of information he reveals.

"It was the daughter of one of the wealthiest, most powerful men in the city. My heart dropped. I walked out of the hospital dejected. There was no reason to even think about her again because I didn't have a chance. We could never be together. But it was all so romantic, right?" He looks at me with warm eyes. "The star-crossed lover's thing. Rich girl, poor boy. I decided to keep the secret to my grave and write a song about forbidden love with that beautiful girl."

"It was you?" I swallow hard as tears fill my eyes. "You saved me?"

"I took you to the hospital." Austin looks at my chest while drawing an invisible heart with his finger. "I think the 'saving you' part is all in my head."

I reach up and place my hand on his cheek. "Did you tuck my hair behind my ears that night?"

"I did, yes." He brings his gaze back to mine. "I wanted to remember your face."

"I knew—when you did that after your set at The Underground. I could feel that you'd done it before. It was surreal. Why didn't you tell me all of this before?"

Austin takes a breath, releasing it as he lifts his eyes to the roof of the van. "I don't know. I wanted to see if this connection was real—and not some kind of obligation because I helped you." He laughs. "I mean, I didn't even do anything. There's nothing to be repaid for. I just—"

"Thank you."

"You don't have to say that." He shakes his head and casts his eyes downward.

"I'm alive because of you, Austin! That's not something we can push aside." I take his face in my hands and lift his head so our eyes meet. "Thank you for saving my life. And for encouraging me and listening to me. Thank you for always making me feel good about myself. I've never had anyone treat me the way you do."

As soon as I say it, I curse myself. Why do I keep playing the pity card in front of him? That's not me. I've never been that person. I've always focused on accomplishments and being strong.

Confidence is not only the number one rule of dating, it's the number one rule in medicine. Confidence, not cockiness. Making someone feel like you're the most in-demand person and they're lucky to have you.

Who am I kidding? I have zero confidence with men. Even after months dating Austin, who hasn't given me any reason to doubt how he feels.

But leave it to me, at the lowest point in my life, to keep digging into a dark hole.

"How is someone like you attracted to someone like me?"

The light that's been on Austin's face, since he told me how he feels about me, dims. "What in the world do you mean?"

I open my mouth, but he continues without letting me answer.

"What do you mean someone like me, Liz? A loser from the wrong side of town, who sold pot in middle school to afford instruments, and barely graduated high school?"

"No. Austin—"

"Why would someone like you—a beautiful, smart doctor—want to be with someone like me? I don't have a safety net, Liz. I'm an uneducated guy with no money in my savings account and zero job skills. If music doesn't work out, I'll be sweeping floors and stocking beer coolers at The Market for the rest of my life."

"It's a job that pays your bills. There's no shame in that."

"I know, I—" Austin closes his eyes for a beat and takes a deep breath. When he opens them, he says, "Can we just enjoy this time with each other, Liz? We're two perfectly imperfect people who found each other. I've had an amazing time with you since the very first moment we met. Being with you makes me happy. You make me feel. You lighten the darkness inside me. You make me want to be a better person—because of the good I see in you. And because of all the good I know you're going to accomplish in your life. You're saving lives—and I'm writing songs."

"You're saving lives too, Austin. I know that for a fact. I've read the posts on social media about how your music has affected people. About how your music has saved them—and I know it because I'm one of those people, Austin. *Open Your Heart* saved me, too."

Now that I know the story behind the song, that's currently holding steady at Number Three on the Billboard Alternative chart, and tearing up Satellite radio, I feel empowered to tell him how much it resonates with me.

"I can't even explain how much that song means to me. From the very first time I heard it, I felt like it was for me. It grounded me. Listening to it brought me back to life over the last few months. Or maybe it brought me to a new life?" I pause. "You saved me. You changed me. You helped me figure out who I really am and what I can give to this world."

"I didn't—" Before he can dismiss my feelings I interrupt him.

"I love you, Austin."

Out of any moment in my life, this is the moment I should be making eye contact with someone. I've never been so sure of my feelings. Not since I decided that I wanted to be a doctor. That I wanted to make a difference.

And yet, I can't look at him because I'm afraid of what I'll see.

"What?" he asks, lifting my chin with gentle fingers.

"I love you," I repeat. This time I say it louder while looking straight into his eyes.

"Fuck, Liz!" he exclaims.

I'd be offended, except there's a huge goofy grin on his face. The grin of a kid who seems flabbergasted to hear that a girl loves him.

"You're telling me this in the back of a smelly tour van?"

I laugh, understanding why he's amused, but he still hasn't acknowledged my declaration. And though I feel completely confident in my words, I'm getting a bit worried that he doesn't feel the same.

It's weird, because I've never said it to anyone outside of family and a few close friends before. I've never been so anxious waiting for words before.

He grabs my hips, then moves one hand to my heart, then brings them both up to cup my face.

"I can't—I—fuck! Just hearing you say that is amazing. I love you, too, Liz."

Relief washes over me. Each word a new wave of acceptance.

"I almost don't want to fuck you like a groupie in the back of the van anymore."

"Really?" I ask. "Because that's exactly how I want to celebrate this moment."

Austin cocks his head, not taking his eyes from my boobs, which I've just remembered are still bare and basically in front of his face.

"As long as you're cool with it." He lifts his hips—and me—off the seat and reaches between us to shimmy his shorts down enough to release his cock.

I bite my bottom lip at the sight—hard and thick and so ready.

"You look like a kid in a candy shop, Liz."

"You've got something very lickable right there."

"You can lick it later, babe. Right now, I want you to take me deep. I want to feel your pussy squeeze my cock as you ride hard." He reaches into the crevice, where the seat back meets the bottom, and pulls out a condom.

I push one leg of the boxers aside and lift myself up so I can slide onto him once he's sheathed. As I lower myself slowly, Austin releases a low moan.

"I fucking love you," I tell him.

It's the only response I have. It's the only truth I know right now. My career—as I know it—is over. My life, which has been planned out for years, has suddenly come to a complete standstill. I don't know who I am or how I fit into the world anymore.

The only thing I have is this moment with Austin.

Chapter Seventeen

AUSTIN

*I*t's festival day.

Our first festival and we're scheduled to be on the main stage. Our time slot is 3:30, but still—main stage. The excitement has my stomach flipping out. So much so that it woke me up at seven and I haven't been able to get back to sleep. Instead, I've checked social media, gone down the rabbit hole of videos on YouTube, and watched the girl I love sleep.

It's taken every ounce of self-control I have not to wake Liz. We were up late last night and today will be long and hot, so I want to let her rest. But I also have all this energy that I need to get out, and fucking her would be the perfect way to do it.

Excitement trumps nerves on the scale of how I feel about today. I know from being at festivals as a fan that people camp out all day at the main stage so they can be front row for the headliner. Nothing about that sounds fun for me as a concertgoer, but as a performer I appreciate that we'll have guaranteed people upfront. I'm more interested in seeing how many people, out of those who wander from stage to stage, come over to see our set. I hate that I'm even thinking about it, because I have no control over it, but I do.

We've got a few interviews scheduled with radio stations before we have to head over to the festival. I'm on my way to meet the guys in the lobby.

"You sure you're okay with hanging out by yourself for a bit?" I ask Liz for the second time this morning. She's got to be annoyed by how nervous I am. I'm annoyed with myself.

"I'm positive," she answers, opening her eyes. "Don't worry about me, Austin. I'm good on my own." She hasn't gotten out of bed yet.

I cross the room and plant a huge kiss on her lips. "I'm off. Text me if you need anything, okay?"

"Go get 'em, babe! I'll see you soon."

I wink one last time before leaving the room. Time to light Atlanta on fire.

ONCE THE BAND before us is finished removing their gear from the stage, we've got twenty minutes changeover time to get our stuff set up. That's a lot less time than we have at a normal show. Thankfully, our tour manager and crew have it down to a science. Still, twenty minutes means all hands on deck and Tim is nowhere to be found.

As Nelson works on my amp, I adjust my mic stand to my height and look out over the crowd to see if I can spot Tim anywhere. When I drop my eyes to the crowd that's gathered already, I see Liz. I haven't seen her for a few hours. We had some interviews and a meet and greet before our set, and she wanted to walk around and listen to other bands while we completed everything we needed to do.

It's refreshing to have an independent girlfriend who can entertain herself when I'm busy with work. But seeing her standing there front and center, bouncing on her toes, makes my heart soar while grounding me in the moment.

"Hey, babe. I like your dress," I say raising my hands to make a heart shape in front of my chest.

Her cheeks flush pink and she lifts her hand in a shy wave.

"I better get more than that when we go on," I tease.

"Austin!" Someone yells, which starts a stream of shouting.

"We love you!"

"Please play *Open Your Heart!*"

Just as I give the crowd a smile and thumbs up, Tim stumbles across the stage, tripping on a wire as he approaches his spot.

"What the fuck, man?" Fozzie yells.

"Yeah! I'm good. Let's go!" He claps his hands, then picks up his guitar and attempts to lift the strap over his head. It gets caught on his head first, then his ear, then it slips from his hand and crashes to the stage. "Fuck."

Both Nelson and I rush to him immediately. It's almost a hundred degrees today and we're all sweating like pigs in the afternoon sun, but Tim's face is ruddy and red; he's sweating profusely. He sniffs. There's no doubt that he's on some kind of drug. I don't know what it is and I don't care. We don't have time for this shit. Not today. Not on a stage this large with a crowd that gets bigger and bigger with every minute closer to the start of our set.

Why didn't we fire him before coming to this festival?

"What's up, Tim?" Nelson asks. "What's going on, man?"

"Nothing. I'm good." He stoops to pick up his guitar and loses his balance. I reach out and catch him before he hits the ground. His eyes roll to the back of his head and he slumps in my arms.

"He can't play like this," I say, panic raising in my voice. "Fuck! Call Jimmy over."

"Jimmy!" Nelson calls to our assistant tour manager. "Jimmy, come over here."

"Yeah?"

"You still know bass for all the songs?" I ask.

He nods. "Absolutely."

"Can you play bass for this set?"

He nods again. "Anything you need, man."

Anything I need? I need someone to smash their fist into Tim's stupid fucking face. But that won't solve anything right now.

Instead of voicing my violent thoughts, I clasp Jimmy's hand and pull him in for a shoulder-bump-bro-hug. "Thanks, man. I appreciate you."

Nelson turns around. "All good, Foz?"

"Yup." He gets up from his drums and heads off stage.

Nelson and I help Tim offstage, leaving Jimmy to finish checking the sound with Clint, our audio engineer, who's at a sound board, which is under a tent about seventy-five feet from the stage. I'm so thankful to have the experienced crew that we have. The mild panic attack that has my heart racing could be a million times worse. Knowing these guys have the experience to handle this kind of shit brings my anxiety down a notch.

If I'm completely honest, I thought our set was fucked when we had to bring in Jimmy last minute. Not because I didn't have faith in his ability, I know the guy is a talented musician and has played with us during practice and sound checks. I was worried about throwing someone—anyone—on stage and how that would affect the vibe. Would I be worrying about him the entire forty-five-minute set? Did anyone in our fan base notice us escort Tim off the stage? Should I say something?

All of my worries wash away during our opening song. Jimmy's huge smile and easy interaction with the crowd are the keys to his amazing stage presence. I'm already impressed, but I could literally kiss him when he walks over to me so we can play and sing side-by-side, just like I would do with Tim.

By the second song, the crowd is jumping and dancing, and the only thing running through my mind is killing this performance. Instead of dwelling on the almost disaster, I use every ounce of anger and frustration I had before our set started and transform it into positive energy. Shit is always going to come up; I've gotta be able to roll with the punches.

We're all buzzing hard-core after our set. The crowd was bigger than I ever expected, and the energy was completely off the charts. I'm humbled by all the people who knew the songs. Our debut album isn't completed yet, though we do have an EP on streaming services and audio versions of our songs on YouTube that get hundreds of thousands of plays, so I guess it's not unlikely that people know our stuff. It's just crazy to me.

When I get to my phone, there's a message from Liz waiting for me.

Liz: You were amazing out there! I'm so proud of you, Austin!
Me: Thanks, babe! Thank you for your support and for being right in front, rocking out with us. Seeing you gave me so much confidence. I appreciate you so much. I love you.
Liz: Love you, too.
Me: We're gonna be a few more minutes. Have some stuff to take care of. You okay?
Liz: Take your time. I'm good. I'm watching Joywave right now.
Me: Cool. I'll text you when I'm on my way and we can figure out a place to meet up. Cool?
Liz: Absolutely. See you soon. Love you!
Me: I love you, too.

I thank my lucky stars again that my girl is independent and strong. I can't even imagine being at this festival with some of the girls I dated in the past. The clingy ones who would've absolutely freaked out if I'd said I had stuff to do with the band. I'm not a complete asshole; in a case like that I would have known beforehand and made sure she had a friend with her to keep her occupied. But I don't even have to think about it with Liz. She does her own thing and understands that this is my job—and my first priority.

"Austin!" Nelson calls. "You ready?"

"Yeah," I answer quickly, spinning around as I shove my phone in my pocket.

Within a few strides I'm at his side. Fozzie flanks his other side. Strength in numbers. My stomach is tied up in knots. All the shitty things Tim's done roll through my head, accumulating like a snowball of anger. Even when it's justified, it's not easy to fire someone. I have no clue how people do this for a living.

"You want me to do it?" Nelson asks.

Yes. I think to myself, but I know that I have to be the one that kicks Tim out. Well, Fozzie and me.

"Thanks, man." I clap him on the back. "We got it."

"Should've done this months ago," Fozzie mutters. I understand his frustration completely.

"Yup, I agree. But we didn't and here we are."

"After you guys tell him, I'll have Clint take him back to the hotel and get his shit," Nelson says. "Want me to book him a flight home?"

"Why should we waste that kind of money on that fucker?" Fozzie blurts, kicking a clump of dirt as we stride across Atlanta's Piedmont Park to the exit where a few guys from our crew took Tim after our set.

"So you want to kick him out of the band and then drive home in the van with him tomorrow? Hungover and coming down from whatever he was on?"

Thank god for Nelson and his level head. Forget the fact that a same-day or next-day plane ticket is gonna cost a load of money we don't have to spend.

"Yeah, that's not an option," I say. "It sucks, I know, but we chalk it up as a necessary business expense and move on. The price of a plane ticket is worth never having to deal with him again."

Kicking Tim out of the band goes a lot better than expected, but I'm chalking that up to the fact that he's barely coherent and can't comprehend anything we say. Still, we did it. Will we have to follow up? Yup. But I can wash my hands of him for the time being and enjoy the rest of the day. I only watch for a second as Clint leads Tim out of the exit and leads him down the street.

Jimmy, who disappeared while we were talking to Tim, nudges me with his elbow and hands both Fozzie and me a can of ice-cold beer.

"Thank you so much, man. For everything. You saved us and you fucking killed it today," I say, taking the beer.

Jimmy's kindness reminds me again how grateful I am to have the awesome crew of guys we have on our side. A day that could have been a complete and total disaster went off spectacularly. The universe was on our side.

Time to find Liz. I dig out my phone and shoot her a message, asking where she is. She answers with the name of the set she's watching, so I head over to the stage. When I arrive at the back of the crowd, I scan the area, looking for her.

"Hey, babe!" Liz calls out, running—or rather stumbling—toward me. When she reaches me, she falls onto my chest. "You feel so good."

"Thanks, love," I say with a smile. "You okay?"

Something seems off. Liz and I have had drinks together plenty of times, but I've never seen her wasted, which makes me wonder how much she's had to drink today. It seems really out of character that she would have spent the day drinking, but maybe she hasn't had anything to eat. Or maybe she's just enjoying herself. This weekend is the first time she's had two days off in a row since I met her, so I can't fault her for letting loose. I'm about to down a few beers and enjoy the day, too.

"I'm wonderful. Absolutely wonderful," she says, rubbing her cheek against my chest. Her hands roam across my back, then slide around to the front, where she cups my junk. I jump, startled. "I want to feel you. Touch me, Austin."

"I'd love to, but not here."

"You guys sounded amazing today! So much energy. And the crowd loved you."

Pride fills my heart hearing her compliment our set while wearing my band's logo across her chest. As she spins in a circle, the wind catches the hem of her tank-top-turned-dress, giving me a view of her bare thighs. Lust takes over. All I can think of is getting my hands on her again. "You want to head back to the hotel?"

"No!" She grabs my hand and leads me toward another stage. "Let's go dance!"

I laugh, amused at her sudden turn of priorities, but it's all good. I'm excited to enjoy the rest of the day with her. I'm ready to let go of all the tension from earlier and let loose with my girl. Or get on her level, since she seems to be pretty loose already.

I'll never get tired of seeing Liz wild and free. She spreads her arms wide and spins around, a free spirit in an open field, dancing as if there's no one else around. It reminds me of the night we officially met. When I watched her from the stage dancing and jumping to my music, then singing and dancing around to Intermission. I love seeing the silly, fun, playful side of her. I wish she would spend more time on that side. I'm sure she will once her residency is over. It can't be easy to let loose when she has to be alert all the time.

After walking around and dancing for a couple hours, I'm dying in the scorching sun and hundred-degree temperature. I've gotta find some sort of shelter and air conditioning soon, even if it means leaving the festival and going to a nearby restaurant for a break. Liz hasn't stopped moving or smiling since I met up with her.

"Hey Liz, let's take a break. You've gotta be dying out here in this heat."

"I'm not. I'm actually kind of chilly."

The words signal an immediate red flag in my head, but before I can question it, she moves closer to me and takes my face in her hands. "You wanna know something, Austin?"

"Always."

"You are the best thing that's ever happened to me. You see me. What's real. You don't treat me like crap just because I can't operate anymore. You know that there's more to me. That I have worth."

My heart expands with each word. It's always awesome to hear someone tell you that they appreciate you and how they make you feel, but it's never felt as good as when Liz says it. I love everything about her. The more time we spend together, the more time I want to spend together. Every part of my life is better with her in it. Even the bullshit —like today—is more bearable because I know I get to wrap my arms around her.

Looking into her eyes, I realize something is wrong. Her pupils are huge—dilated so much that I realize it couldn't be alcohol that caused it.

"Babe, are you okay?"

"I feel great. I need more water though. I'm so thirsty." She's already gone through two water bottles, which I attributed to the intense heat and staying hydrated. Now I'm thinking it's something completely different.

"Babe." I grab her face and hold it so she can focus on me. "Did you take something?"

She bites her lip. "I had a headache. Tim gave me—"

"What did Tim give you?"

She shakes her head out of my grasp. "Ibuprofen."

"Bullshit!"

She doesn't look at me.

"You're a fucking doctor! You fucking knew whatever he gave you wasn't Ibuprofen."

Fuck. Fuck. Fuck. Tim gave Liz Ecstasy. I'm gonna fucking kill him.

"I'm just trying to fit into your world, Austin. Be one of the party girls you like so much," she says.

"Fuck that! You know I don't do that shit. When have you ever seen me do anything other than smoke weed?"

What the hell was she thinking? I've never done any kind of hard drugs in front of her. And I've never shown any attraction to "party" girls who snort coke and swallow pills. What would possess her take drugs?

Her eyes are glassy and I know nothing I'm saying is registering with her. As if screwing up our first major festival set and kicking our bassist out of the band wasn't enough stress today, now I have to monitor my girlfriend. If I would have known she was rolling, I could have watched out for her.

"Let's get back to the hotel. It's too hot out here and you can't have any more water." I reach for her hand.

She shakes her head and pulls away from my grasp. "I don't want to go. I want to listen to music and dance."

"I'm not leaving you here by yourself."

"I'm not by myself. There are thousands of people around."

"Jesus Christ! Come on, Liz," I plead. I'm hanging by an invisible rope, severed to a thin string. I honestly can't handle one more thing today. I'm on the verge of a nervous breakdown.

"You're such a buzz kill," she mumbles, but doesn't resist when I slide my fingers through hers and lead her to the closest exit.

There's no way I would have left her out here by herself. Not knowing that she was on X. She may be a doctor, but I'm pretty sure she doesn't know anything about the effects of that shit on her body. I've seen enough people on it to know what to look for and how to watch out for someone.

Once we're back at the hotel, she starts walking in the opposite direction of the entrance.

"Where are you going?" I ask.

"I'm going to get something to eat. Right. Over. There." She points to the Applebee's next to our hotel. "Am I allowed to get some food, Dad?"

I glare at her, then start off toward Applebee's. "Fine."

"What are you doing?" she asks.

"I thought we were going to get something to eat?"

"*I'm* going to get something to eat. *You* can go back to the hotel room."

I open my mouth to protest, then stop, because I can't take it anymore. I know I should protest, but I'm pissed and hot and tired, and I can't deal with this bullshit right now.

"Please don't drink any more water!" I call to her as she walks away.

"Yes, Dad." She salutes me with a middle finger and keeps walking. If I weren't so irritated, I'd laugh.

I wait a minute before following her into Applebee's and asking the hostess to point me to where she seated Liz. Then I grab a spot at the bar where I can keep an eye on her. I'm trying to be stealthy, but I'm so exhausted, I couldn't care less if she sees me. At least she'll know I never left her.

THANKFULLY, Liz didn't drink any more water at dinner. She just scarfed down a burger and paid her tab. I follow her out the same way I followed her in—far enough away to give her space, but close enough to keep an eye on her. As she walks, she taps away on her phone. I expect my cell to buzz, but it doesn't. Instead of stopping when she gets to the door to our room, she passes it by and knocks on Fozzie and Jimmy's door.

What the fuck?

I'm a second away from going ballistic when I get a text.

Fozzie: Your girl said to tell you she's safe and she wants you to stop following her.

Me: Fine.

I stalk back to my room and slide inside, slamming the door closed behind me. I'm so angry I could punch a hole in the wall—but I don't want to get fined. This was supposed to be the best day of Drowned World's career, and it's turned into absolute shit.

I slide my damp, white T-shirt off and whip it to the ground. Then I unbutton my pants and try to pull them down, but the leather sticks, suctioned against my skin. Any other day, I would take my time, because I know how hard it is to get them off when I'm sweaty. But today, I'm frustrated and angry. I tug and tug, getting more pissed when they don't give more than a tiny inch each time. I waddle across the carpet to my duffel bag. I know I have baby powder in there, which will absorb some of the moisture and allow them to come down easier.

Once my pants are off, I leave them in a heap on the floor and enter the bathroom. A long, hot shower will wash away the bad vibes of the day.

After my shower, I climb into bed and grab my phone, hoping to see a message from Liz.

Nothing.

Instead of get worked up again, I check our social media accounts and reply to some of the photos and videos fans posted from our set at the festival. Watching the videos gives me validation that we really did kick ass today, despite all the drama with Tim. If you didn't know there were issues going on behind the scenes, you'd never be able to tell. Jimmy fit so well; I'm not sure why we didn't fire Tim sooner and get him up there before any of this went down.

I set my phone down on my stomach and look up to the ceiling. I take full responsibility. I need to be stronger when making the hard choices before it leads to bigger problems.

Just as I'm about to go over all the bad decisions I've made over the last five years of my life, my phone buzzes.

Fozzie: Open your door. Liz is taking our room tonight.

The tension I washed away in the shower comes right back to my neck and shoulders. I lean back into my pillow and groan in frustration.

Me: Just send her over here.
Fozzie: She said she doesn't want to be around you.
Me: Jesus, Fozzie! Just—

Another message pops up as I'm typing.

Fozzie: Let her be, man. Give her space.
Me: I need to talk to her.
Fozzie: Not tonight. Now unlock your fucking door unless you want us to sleep with your girl.
Me: Fine.

I get up and unlock the door, then return to bed. Fozzie and Jimmy slip in a few minutes later. Neither one says anything. Jimmy goes straight for the couch and collapses in a heap, while Fozzie shuffles to my bed.

"You know she's tripping on ecstasy, right?" I ask him.

"Yup." He climbs into bed next to me and pulls the covers up.

"Is she okay?"

"Yup." He rolls onto his side and I realize by his long, deep breaths that *"yup"* is the last word I'm getting from him tonight.

We've all had a long, stressful day, so I can't blame him—or be annoyed. I should have thanked him for letting Liz stay in their room when I know they're just as exhausted as I am. My head is all over the place. Stress meltdowns will do that to a person.

LIZ FINALLY CREEPS into our room at 4:17 a.m. I know because I could barely sleep. I think I got an hour total, maybe two. Between Liz not being next to me, Jimmy snoring louder than an English bulldog, Fozzie hogging the comforter, and all the other thoughts racing through my head, it was impossible to get my mind to settle down.

"Hey," I call out in the darkness when the flashlight on her phone illuminates up the floor.

She doesn't answer—or even acknowledge me—just follows the beam to her duffle bag. I watch her silhouette drop to her knees and begin shoving clothes into her bag.

"Liz, please." I spring out of bed and kneel next to her. Anger radiates from her every pore, but we need to talk, so I set my hand on her forearm. "Can we please talk this out?"

She bats my hand away. "I don't feel like talking right now."

She stands up and rushes to the bathroom, leaving me on the floor in confusion. I'm not letting her walk away without talking to me. I need to know what the hell was going through her head.

"Well, relationships aren't a one-way street, and I think we should talk about it." I follow her to the bathroom and lean against the door frame, watching as she grabs the tiny bottles of face and hair products and makeup off the sink and drops them into a pink-and-black leopard-print bag. "I don't understand why you'd take that shit. You of all people know how much even one hit can mess up your head. Help me understand."

"Do you really want me to explain or do you want to keep chastising me for taking drugs? Wasn't yesterday's berating enough?"

Jesus.

It's not like I was an asshole to her yesterday. Sure, I was more pissed than I normally would have been because of how stressed I was, but I didn't 'berate' her. "Look, I'm sorry I was frustrated. Tim was so high he couldn't even hold his guitar. If Jimmy hadn't been able to play bass for us, we would've had to cancel our set, right then and there, in front of all those people. I had to kick Tim out of the band. I was devastated, Liz. I didn't know what we were going to do—I still don't. And then I got to you—the person I can count on—and you were out of your fucking mind."

Rehashing yesterday's events sparks the anger and frustration. I still have no clue what's going on and how we're going to move forward as a band. How could I have made such a huge mistake not firing Tim before it even got to this point?

Liz snorts, taking me out of my divergent train of thought and bringing me back to the present. "I get it now. This isn't about me taking drugs at all, is it? This is really about you being pissed at Tim and taking it out on me. Gotcha!"

She elbows me out of the way as she exits the bathroom. Then she places her toiletry bag into her duffel and zips it up.

I spin around and follow her. "No, this not about me being pissed at Tim. It's about how irresponsible and bratty you were yesterday. I was stressed and frustrated and your behavior sure didn't help, Liz."

"Irresponsible and bratty." She repeats with a faint laugh. "Good to know how you feel about me. I'm done letting other people tell me how I should act and what I should do. I thought you, out of all people, would let me enjoy the moment. I thought you'd laugh and dance and let me be me."

"Bullshit! That wasn't you." I roll my eyes. She's not going to spin this. "You're going to stand here and tell me you thought I'd be okay watching you fuck your head up with chemicals? If you wanted to get out of your mind, you should have come to me and we could've smoked some stellar weed together. But for you take a random pill from a dude you barely know? No, I'm not gonna sit by and act like I'm cool with that."

She stands up and looks me in the eye for the first time this morning. Despite the anger in her voice, she looks like she's about to cry. "You want to know the reason I took it, Austin?"

"Yes."

"Because I have been in a downward spiral of despair since my car accident. I am no longer a Surgical Critical Care fellow. I am no longer in my surgical residency. All I am is a complete and total failure."

Fuck.

"Liz, I—" I try to console her, but she's not having it.

She raises her finger to my lips and shakes her head. "Oh, no! You asked me why I took that pill and I'm telling you." Then she continues, steamrolling me with every word. "I came here excited to support you and cheer you on and enjoy this weekend with you. So when Tim offered me that pill, I thought about it as a medical professional for a split second, then I bit it in half and swallowed one of the pieces because it seemed like the easiest way to get out of my head for a few hours." She lifts her duffle bag over her shoulder.

"I get it. I don't agree with it, but I get it," I say, trying to diffuse the situation. "I'm sorry I—"

"I don't want to hear it right now, Austin. You said you wanted to talk. You asked why I took that pill, I told you. Now please let me have some space."

"You can leave your stuff in here, ya know. We're leaving as soon as everyone gets up."

"I'm going to the airport."

"What? Liz, come on!"

She tugs the door and exits without looking back.

What the hell is going on?

I grab a pair of jeans and step into the legs, hopping from foot to foot as I pull them on, while trying to get to the door.

I follow her out the door in my bare feet. She doesn't look back as she glides over the sidewalk and into the parking lot where a yellow cab waits at the curb, engine running. The driver scrambles out of his car when she wheels her bag to the back of the car. He lifts it easily into the trunk.

I'm out of breath when I catch up to her. "Liz, please stay. Please—"

"The last thing I want is to be crammed into a van with you and your bandmates right now. Give me some space, okay?"

"Are you sure you're okay to travel alone? Do you—"

"I'm an independent woman. I think I can handle it."

"I mean, are you feeling okay? You might have some withdrawals or something."

"I'm fine."

"Okay." I sigh, feeling defeated. "I guess I'll talk to you when we get home."

She nods and ducks into the cab. No kiss. No hug.

I watch the cab pull away from the curb, hoping she'll look out the window and acknowledge me. I need the peace of mind. She doesn't even look up. I watch until the car turns onto the main road and drives out of sight. The farther it moves away, the further my heart drops.

Normally, all of the ways I could have handled the conversation differently would be racing through my head.

But that's not happening right now.

My stress level is at maximum capacity. My band is falling apart because I couldn't make a decision that needed to be made before we even came to this festival. I should have kicked Tim out of the band months ago.

The career I worked for my entire life is falling apart, and I just fucked things up with the girl of my dreams.

Chapter Eighteen
LIZ

*L*ashing out at Austin because of my own issues and insecurities was a completely horrible thing to do. I think about how unfair and selfish I've been the entire plane ride home.

I was in the wrong. He had every right to be angry with me for taking drugs from Tim. What the hell was I thinking? I still can't believe I gave into the temptation, knowing it was such an ignorant thing to do. I've never researched the effects ecstasy has on the body because I've never even thought about taking it before. Now, the more I think about it, the more upset and paranoid I become. My entire body shakes while the thoughts swirl in my head like a tornado. I can't tell if it's a reaction to the chemicals leaving my system or my nerves.

Austin had one of the worst days of his life yesterday, and I couldn't even get past my selfishness to console him. What kind of girlfriend am I? Is this the way I handle hardships? What does it say about our relationship if we both lash out and can't stop to understand the other when we're both going through a difficult time? It's bound to happen again. Life is constant change, obstacle after obstacle. Maybe our bond isn't as strong as I believed it to be. Maybe the similarities in our personalities are more troublesome than cohesive. Maybe we aren't able to be there for each other.

The thought depresses me. It's not true. We both needed to step back and talk about it as adults. I embarrassed myself and I took it out on Austin. He had every right to be pissed at me. He made complete sense when he said I should have gone to him and asked to smoked pot with him to get out of my head. I trust him. I know that he would keep me safe. We could have enjoyed the night; despite us both having career-devastating issues to work through, we could have tackled our problems together in the morning.

Instead, I made a stupid decision and screwed everything up, thinking I knew what was best for him. Why did I think I couldn't tell him about leaving the fellowship? We'd talked about the next steps in my career. We'd come up with a plan that I was excited about.

Then my ego got in the way, and all of the new ideas for moving forward fell by the wayside. I made a stupid decision because I still couldn't accept that my career is over. And starting over sucks.

As soon as the wheels hit the runway, I pull my phone out of my pocketbook and switch it off airplane mode. I need to text Austin and apologize. Hopefully he'll see me today. Hopefully, I haven't screwed it all up with my poor choices.

As soon as I have service, text messages pop up. Hope fills my heart that it's from Austin.

No such luck.

Out of the three texts, two are from Mama asking where I am and why I'm not at brunch, which is a Sunday staple in our house, and the third is her telling me she's worried and demanding I call her as soon as possible.

It's my own fault. I'm the one who mentioned that I had Sunday off, which has been rare over the last few years. Working weekends—or at the very least, being on call—has been part of my life for years. I'd forgotten to let her know that I would be out of town and not able to make family brunch. Or, I purposely forgot because I didn't want them to know I was going to the festival with Austin.

Tapping the screen with my thumbs, I text out a note to Mama.

Me: Hi Mama! Sorry I missed brunch. I've been out of town. On my way home now. Sorry I forgot to tell you.

Mama texts back immediately as if the phone is glued to her hand.

Mama: You had us worried, Elizabeth! You said you had
Sunday off. I assumed you'd be here.
Me: I know, Mama, I'm sorry. Slipped my mind. How about I
stop over for dinner tonight?
Mama: I just finished making an enormous meal no one
showed up for. I'm not cooking again tonight.
Me: You don't have to cook, Mama. We can have leftovers.
Mama: Leftovers? I sent the food home with Maria. At least
her family will appreciate it.

My head is so messed up, I can barely think straight. The only time
Mama uses leftovers is after Thanksgiving dinner. Her turkey sand-
wiches are another meal in itself.

Me: Pizza then?
Mama: Fine. I'll invite your sister, as well, since she couldn't be
bothered to make it either.
Me: Emily?

Emily hasn't been at brunch since she was fourteen. It seems silly
that Mama would be annoyed at her. But the only Sunday brunches
Maddie has ever missed are the ones where she was away at college.

Mama: Madeline.

Oh dang! Maddie didn't show up. And she didn't even tell Mama?
That's big time. Wonder what's going on with her.

Me: My plane just landed and I've gotta grab my bag. I'll see
you soon, Mama.

Instead of waiting for her response, I shove my phone back into
my bag.

Texting Austin can wait. I can't think straight and I need to gather my senses and prepare for a difficult conversation with my parents. I have to come clean about my fellowship and residency. If I don't tell them, they'll hear it from someone through the grapevine of gossip, and that's way worse to handle. Imagine their embarrassment if someone random broke the news to them. Seeing Mama scramble for composure and faking like she already knew, would be priceless, but I'm not interested in embarrassing my parents. Not when I'm an embarrassment enough.

All I can do is hold myself together and try not to cry in front of my parents. The only thing worse than being a disappointment is being a gigantic baby who can't control her emotions about that disappointment.

"What's wrong, Elizabeth?" Mama asks as I grab the salad dressing out of the fridge.

"Sorry?" I turn around and look at her.

My head is pounding and I can barely keep my eyes open. I wonder if crashing hard is part of the effects of coming down off ecstasy. I should've done the research before I headed over to my parents' house.

I never should have offered to come over for dinner, but I felt an obligation. Ever since Maddie's party, when they both made it clear that they weren't happy with me dating Austin, I haven't spent as much time around them.

It's annoying that they won't even give him a chance. They have to see how happy I am with Austin. Yet instead of caring about things like that, they push me toward boring guys I have no attraction to. How is someone I don't even like being around a better option than a kind, hardworking guy—who happens to be a tattooed musician?

"You look like death. Are you sick?" She touches a lock of my hair, still wet from the shower I'd taken twenty minutes before I left for their house.

The disappointment shows in her disgusted frown. Southern ladies do not leave the house with wet hair or a plain face. I've known that since I was a little girl. Even in case of fire. You stand there and let the flames surround you while you finish your hair and makeup. Maybe by that time a good-looking fireman will have appeared at your window to save you. Because all women want—no, *need*—is to be saved by big strong men.

Which is heavy sarcasm, obviously.

"No. I—"

Internally, I wrestle with whether to tell them I was at a music festival with Austin. I already know they're going to be pissed. Better to come clean than get caught in a lie. I don't want to lie about my relationship with Austin anymore. I want to be able to bring him around my family again—someday.

"Austin played a huge music festival in Atlanta yesterday. I just got home this morning."

"I thought we talked about him, Elizabeth." Mom sighs.

"We did talk about him. I told you how well he treats me and how kind he is and how happy I am to be with him."

"That's very nice, but he's not someone you could have a future with."

"Why not?"

"We discussed this."

"Because he doesn't come from money? Is that the problem?"

Mama rubs her face with both hands. "Yes, Elizabeth. That's exactly why. He will never fit into your life. Do you remember what happened at your sister's party? Do you think he likes feeling out of place?"

She stops talking when Daddy enters the room. I wonder why because she usually doesn't filter herself around Daddy.

"Please take this to the dining room." Mama thrusts a huge bowl of salad at me. I grab it out of her hands and head out of the kitchen. After setting it on the table, I go back to see if there's anything else I can help with.

I stop before I enter the room because she's talking about me. Let's hear what she has to say to Daddy about Austin.

"It's getting to be too much. She hasn't spent any time with us recently. Now she's sneaking off to music festivals. You know that means they spent the night together."

"Don't be naive, Cookie, she's twenty-six years old. Let her get him out of her system."

"What about the auction? It's her big event and she doesn't even know what's going on with the planning. How do you think it's going to turn out if she hasn't paid any attention to it?"

"She's got a lot on her plate, but she always makes it work, don't worry."

"You don't think she'll bring him, do you?"

"Shhh, Cookie." Daddy lowers his voice and I have to take a step closer to the door and lean over to hear. "Don't worry. She'd never bring him to something like that. She'll realize that someone like him doesn't fit into her life. It'll all work out."

"I thought you took care of it, Harris?" Mama says in an angry whisper. "I thought his mother took the money to get him to stay away from her."

What the heck?

"We're all on the same page, Cookie. She said everything was taken care of. I can assure you that she doesn't want her son with Elizabeth just as much as we don't want her with him. He feels inferior when he's around her—and us."

He pauses and I hang on every second of silence. "Elizabeth is a distraction. Austin doesn't really feel anything for her. She's a conquest unlike any he's had. At least he's smart enough to realize that."

A conquest. I'm just a conquest?

My stomach tightens and I swallow hard, trying to push back the anger and confusion.

If I was just a conquest, why would he tell me he loved me? Why would he waste so much time with me? I'm not exactly the coolest person to be seen with.

"I wish she were thinking straight. It really chaps my rear that she's throwing everything away for this guy," Mama says.

"Don't worry. He's going on tour soon," Daddy says, using his fingers to put 'on tour' in air quotes.

"What does that mean?"

"It means he's leaving town."

"Oh, thank the good Lord for small miracles!"

"We'll have our level-headed girl back soon."

"I hope so, Harris. This injury has really taken a toll on her. I'm questioning her choices. Should we suggest a therapist?"

Daddy crosses the room and puts an arm around Mama's shoulder, giving her a squeeze. "Let's hold off on that. Once this phase is over, she'll be back to her old self."

"I hope so."

I don't know if my parents could be any more dramatic about me dating someone. It's as if I'm going through a horrible illness.

A beat passes before I call into the kitchen to make my presence known, "Anything else I can help with?"

I figure announcing myself is better than barging in. They'll get paranoid, wondering if I heard anything. Daddy's always been a very private person. He has most of his discussions behind closed doors—including those with Mama about our family. Choices made for us to keep up appearances. Or stop us from embarrassing the family.

This should have been one of those conversations. I'm obviously embarrassing the family.

No wonder Emily wants nothing to do with us.

I enter the kitchen as if nothing is wrong, as if my heart hasn't been torn apart, hearing that Daddy paid my boyfriend's mom to keep him away from me. As if hearing that all I am is a silly distraction for the only man I've ever loved isn't breaking me into a million pieces inside.

"I think we're all set, dear," Mama says, lifting her fingers to her fix her immaculate hair and stepping away from Daddy's embrace.

"Hope you're hungry," he says. "Your mother outdid herself on this meal."

"Harris," Mama warns. Daddy's joke about her ordering pizza doesn't take well with a proud Southern woman.

"Come on, Cookie! I'm kidding," Daddy says, grabbing the pizza box before following me into the dining room, where I've already set the table.

"She made the salad," I offer quietly even though the last thing I feel like doing right now is standing up for either of my parents. I pull my chair out and sit, though I'm not hungry in the slightest.

"How's physical therapy going?" Mama asks, as she scoops a heaping portion of salad onto Daddy's plate.

"About the same." I can't lie to make them feel better. I can't pretend anymore. As of this moment, I have nothing left.

"What do you mean?" Daddy nods slightly to tell Mama he has enough. She passes me the salad bowl and puts two slices of steaming cheesy pizza in front of him, before taking her seat at the table. It doesn't seem weird that she plates his dinner for him. It's kind. And it seems to make her happy. Doesn't mean I think all women should do that.

Even though my parents pushed me into a career in medicine, one of Mama's top priorities was teaching me how to take care of a family. Because I'll be doing it all: Working eighty hours a week. Making dinner. Taking care of my husband. Taking care of the kids. Running the entire household. It's all on me.

And it sounds absolutely dreadful.

It's at this exact moment, I decide I'm done. I'm done busting my ass to attain someone else's definition of the "ideal" life.

"It's not getting any better. I'm not going to be able to perform surgeries again." It's blunt, but it's honest.

"Elizabeth! Don't talk like that!" Mama scolds.

"I'm telling you the truth, so you're prepared when Dr. Crowder and Dr. Sharma and Vik all tell you the same thing. It doesn't matter who my physical therapist is. I can function normally, but I will never be able to do anything as specialized as surgery again."

My parents are speechless. I'm not sure if it's because I finally admitted my greatest fear or because they're coming to terms with the fact that this is the end of their daughter's prestigious career.

Either way—the silence is thicker than morning fog in London.

I spear a piece of romaine with my fork and bring it to my lips. That's when I realize, I can't do it. I can't sit in their presence, knowing what kind of plan they orchestrated. I can't look them in the eye and make small talk, knowing they used their money and influence to squash the only thing that brought me any kind of happiness over the last few months, as the life they wanted me to have came crumbling around my feet.

"What's going on with you, Elizabeth? What do you mean you won't be able to perform surgery?"

"I can't completely grip the scalpel or the laser. I can't hold it tight enough." To demonstrate, I lift my knife and hold it against a slice of pizza as I would a human body. The only way I could cut the pizza is with a really sharp blade because my grip sucks and I can't press hard enough. "And when I try—every time I try—my hand shakes too much. I cannot get control when it comes to making precision cuts. My hand recovered quickly, easily, for everyday tasks, but I cannot go back to surgery." I toss the knife onto my plate with force, causing a loud clunk.

Mama gasps.

"I'm not going to be the prestigious surgeon you can brag about anymore." I push my chair back from the table and stand. "That's my reality. I have to start over. What will you tell everyone? How does it feel to have a failure as a daughter?"

"Elizabeth, stop this nonsense," Daddy says. He rises from his seat and moves toward me. He places his arm across my shoulder, trying to comfort his hysterical firstborn.

"It's not nonsense. I was dismissed from the fellowship and my residency weeks ago. I've been finishing up with patient care. How do you think I had this weekend off?"

My parents are silent for a full minute. Then Daddy says, "We know how devastating this must be for you."

His actions and words should be comforting coming from a parent, but I see through it now. It's all fake. It's another way to control me.

I shrug his arm off. "Do you? Or are you projecting your feelings onto me? Are you talking about how devastating this is for you?"

"This is exactly why we didn't want you spending time with that musician, Elizabeth," Mama interjects. Everyone assumes Daddy is the hard-ass because of how ruthless he is in business, but they're wrong. Daddy was always there to give us a hug or an encouraging word—even if it's fake.

Not Mama. She is cutthroat. She'll tell me to suck it up through clenched teeth and a plastic grin. She's never been the warm and fuzzy type.

"You've always been focused. The Elizabeth we raised would be seeking solutions. Maybe you can't go back to surgery, but what can you do? They can't cut you out of the fellowship; that doesn't require you to perform surgical procedures. Ugh! You started hanging around that lowlife with no goals and you lost yourself."

"He's not a lowlife!" I yell. "He's genuine and kind and passionate. He's driven and smart. He's traveling the country, opening up for one of the most popular bands in the world. He is more successful than I am right now! More successful than I'll ever be!"

Tears well up in my eyes. I didn't want to cry because crying in front of my parents is a sign of weakness. "But you can't see that. All you can see is the neighborhood he grew up in and the amount of money in his bank account. That's not how I want to live my life. You're right Mama, I *could* go into critical care. But I don't want to. That's what *you* want for me. Not what I want. As of this moment the path you chose for me is over; I'm taking my own path. You might not like the one I choose. And I don't give a fuck!"

"Elizabeth!" Daddy scolds. "Your attitude and tone are absolutely unacceptable."

"It's totally acceptable. I'm a grown-ass adult. I can say what I want. I can do what I want. I can date who I want." I stride toward the door. "And I can leave when I want."

As much as it tears me apart to hear, I honestly don't blame Austin's mom for taking money to break us up. My family throws money at people to solve problems. It might seem like taking it is a shitty thing to do, but who in their right mind would want their son to be part of this family? I probably would have done the same thing if I were in her place.

Austin is the best thing that's come into my life in a long time. He helped me see that I didn't have to follow my parent's plan if that wasn't what I truly wanted. His encouragement gave me the confidence to take control over my career and my future.

Then there's me. I've been the dark cloud over his life since we met. His friends don't like me. I brought him into a family that will never accept him. And I ruined the biggest day of his career with my irresponsible and selfish behavior.

Chapter Nineteen

AUSTIN

Getting ready to embark on a major three-month tour is no joke. Thankfully, we've done it on a smaller scale so our team knows what to do. Still, it's stressful making sure everything is in order. From having all of our gear packed into the trailer with care, to driving schedules and sleeping arrangements.

It's even more stressful knowing I'm leaving in a few hours and I still haven't heard from Liz. The one thing that could take my mind off the stress is spending my last night in town with her. I need to hold her in my arms. Feel her heartbeat against my chest. Her peacefulness calms me. Before I leave I need to know that we're okay.

But it's been three days since I saw her and she hasn't answered my texts or calls.

I'm trying to keep my shit together. I know I need to set it aside and focus on the tour. As much as I love her, my career is my main priority right now.

But I can't stop thinking about her. She knows we're leaving. Why would she wait until the last minute? Is she even going to make time to see me? Was our fight really that bad?

I can't think that way. She's going through her own shit. It's not about me. There's no reason for me to be so selfish. She told me how devastated she is right now.

When Liz finally texts me and says she needs to talk, I'm overcome with relief. As much as I knew I had to give her the space she needed, I've been dying to hear from her. I need to hold her and apologize, and let her know that nothing we go through is too much. We can work through anything.

My heart practically bursts out of my chest when I open the door and see Liz standing on my porch.

"Hey babe," I greet her. I can't keep the stupid-ass grin off my face. I immediately lunge toward her, with my arms extended, ready to sweep her off her feet. She leans back and holds up a hand, stopping my advance.

"I need to apologize for how I acted and how I treated you," she begins. Her eyes are vacant. Her face is pale. Her voice is robotic. She seems really out of it. "I had no right to get angry at you. What I did was irresponsible and selfish. I'm so sorry for the way I acted."

"It's okay," I say softly, reaching out to touch her arm. She steps back. "What's wrong, Liz?" I ask.

"I've been thinking a lot since Atlanta and—" She stops to lick her lips. "I think we should break this off."

"Excuse me?" I ask, completely puzzled. Maybe I hadn't heard her correctly.

"I told you from the start that I have expectations from my family that I have to uphold." Liz's gaze drops to the floor. At least she's nice enough to avert her eyes instead of lie to my face.

"Fuck your family's expectations, Liz! I thought that—" I rest a hand against the door frame, which serves two purposes; keeping my body open to her while holding myself up. "I thought what we had would make you forget about all that shit."

She hasn't forgotten, despite countless conversations. And by the vacant look on her face, it seems as if she knew our relationship would never turn into more. How had I never noticed that before? Had she always been indifferent? Had I been making everything up in my head this entire time? Romanticizing the depth of our relationship?

"I can't just forget, Austin. It's my family. They aren't going away. They aren't going to make this easy."

I drop my arms and take a step toward her. "I know that. Nothing worth fighting for is easy. Once they see how much we love each other and that we aren't giving up, they'll just have to learn to accept me, right?"

"It doesn't work like that, Austin. We come from two different worlds. I don't have the time or energy to try to mesh them."

Her words leave me speechless, confused, and hurt.

"So that's the real story, eh? You don't want to make the time for me—for *us*."

"I'm trying to make this as easy as possible."

"Easy? You think this is easy? I love you, Liz. I have never loved anyone the way I love you. And you're dropping this on me the day I leave for three months."

Today started with so many wonderful possibilities. It should have been the best day of my life. Instead, it's morphed into the worst.

Mom warned me about this. Focus on my career, not the girl. Don't let my heart get in the way of my dreams. I thought I could handle both, but I was wrong. She was right. She's always right.

"I'm sorry about the timing, but I didn't want to do this over the phone or text."

"Come on, babe. I thought we were in this for the long haul. I thought we were going to make a life together. Jesus, Liz, I see myself having a family with you."

She closes her eyes for longer than a blink. "You'll never be able to give me the life I'm used to, Austin," she says. "But you can have a nice life for yourself with the money my father gave you to stop seeing me. You won't have to worry about making ends meet."

"What? What are you fucking talking about? Your father didn't give me any money."

Is she delusional? I've heard people talk about "suicide Tuesdays," which is the nickname for the effects someone, who used ecstasy over the weekend, feels when they fully come down from the high. The depletion of endorphins causes an extreme sense of hopelessness, depression, fatigue—maybe delusions? I don't know. I've never done X, so I can't even speak from experience. Are the drugs fucking her head up this much?

"Just let it go, Austin. Let everything go. You don't have to pretend anymore. Just forget it. You won't have any trouble finding someone else." She turns around and starts down the steps. "You'll be better off with someone else anyway."

"Liz, you gotta help me out here. I have no clue what you're talking about. You're not making any sense."

She won't even look back at me, let alone answer me.

My phone, which has been ringing constantly since I woke up this morning, goes off again. I check the screen quickly. Nelson again.

"Look, I've gotta talk to Nelson. We've got so much to do today before we leave. Can we please talk about this tonight?"

"There's nothing left to say." Liz looks up at me, finally meeting my eyes for the first time since she got here. "Kick ass on tour," she says before continuing down the walkway.

It's the first time I've ever heard her swear—so minor, yet the words are a sword slicing my heart.

"I don't care what your family thinks of me. I have no clue what's going on right now, but I still love you, Elizabeth."

She doesn't turn around. Doesn't acknowledge me at all. Just jerks the door open on her shiny new SUV and climbs inside.

Rain starts to fall, pelting my head as I stand in the driveway, watching her vehicle get farther and farther away.

I shouldn't be surprised. Shouldn't be hurt.

Elizabeth Commons was never mine. She'll always be tied to the expectations and obligations of parents who have control over their daughter's minds. She'll always be tied to the way of life she grew up with—unable to find happiness with someone who doesn't fit that mold.

I should be relieved to be rid of all the complications that came with dating her.

Instead, darkness flows into my blood, my heart pumping it through my body fast.

I don't even have time to deal with the shock or grief right now. My world—the world I spent years working my ass off to create, to get to this very moment—is still turning. My stomach lurches as I shut my emotions off and switch into the lead singer of Drowned World.

Tonight, when I'm in the back of the van, staring out the window, as we drive to the first city to meet up with Walk on Mars, that's when I'll be able to overthink and analyze and grieve.

Chapter Twenty

LIZ

Hey! I told Mama and Daddy my surgical career is officially over. Then I cursed them out. Oh, and they offered him and his mom money if he agreed to stop seeing me, so I broke up with him. My life is fucking amazing right now. How are you guys?

*B*oth of my sisters dropped whatever they were doing and met me at my house in response to the text I sent them. I didn't want to get them involved, but the more I thought about it, the more I realized I needed someone to talk to. I couldn't turn to Austin. My sisters, no matter how different we are or what we're going through, have always been there for me when I needed them.

Maddie entered dramatically, pushing the front door open with her backside so she wouldn't drop the massive amount of clothes and shoes gathered in her arms. Because that's Maddie. When she's upset, she shops. So she thinks the shiny new things that make her feel better will make other people feel better too. I can't be mad at her for loving me the way she knows how.

Emily came with lip gloss and ice cream. Again, things that make her feel better. Huge props to Em for knowing her audience. Unlike many of her friends, I can't be consoled with weed and her tattoo machine.

"I can't believe you said fuck in front of Mama," Maddie says after I've rehashed the entire story of dinner at my parents' house. She digs her spoon into her pint of Coffee Caramel Fudge. Yes, I said *her* pint. Emily brought one for each of us.

"I can't believe you said fuck at all. I didn't think you swore," Emily says.

"I do in my head," I defend myself. "I learned to control my swearing. Can't go dropping the f-bomb in front of patients or their families, ya know?"

As my sisters enjoy the ice cream, I twist the cap off the gorgeous, deep-red lip gloss that Emily brought. It sparkles like diamonds in the tube; any other day I'd be dying to see how it looks on my lips.

Suddenly my phone rings, breaking me out of my thoughts. It's Ariana, the event planner I hired to take care of the details, for the event coming up in two days at the auction. I lift a finger and tell my sisters, "Hang on, I need to take this."

The call lasts less than a minute. I set my phone down, then dig into my ice cream. Stabbing the spoon into the carton as if there's something to kill in there.

"What's up?" Maddie asks.

"The band we had booked for the auction just cancelled. The singer has mono. We're two days away. Everyone good will be booked at this point."

Another issue I don't have the energy to deal with right now. Why can't anything go right? Where's my good karma?

"Do you want me to call around? Maybe find a DJ?" Maddie asks.

"No, but thank you. Ariana is on it. She just wanted to keep me informed."

"Well, that's piss poor. She should've called with a solution, not the problem," Maddie says. I roll my eyes because it's one of Daddy's favorite things to say.

"Okay, back to the story. You cussed out Mama and Daddy. That was a long time coming," Emily says. "Let's talk about the money thing. What do you mean they offered him money to stop seeing you?"

"I heard Mama and Daddy talking in the kitchen. And—"

"Whoa! Wait!" She holds up her hands and waves them in front of her. "You're basing this on something you overheard? You know they don't say anything important in public. Maybe they were hoping you were listening. Trying to piss you off or get you mad enough to break up with him yourself."

They wouldn't. Would they? I hate thinking about our parents being so deceptive, but I know they are. Though I don't normally see that side, I've heard about it. I've tried to ignore the stories because they're my parents. I appreciate what they've given me, even if I struggle with living my life as they want me to, versus the way I want to live.

"Well—"

"Maybe you need to talk to Daddy about the money thing," Maddie pipes up.

"Why would I do that? That's absolutely—" As I speak I search my sister's face. She's biting her thumbnail and averting her eyes. She almost looks guilty. "Maddie, do you know something about it?"

"No! I swear, Liz! I just—I know something about Austin's family and the money you might be talking about."

Emily and I both stare at Maddie. Imploring her to tell us what she knows. I'm a bit offended that she's been keeping something about Austin a secret from me.

"Is Austin's last name Williams?"

I nod.

"Well, Daddy—" she stops. "I shouldn't even be telling you guys this."

"Madeline, spill your guts or I will dye your hair purple while you sleep," Emily threatens her.

Maddie's eyes darken. Messing up her gorgeous blond locks is probably the worst torture she can imagine. "Daddy didn't come up with the idea for the Commons store. And he didn't even design the first clothing line. Charles Williams did."

"Who is that?"

"Austin's dad."

"What?" I ask, wide-eyed. "How do you know this?"

"A few weeks ago he had a lawyer draw up some paperwork. I happened to be there when the courier dropped it off. I thought it was a contract we'd been waiting for, so I opened it. And read it." She looks so disgusted with herself, I feel bad for her. It's not a situation any of us ever expected to be talking about.

"What does that have to do with Austin's dad?" I ask.

"It was a contract offering his mom money for the ideas his dad came up with for the business. Like, giving her compensation that they never received. It seemed really weird that they would have a contract drawn, up out of the blue, after not compensating the Williams family for all these years. I can only assume Mama told him to try to buy Austin off, and that's how he did it. I doubt he walked up to Austin or his mom and offered them money to stop seeing you. Mama might do something that callous, but Daddy never would."

Emily snorts. She thinks both of our parents are completely capable of that kind of behavior.

"The funniest part is that I was only offended that Austin may have taken the money for a split second. He needs the money. He doesn't need me. He can find another girlfriend—one who doesn't have parents who think they can do shitty things to get their way."

"You're right, Liz, he *can* find another girlfriend. But he won't find another soul mate." Emily says.

"Soul mate? What kind of soul mate accuses their boyfriend of taking money from her parents to stop dating her? Why the hell would he want to be with me after that? It's the most offensive thing I could have ever done. Especially given how big a deal the wealth difference was at first for both of us."

Why didn't I talk to Austin before I ran my mouth? Why didn't I call my sisters before I did anything?

"It was shitty, but if you tell Austin the truth, I think it's salvageable. He really loves you, Liz," Emily says. "You've been a completely different person since you met him. You've come out of your shell and done things that you normally wouldn't do. It's like you found your true self."

"I agree with Em," Maddie says. It's a surprise not only to me, but to Emily, as well, judging by the startled look on my youngest sister's face. "It's obvious Austin loves you. He brought you out of your shell and into yourself. I know you've felt hopeless since the accident, like everything you've ever known was flipped upside down. But now, it seems like you've finally realized that you don't have to be what other people want you to be. And I think he helped you realize that."

Wow. I didn't expect that observation to come from Maddie. I really thought she would be angry with me for not falling in line to what our family expects of me. "So what do I do? He's gone for the next three months."

"Go to him, Liz! Check their tour schedule and show up at a show," Emily says.

Maddie takes out her phone and begins tapping away at the screen.

I contemplate Emily's suggestion for a minute, then shake my head. "I don't want to show up unannounced at a show. That might throw him off and I don't want to mess with their set."

"They're off tomorrow night," Maddie announces, holding up her phone. The screen is filled with a list of Drowned World tour dates.

"The auction is tomorrow. I can't miss it. I've failed at a lot recently; I'm not going to mess up the fundraiser. It helps a lot of people."

"First"—Maddie says, lowering her phone—"you aren't a failure and you've gotta stop with those kinds of thoughts."

"I—"

"Second, I agree about not missing the auction. They've gotta have another night off soon, right?" She drops her gaze to her phone again.

I nod. "They usually play a few days in a row and have at least one off in between, for rest and drive time."

"Maybe you should call him?" Emily suggests.

She's right. I should have my phone in my hand right now. But it seems like one of those things I should apologize for to his face. And I honestly don't even know how he'd react if I called him.

"After the auction. Once that's in the books, I'll call him and tell him how stupid I was," I say, hashing out the plan in my head. "And if he won't take my call, I'll go to him—wherever he is—and beg for forgiveness."

"On your knees," Emily adds. "Definitely be on your knees."

I roll my eyes, but make a mental note to give head if necessary.

"You're so crude." Maddie scowls.

"Oh, come on! Doesn't Trent like blow jobs?" Emily teases. "I would've thought the stick up his ass would make it extra enjoyable."

Maddie slams her ice cream carton on the table and stalks out of the room.

She's been a different person since Trent moved back to Charlotte from Georgetown. She's been moody and distant and sad like I've never seen from her before. Maddie is usually bubbly and energetic. And she never would have eaten an entire pint of ice cream in one sitting. I think they had a better relationship from a distance. Maybe she's finally opening her eyes to what a controlling asshole he is.

Chapter Twenty-One

AUSTIN

"What's going on, Austin," Mom asks.

"Nothing."

"Don't nothing me. You never call me this much when you're on the road."

"Feeling a bit homesick and I wanted to hear your voice."

"I know something's wrong. You're mopey and you haven't mentioned Liz once."

"No reason to mention her. She broke up with me."

Part of me wanted Mom to ask. I didn't want to call her crying about Liz breaking up with me. I honestly thought the whole thing was a weird fluke. I've been replaying the things she said in my head. And I just couldn't comprehend some of it.

"What?"

"We got in a fight at the festival. It sucked, but I didn't think it was that big of a deal. But I didn't hear from her for a few days, and when I did, she comes over to tell me it's over. All this bullshit about being from different worlds and not being able to give her the life she's used to. Then she started saying crazy shit about me taking money from her father to break up with her. I have no clue where she even got that idea. I've never had a conversation with her father."

"Wait. She said her father gave you money to break up with her?"

"Yup." It still sounds so ridiculous, I can't even believe I told Mom. I just don't know how to process it.

Mom is uncharacteristically silent on her end.

"Mom?" I ask tentatively, knowing that what I'm about to suggest could piss her off royally. "Did Harris Commons offer *you* money to break us up?"

"Austin Charles Williams! What kind of person do you think I am?" *Shit.*

It's not like I believed she did it, but I had to ask because I don't know why Liz would say something so absolutely outlandish to me.

"Sorry, Mom. You know I don't think you're the kind of person who would accept something like that. I'm just searching for answers."

She's quiet again. It's concerning, because I expect more anger after suggesting something so offensive to her character.

"Harris Commons offered me money a few weeks ago."

I straighten up in bed. "What?" I ask loudly. "Why?"

It must be a little too loud, because Fozzie glances over from the bed beside me, giving me a dirty look before jerking a pillow over his head and burrowing into the covers.

"As compensation for the business idea that he stole from your father. And for a clothing line that I helped design," Mom says as if I'm supposed to understand that at all.

"What in the world are you talking about?" I'm so confused. Mom could barely put together my homemade Halloween costumes. How could she design a clothing line?

"Your father and Harris met in college. They became friendly, not necessarily friends, but they had some business classes together. Your father always had ideas for businesses. He was brilliant, but didn't have the financial means to pursue them. That's where Harris came in. They brainstormed the concept of the Commons Department Store together. Your dad even came up with the slogan because he knew Harris's family would be the ones funding the business. They asked me to help design a chic yet cheap clothing line to start it off. I was sewing a lot of my own clothes back then. I'll admit, I was never the best designer, but I knew where to get fabrics and put together a cute line that wouldn't cost too much for the business and the consumers."

Mom pauses. Which gives my swirling brain a chance to catch up to this *what the fuck* moment. My dad helped come up with the Commons concept? How did I not know this?

"We were naive and trusting back then. Stupid, is what I call it now. We thought we were working with Harris. It never even crossed our minds to protect ourselves with a contract or something written to state that we were cocreators on the ideas. We put together the concepts and gave him the sketches for the line. He took all of it to his father to get a loan to start the store." Mom sighs. "And that's when everything changed. We never heard from him after that. He wouldn't return our calls, wouldn't meet with us. He started the store without us. Without ever giving us any credit or compensation. We certainly didn't have the means to fight him. Who could fight the Commons family? They had all the money and influence behind them. We had nothing."

The animosity Mom's had for Commons stores for all these years becomes crystal clear. Why didn't she ever say anything?

"So, after almost thirty years, Harris Commons offered you money to compensate you out of the blue. That didn't seem odd?"

"It absolutely seemed odd! I almost fell off my chair when I got the call. But I thought—hoped—that he might have found his conscience because you were dating his daughter. How could someone look into the eyes of the son of the person, who created the concept where he made millions, and not feel any remorse? When he offered, I sure as hell wasn't going to turn down the money, Austin. I never imagined he'd—"

"I'm not blaming you, Mom. I think you should take every penny. He probably lowballed you anyway."

"The amount we agreed on doesn't matter. It was never about the money for your father and I. It was about the deception."

"I get that. Totally. But the timing of his change of heart is suspicious."

"I'll bet that bastard told his vile wife he used the money to pay me to break you up. She never would have agreed to give me compensation for the business. Cookie Commons is a different breed. She didn't come from money, but she sure hoards the fortune she has now."

"Fuck," I groan.

"I'm sorry I didn't tell you, Austin. I was surprised by the contact, but I didn't realize he would ever do something so awful to his own daughter. Just to get her to stop dating you? What a sad state of affairs when humans put so much weight on wealth and not a person's character."

"Well, from what you just told me, they don't have a whole lot of character in the first place. Money can't buy class."

"Austin, have you wondered why she would believe that about you?"

I sigh and scrub my face with one hand. "I have. I've been going over it a million times, Mom. First, I was offended and pissed. But then I was just perplexed. Liz has a heart of gold. She's not like her parents. So I honestly can't see her believing I'd actually take money to break up with her. It's like she had some other thought behind it."

"Do you think she thought she was helping you? Maybe she thought you'd be better off without her?"

"Why would she think that?"

"She's embarrassed by her family, Austin. How would you react if someone did that to you?"

Shit. Did Liz really think she was doing me a favor by breaking up with me? Was she trying to shield me from her deceitful family's bullshit?

It makes a hell of a lot more sense than her really believing that I would take money to break up with her.

"Do you want to get involved with a family like the Commons?" Mom asks softly. "Is she worth it?"

"Absolutely," I answer with zero hesitation. "I'd let someone rip out my vocal chords if it meant being with her again. I don't care about her shady-ass family. She's nothing like them. She's everything to me. Absolutely everything."

"As long as you're aware of what you're getting into."

"I know. I can't say I like it, but I know."

I may not have the net worth or the all-American look of the guys Liz's parents expect her to be with, but I have integrity.

Liz and I were brought to each other for a reason. If we can filter out the bullshit brought on by others, we can get through anything.

I shove the covers off and run to the bathroom. It's about time to show Liz that we're meant to be together. All we need is each other. All of this bullshit is ridiculous. I'll always be here for her. I already saved her once. And I'll do it again.

Chapter Twenty-Two

LIZ

I've never felt so out of place surrounded by so many familiar faces.

I should be the belle of the ball, working the room of the fundraiser I started, but I don't feel like talking to anyone. They aren't all bad people—on the contrary—everyone in attendance has generously donated a large amount of money to be here. I'm just annoyed at what a night like this represents. Being at a fundraiser like this is something I used to enjoy. Something I used to look forward to. Picking out a fabulous gown and getting my hair and makeup done with Mama and Maddie was one of those silly pleasures I actually looked forward to.

But that was then, and this is now.

Tonight, I'm bored and annoyed. When I started brainstorming this event a few years ago, I wanted something small, but Mama insisted I had to go big in order to bring out the power players. She even set me up with Ariana Rogers—event planner to the stars. The silent auction boasts prizes like private-jet excursions and a weekend in St. Bart's. The meal is a seven-course dinner from a Michelin-star chef Daddy knows, who flies in from New York City.

I'm excited that the event draws such a great crowd, but I can't help think about how much money we'd be able to give if I didn't have to waste so much to get the people with money to be here? I'm torn between appreciation—which I absolutely have—to the sick feeling that many of the people are here tonight for the laughing and dancing and drinking, and barely register the reason they're here—the families who benefit from their generosity who are struggling. Is it just a donation tax credit for them? Or another philanthropic cause they can brag about at the country club while drinking "chaahh-mps" (the annoying nickname some people use for champagne)?

I hope not.

Speaking of chaahh-mps, I grab my fourth glass of bubbly from the teetering serving tray that passes me. If I can't beat them, might as well join them.

"Do you really need another?" The sultry voice of my favorite singer rings out from behind me. I spin and come face to face with Austin.

The sight of him makes me gasp. Not just because I'm surprised that he's right here in front of me when he's supposed to be in DC for a show tomorrow, but also because he looks absolutely magnificent.

He stands tall, confident, and absolutely flawless in a tuxedo, perfectly fitted to his muscular frame. His hair is gelled; luscious pink lips are surrounded by a freshly trimmed ten o'clock shadow. He looks impeccable—like he wears a penguin suit every day.

Austin takes the flute from my hand and brings it to his mouth, tipping it back and draining it in one slug. Champagne wets his lips which makes me want to sweep my tongue over them to taste him one last time.

I can't take my eyes off him. He's always handsome. But I've never seen this side—dashingly dressed to the nines. He doesn't seem uncomfortable at all. He looks as laid-back as he does in a white T-shirt and leather pants.

What I wouldn't give to see him in leather pants again. To drop to my knees and slide those pants down his thighs.

"What are you thinking about, Miss Honey?" he asks, jolting me out of the lewd fantasy.

My eyes must have dropped, because he lifts my chin with his fingers, tilting my face up so our gazes meet.

"You don't want to know." I shake my head and turn away as I feel the heat rise from my core to my cheeks.

He takes a step closer, places his hands on my hips, and dips his head to my ear. "I do, but there's one thing I want to know more than what you were just thinking about."

"What's that?" I ask tentatively. My heart revs in my chest. I feel like it will carry me away if I'm not careful. I feel unprepared, even though I planned on leaving first thing in the morning to meet up with him in DC to let him know how much I need him.

"I want to know if you love me. If you ever loved me."

"I—" The words stick in my throat.

My heart pounds against my chest. Austin is here, standing right in front of me, asking me if I ever loved him. I'm saddened that my ignorance and insecurity caused him to have any doubt.

Of course I love you! You're the only man I've ever loved. I want to scream, but I hold back. I'm trying to suppress the overwhelming urge to throw myself against his chest and wrap my arms around him. I love this man with every piece of my soul, but I hold back because I can't understand how he'd want to be with me after I accused him of taking money from my father.

"What are you doing here?" I ask.

"I just told you why I'm here." He sets the empty glass on another passing tray. The servers don't have faces, hidden by ornate purple, green, and gold Mardi Gras masks which follow the theme of the party. Each one mocking my misery as they stroll by, fake with plastic smiles, jovial as Bourbon Street on Fat Tuesday.

"This benefit has been sold out for months. How in the world did you get in?"

"I was invited. Emily said your band canceled, and I couldn't let you use a shitty DJ you found last minute for such an important event." He looks over his shoulder toward the stage where Emily is talking to the DJ Ariana found last-minute. Behind them there's a flurry of activity as Jimmy from Austin's band sets up equipment. "Lucky for you, I happened to be free tonight."

"Austin, you should be in—?" I'm totally confused at what's happening right now.

"Right here with you is the most important place for me to be. We need to get the bullshit misunderstanding out of the way before we can move on." Austin grabs my hand. "You were right, my mom did take money from your father, but it wasn't to get me to break up with you; it was for a bunch of shit that happened years ago."

"Yeah, I—" I close my eyes and shake my head, ready to explain.

But Austin keeps talking, "Not saying your family isn't shady as fuck, because your mom actually did ask your dad to pay us off, but that's not what we took money for."

"I know. Maddie told me." I reach up to brush my hand through my hair, but stop when I remember it's being held back by an antique silver comb.

"Did you really believe that I could be swayed into breaking up with you over some cash?"

"I wasn't thinking straight. I wasn't feeling like the best version of myself at that point, and I didn't know what to believe, Austin."

"I get that. You come from a family who thinks they can control people with threats and bribes, so it makes sense."

I nod. Because it's true and it usually works. Most of the people my father bribes can't resist the money. The rich get richer and the poor— well, the poor get a desperately needed windfall.

"My family doesn't work that way. My mom isn't desperate enough for money to be that shitty of a person. But she will accept compensation for an idea that she and my father should have been compensated for years ago."

His words slice through me like a double-edged sword. An insult to my family, capped with the insinuation that I think his mom is a horrible person.

"I know, Austin. I know my family plays in a totally different league."

Out of the side of my eye, I notice that we've gathered an audience. Curious eyes watch with intent interest. The elevator-style dinner music blends with the laughter and chatter in the room, but in our vicinity the noise has decreased dramatically.

My parents are around here somewhere, shmoozing with someone. I'm sure they've seen the crowd gather and they'll be at my side at any moment. They'll be pissed when they realize that Austin and I are talking about this in public, causing a scene at an event attended by so many of their friends. There's a reason Harris Commons does all of his business behind closed doors.

"When you left me I was shocked. Heartbroken. Pissed. So completely pissed. I couldn't believe you would just walk away, out of the blue, with no warning. It was a complete slap in the face.

"Then I talked to my mom and she explained what happened. And right away the flip in my brain switched from anger to confusion. Did you break up with me because you thought giving me up would be better for me?"

I bite back tears as I nod. I hate coming across as such an insecure idiot, but that's the way I portrayed myself, so I have to face the consequences.

"I think you did that because you love me. You thought your sacrifice was worth the pain." He pauses. I open my mouth to respond, but he continues before I can utter a sound. "And that's a fucked-up way of thinking."

Stunned into silence, I lift my eyes to his.

"You grew up in this life where money can buy anything. Homes. Cars. Feelings. People. I can't blame you for how you were raised. I can't blame you for being confused by the tug of war between your family and your heart. But damn!" He closes his eyes as if in pain. Which makes me want to cry. "It pisses me off that you thought I might be lured by money. Not everyone can be bought. You don't have to sacrifice your own happiness to offset your family's fucked-up politics."

"You're right, I should have talked to you instead of giving up. I was tired and angry and absolutely embarrassed. Why would you even want to be involved with me—with us?" I say, conflicted because even though I know my family can be shady, I still love them. Mama and Daddy aren't horrible people, but they won't hesitate to use their power or money to influence a situation. They think they're doing it for a greater good. Too bad the greater good is their own personal interests.

"Why? Because I love you. And I see you for who you are, not as the family that you came from."

"We're intertwined. I'm part of them."

"Well, sure, but you have free will. And I'm pretty sure you would never bribe someone to get your way."

"I'm sorry I didn't put up a fight. I wish I would have handled it differently. I wish I would have talked to you instead of assuming I knew the best thing for you."

"I wish you would have, too, because one of the things I love about you—about us—is that we can talk about anything—even things that are uncomfortable. Nothing is off-limits. My fucked-up brain is completely open and free around you, Liz. And we need to keep that communication and trust going."

I swallow hard and nod.

"Forget all of these complications—the miscommunications, the insecurities, the obstacles that we keep creating because we're scared. Because all of this is actually very simple. No one—*nothing*—will stop me from loving you."

I stumble backward, suddenly unsteady in my heels. He grabs my waist and I raise my face to his, my gaze locked in his just like that first night we met.

"When I'm looking in your eyes, everything else goes away. All I see is you and me. That's all we'll ever need. We can handle anything as long as we remember it's just us. Right here. Right now. Forever."

I nod. Which causes a few tears that had been building up to spill onto my cheeks. "So you forgive me?"

"Of course I do. We all jump to conclusions. We all make mistakes. I've made more than my share. But I need to know if you're all in, Miss Honey. 'Cuz I need you. I need you so much my heart aches when you're not around."

"I'm in," I say firmly with complete sincerity.

"Do you love me?"

"I absolutely love you."

"Will you dance with me?" Austin offers me his hand.

"I will always dance with you." I slip into his arms without hesitation and he wraps me in his embrace. His facial hair tickles my cheek as I rest my head on his shoulder and nestle into the crook of his neck. Inhaling the spicy scent of the beard oil I bought him floods me with warmth. He smells like home—or my new mindset of what I want home to be.

"Elizabeth," Daddy says sternly from behind me.

"I'm dancing, Daddy. I'll talk to you later," I say. Then I close my eyes and relax in Austin's arms. I refuse to let my family interfere with us anymore. This is the first step on a long road of change.

We sway together silently for two songs. Emotions flood every cell of my brain. I almost lost it all. My career. My love. Myself.

"This is everything," I murmur, unsure if Austin can even hear me. "This is all I'll ever need."

"You'll have this for as long as you want it. But let's talk about the immediate future."

I try to lift my head, but he takes one hand off my hip and presses it back down. He strokes my hair as we sway. I smile against his shoulder.

"I know you're confused and hurt. I know it sucks to have to start over. But no matter what program you choose, you'll have some time to kill until the new one starts, right?"

"Yes."

A lump forms in my throat. The discussions I had with Austin led me to the program I chose. After speaking with Dr. Crowder and a few trusted coresidents about what I really want to do with my medical career—and where I would fit best—I decided to apply for the family-medicine residency. With that, I can move forward with my personal goals as a physician.

"I think you should use the free time for an epic adventure," he says.

The power and confidence in Austin's voice brings me back. He tethers me to reality.

In the months before I met him, my head was a mess—swirling with confusion and hurt. What I truly wanted from my career got buried under a mountain of expectations I was too ashamed and insecure to confront. Instead of having a conversation with my parents, I allowed the perceived disappointment and failure to weigh me down.

I'd been so buried by guilt, that I would never be what they expected of me, that I couldn't see my injury as a blessing in disguise. Until Austin.

"What kind of epic adventure?" I ask.

"Come on tour with me and be our merch girl."

"You want me to come on tour with you?" I ask. This time I lift my head and look at him with wide eyes.

"Absolutely. I don't want to live without you, babe. I want you next to me every fucking time I wake up."

"And I want you fucking me every time you wake up." I pinch his waist teasingly.

"Every time?" His smile widens.

"Within reason."

"Deal," he says and presses his lips onto mine.

I wrap my arms around his neck and pull him closer. When the songs ends, he says, "I should probably get up there, eh? This music blows."

"Are you sure? You don't have to do this, you know."

"I know. I want to do it. I will be here for you whenever you need me, in any way that I can be. When one of us is down, we help the other rise up."

"Thank you." We intertwine our fingers and shuffle through the crowd, making our way toward the stage.

"Do you mind if I take this jacket off?" Austin holds his coat open like he's got a superman logo underneath and looks down with a frown.

I grab the jacket, slide it down his arms, and fold it over my forearm. Then I remove his bow tie and undo three buttons on his crisp, white shirt so his neck and chest tattoos are clearly visible. I stop to take in his appearance and decide it's not quite right. Reaching out, I un-cuff each sleeve and roll them up three quarters. Biting my lip, I inspect him one final time.

"Now you're ready," I say.

"I'm not gonna lie. You undressing me in public is fucking hot."

I wink before walking up the two stairs to the stage. Taking the mic in my hand, I greet the crowd. "Good evening, everyone. For those of you who don't know me, I'm Liz Commons, the founder of the *For*

When It Rains Foundation. Thank you all for being here to help us raise money to assist local families with catastrophic medical-care bills. Over the last three years, your generosity has helped almost one hundred families in the Charlotte area." I pause, smiling graciously as I allow the crowd to applaud the impact of their donations. "There's an old saying, 'when it rains, it pours.' That's where I came up with the name for the foundation. We could all use a little help when it rains, right? When it feels like nothing will ever go right and there's no light in sight. It started sprinkling on me a few days ago when the band we had lined up to play tonight had to cancel due to illness. Thankfully, a beautiful friend stepped up to help me out. Please welcome Austin Williams, the talented singer of Drowned World, the love of my life, and the person I can always count on to keep me afloat."

Austin's head snaps up, obviously surprised that I introduced him that way. He's beaming as he crosses the stage. I start to move away from the microphone to let him take over, but he grabs my hand and pulls me into his arms like we're ballroom dancers. Then he wraps an arm around my back and dips me, planting his lips on mine as the blood rushes to my head. I'm dizzy and exhilarated—and alive!

And for the first time, I truly don't care what anyone in this crowd thinks about it—or him. I've found my happily-ever-after with my soulmate, and I'm ready to embark on all the adventures life will bring.

EPILOGUE

Liz

THREE MONTHS LATER

*M*addie calls just as Austin unlocks the door to my house. It's our first time home after three arduous months on the road. All I can think of is climbing into my bed, curling up against Austin, and sleeping for a week.

Instead I answer the phone, because I know she just wants to make sure we got home safe. Our week-long sleep can wait five more minutes.

"Hey, Maddie!" I greet her.

Austin enters behind me, wheeling my suitcase in, before setting his Tumi bag on the floor next to the door. I can't understand how he's still standing. I was just the girl selling merchandise at the show. Austin was running around the stage, night after night, expending more energy than a toddler who got into some coffee espresso beans.

Since he's a seasoned professional, I followed his lead the entire time. Even though we went to bed as early as we could most nights, worked out whenever we had the chance, took plenty of naps, and ate a fairly healthy diet, the entire trip was still utterly exhausting.

"Are you home? Or still at the airport?" she asks.

"Just walked into my house." I glance at the stacks of mail on the counter. Emily and Maddie have been coming by to take in the mail and feed my cat. Speaking of Oliver—I'm surprised he hasn't run out to meow his displeasure at us for leaving him so long, while weaving between our feet to trip us into falling onto the floor to pet him.

"I'm so glad you're back! I missed you! How was it?"

"Amazing and exhausting." I kick off my sneakers.

"I thought you just went to a yoga retreat?"

She's right. After a grueling three months on the road, we bid the guys and the van adieu and stayed in San Francisco for an impromptu weekend yoga and meditation retreat. I've never meditated in my life, though I do believe in the benefits of it. Before, I could never get my mind to slow down long enough for it to work. The fact that I was able to relax so easily in the classes was a huge sign about how much taking a break from the medical program has helped my stress levels.

"We were, and it was amazing, but you wouldn't believe the toll three straight months of being on the road takes on the body."

"Almost like three straight years of a residency, eh?" she quips.

I manage to squeak out a tired laugh. "Might have been worse. I can't believe I thought I had it rough."

Had Austin suggested we end the trip with a few whirlwind days, walking the hilly streets of San Francisco, I would've thought he was crazy, but the retreat was perfect—just what the doctor ordered for our weary minds and bodies. Plus, it gave us some much-needed alone time to reconnect on a completely different level. I wouldn't trade that peaceful, romantic getaway for anything.

"I'm laying by the pool right now. It's nice and relaxing. You guys should come over later."

Austin comes up behind me and grabs my hips. Then he pulls me back into his chest and places soft kisses along my neck. I tilt my head to give him better access.

"I would love to, but I'm so completely exhausted right now, I just want to pass out." She doesn't need to know that I'll pass out completely satiated after sex with my Energizer Bunny boyfriend.

"No worries. Trent just got here anyway."

"I'll call you—" I begin, but stop abruptly when I hear distant yelling on the other end of the line.

"How could you do this to me, Madeline?"

The tone of Trent's voice makes my entire body stiffen. Over the years he and Maddie have been dating, I've seen how angry and intense he can be. Though I'd never seen him hurt her physically—and she's never said that he has—his temper has always freaked me out.

I've noticed a pattern with Trent. When he yells at her, he's usually wrong—and drunk.

"Maddie?" I ask firmly.

"How could you fucking do this to me?" Trent yells.

Maddie's voice shakes when she answers, "Do what, Trent? I—"

"This is the last fucking time you will ever—"

Suddenly there's a crash on the other end and I jump.

"Maddie?" I ask. I swallow hard and my heart pumps faster. "Madeline?" I ask, using her given name instead of her nickname.

But there's no response from the other end. No sound at all.

"Liz?" Austin asks. "Is everything okay?"

My exhausted body is on high alert. Our eyes meet when I spin to face him. "We've got to get over to my parent's house. Now."

"Let's go," he says.

I shove my phone into the back pocket of my jeans and bolt toward the counter to grab my keys. Austin doesn't hesitate to follow or stop me to ask more questions. He knows me well enough to understand that if I'm dropping everything right now—something is very wrong.

The Material Girls series continues with
Maddie's story in **LIVE TO TELL**

Secrets. Lies.

Webs I vowed never to weave because of how many I've been
caught in.

But when I told the truth, it didn't set me free…it set me on track for
deportation.

So when Madeline Commons, heiress to one of the country's largest
department store chains offered to help me with my situation, I
agreed.

I needed a way to stay in the country.

She needed to get away from her abusive ex.

A fake relationship seemed like the perfect solution for both of us.

But there's a massive problem with our plan.

Being with Maddie has been my fantasy since the first time I laid eyes
on her.

The biggest lie isn't our relationship, it's telling myself I can keep my
feelings casual.

Before I started this crazy facade, I thought losing my business and the life I built over the years would be the biggest consequence of our deception, but now I realize...

it's losing Maddie that will break me.

LIVE TO TELL is a sexy, standalone novel in the Material Girls series. Happily Ever After guaranteed. No cliffhanger for Erik and Maddie...but you may be lured into the next book of the series. ;)

Read LIVE TO TELL now!

eBook and Paperback Available on Amazon

DEVIL IN DISGUISE

"The past is never dead. It's not even past."
~ William Faulkner

What do you do when the man from your nightmares comes to life?

It's been four years since my brief tryst with the mysterious Russian mafia thug who saved my life.

Four years since I emptied his American bank account—the money he'd been saving to move here and start a new life.

Four years since I opened my heart and fell in love with a wonderful, new man who makes all of my dreams come true.

Four years of restless nights as the one secret I keep from the man I'm crazy for haunts me.

After four years, I thought I was in the clear.

Then the man from my nightmares storms back into my life demanding the fifty thousand dollars I stole.

Despite having everything I've ever dreamed of--all I want is him.

DEVIL IN DISGUISE is a standalone, second chance romance. This steamy story, is a crossover between USA Today Bestselling author Sophia Henry's Material Girls series and Saints and Sinners series.

One click for twists and turns, ups and downs, and a curveball you won't see coming.

**Turn the page to start reading
DEVIL IN DISGUISE Now!!**

DEVIL IN DISGUISE EXCERPT

Material Girls/Saints & Sinners Crossover Novel

CHAPTER 1

COOKIE

Charlotte, NC

I never really liked our apartment. By 'apartment', I mean the one room that my mother and I share in a run-down building with almost sixty identical apartments.

Neither Mama nor I cook so the lack of a working stove for the last five or so years doesn't matter much. The bathroom is barely larger than a telephone booth, but it works for us. 'Works' is a bit of an ironic word, since the shower hasn't functioned properly and we can only take baths. Most people might be annoyed by the constant drip of the faucet, but not me. That's been my personal lullaby since I was a kid. Maintenance has never been able to fix it—which says everything you need to know about our maintenance people. But, at this point, I might have sleeping problems if they did.

The squeaky ceiling fan is a constant reminder of how much I want to be rid of such an undesirable existence. In twenty years, when I'm telling my kids about the sounds of my childhood, I swear the sound of that fan and faucet are the two things I'll remember. If only I could remember the voice of my father the same way—but life doesn't always work out the way we plan it.

But you have to have *had* a father to remember his voice.

"Suck it up and move on," Mama would snap whenever I got into one of my melancholy moods.

I've never been much of a complainer. Not even when the greasy odor from the fried chicken restaurant next door wafts in through the windows and almost makes me choke. I take it all in stride.

Inside, I might be seething darkly under my breath, wishing we lived next to that cinnamon bun factory off Tryon instead, but I never let it show.

Somehow, Mama could always pick up on my foul moods. Maybe because 'foul' is her default demeanor.

"This one tonight is a good one, Katrina," Mama says in her thick Southern accent as she swipes lipstick onto my lips. She always praises my full lips—a carbon copy of her mother's. "Your Grandmama was a beauty." She likes to boast whenever she dresses me up for a job. "And you are five times more beautiful that she ever was."

Being a bit of a drama queen, my mother likes to pull all the stops when reminiscing on the past, looking lost in her memories and what not.

Any other daughter would be sympathetic. I *should* have some sympathy for her. But I'd have to chip away through too many years of pain to uncover any.

"You should have seen me back in the day," she says now as she moves away to inspect my lips.

"I know, Mama. I hear people talking about you all the time," I say, hoping it comes across as a compliment, though she must hear the sarcastic tone.

The bright red lipstick smells like melted plastic and tastes like wax. It's a slightly lighter shade than the cherry-colored dress that clings to every curve, so tight, it looks like it's been painted on.

"Don't fuck this one up, ya hear?" she continues, spraying me with perfume.

Mama's never been mushy like most mothers I see in school. Oh no, Mama has balls of steel and is very cutthroat when it comes to getting things done, including setting me up with cigar smelling, rich old men.

Speaking of smells, the lavender perfume is overbearing, but there's no point saying anything. So, all I can do is steel my already frayed nerves and let her finish up.

She squints at me, scrutinizing my face as though she wishes she could change it, then resumes her task of painting my lips. I guess she wants to make sure that every inch gets covered with the disgusting—possibly radioactive—lipstick.

"No one is going to kiss me with this nasty shit on my lips, Mama." I retort, looking at myself in the mirror as she continues to fuss over me. "Can't you smell it?"

It's a 'new' dress from the thrift store, but the same old drugstore lipstick.

Mama steps back, scowling as she stares at me like she didn't hear a thing I said.

"By all means, Katrina. You can run to the store and grab us a good smelling lipstick with all the money you have in your bank account," she finally says with a flat look on her face.

All I can do in that moment is press my lips together, already cringing as I remember the reason why I have to do this in the first place.

"What makes this one so special, Mama?" I ask, trying to keep from rolling my eyes. "How is he different than the rest?"

Mama crosses her arms and shakes her head like she's exasperated with a little child. Ever since she got sick, the revolving door of men she brought home came to a screeching halt and I had to pick up the slack.

Other girls get amazing birthday cakes and special treats on their sixteenth birthday—maybe even an over-the-top Sweet Sixteen party.

But not me. Nope. Instead of parties and treats, Mama decided pimping me out to rich old men was the best way to kick start my sixteenth year on the planet.

Then again, we had to sustain ourselves. And using men for money is all she's ever known.

Ever since I can remember, my dream has been to go to college, get a degree, and get a good enough job to take myself out of the slums of Charlotte, North Carolina. Several years later and the dream remains unwavering, but sometimes I can't help but wonder if it will ever happen.

"It's highly unlikely that either of you will amount to anything," I remember Mrs. Hodge saying during Biology class a few years ago.

It's funny how, despite years of mostly straight A's and breezing through my schoolwork, one comment can stick out in my head above any of the other accomplishments.

The comment hadn't been directed at just me. No, she included Andre, my black best friend, too. Though it hurt, it was downright offensive to hear her say that about Dre, because school didn't come as easy for him. He worked hard for every B. But that was life at our high school. Instead of the awesome dude from the *Lean on Me* movie, we got shitty teachers who didn't care. They were people who could never get a job teaching anywhere else, just filling an open job position because no talented instructors wanted to be at our school.

At least most of the people in school don't know that I turn into a 'mistress of the night' and not the quiet girl that loves sitting at the edge of the classroom, taking it all in, but ready to bolt at any second.

How will you ever amount to anything when you're nothing?

The thought crosses my mind as I stare at Mama's retreating figure. For a moment, I thought she was the one saying those words, but after paying closer attention it turns out she had been coughing for the past couple of seconds.

At this point, all the enthusiasm I had managed to put together washed down my spine like an ice-cold waterfall.

"Are you okay, Mama?" I ask, running toward her, my heart pounding in my chest as she begins to hack. "Don't die on me now," I mutter under my breath.

Mama is still doubled over when I reach her, but she shoos me away gently and straightens up slowly. "I'm fine, Katrina," she says, her cough subsiding.

I try to smile but my lips fail to move. Mama is the only family I've got.

"Stop fussing over me and get going already," she says sharply, like she didn't just sound like her lungs would fall out. "You're gonna miss the bus."

"Alright, alright. I'm going," I retort, moving to sit on the couch so I can put my scuffed heels on. In minutes, I have the door shut behind me.

I always thought mothers are supposed to make sure that their children have a better life than they had. But that hasn't been my experience. Maybe she really does want the best for me, and prostituting me out to rich men is her misguided way of setting me up for the future.

"Someday, I will have a successful job, make a lot of money, and get out of this shithole," I whisper to myself as I adjust my dress.

Self-consciousness takes over as I shuffle down the hallway toward the stairwell. Imagine what it's like waiting for a bus in a skin-tight dress in a neighborhood like ours. It's like having a bullseye on my back.

People tend to stare at me whenever Mama dresses me outrageously for certain kind of clients, but I never let them see the swirling emotions. Once I step out for work, I become someone else; cold, calculating, and set on completing the task at hand.

Sometimes, I pray silently that this second persona doesn't become permanent. At the same time, it's been extremely effective in getting me through tough times and pushing me to my goals.

"Hey Kat!" Dre calls as I step outside. I haven't seen him yet, but I'd recognize my best friend's voice anywhere.

"What's up, Dre?" I reply, shivering lightly though it's probably still eighty-something degrees out.

"I'm good. Your mama put you on duty tonight?" he asks.

"Rent's coming up," I reply like he's asking about the weather.

Dre knows everything about my life, not just because we grew up together, but because he's the only friend I have, and he's always been there for me, especially during some of the darkest moments. His mom is joyful and loving—the mother I never had. Despite having four of her own kids to feed on her meager salary from Kmart, she kept me fed during times my own mother hadn't.

Despite seeing me at every phase of life, and knowing what Mama makes me do, sometimes I think he wants more than just friendship. Maybe he thinks he can save me.

Too bad he can't afford me.

Any other eighteen-year-old girl in our neighborhood would be ecstatic at the idea of having Dre interested in them. In fact, some of them have threatened to kick my ass just because they want the attention he gives me. I'm not completely immune to his good looks and charm—with his curly black hair, gorgeous smile, and lanky, baseball-player's build. He actually resembles the guy who plays Willis in Different Strokes.

But I'm the Arnold to Dre's Willis—meaning, I'm shorter, plumper, and—we're like siblings. I don't have any romantic feelings for him. And he doesn't have the guy who plays Willis' bank account.

If he can't get me ahead, I have no time for him because I'm not the average eighteen-year-old girl in the neighborhood. No other girls in my senior class have to snuggle up with old, ass men—do whatever they ask—and still come home and maintain an almost-perfect grade point average.

A boyfriend is the least of my concerns when I have the weight of keeping a roof over my head on my shoulders.

Getting into North Carolina University is number one on my list of ambitions, and I need a lot of money to achieve that by Fall.

"You need me to wait with you at the bus stop?" he asks with concern. Our gazes meet briefly before I glance away. I appreciate his concern—I always have.

I shake my head. "I'm cool."

His friendship is a relief. He doesn't judge me even though everyone else who knows about my family's situation treats us like outcasts. It's funny, because I know a lot of people in this building are doing illegal things like selling drugs or committing robbery, but I'm not treating them like they're dog shit on the bottom of a shoe.

The opinions of sheep don't matter. We all do what we have to do to get by.

"See you in class then?"

"Definitely," I say, bumping his shoulder with my mine. Before I leave, I pause. "Are you good?" I ask.

Dre has a thing for always bottling up his emotions because he feels like that's how a 'real' man should behave, but sometimes I can get the issue out of him. I haven't been a great friend recently.

"As good as any of us in living this shithole ever are, Kat," he replies with a soft laugh.

"Word," I agree, before patting his shoulder and heading to the bus stop.

Don't fuck this one up, Katrina, Mama's voice rings in my ear as I wait on the bus to South Blvd.

As if anything I do could fuck up our life any more than it already is.

READ **DEVIL IN DISGUISE** NOW
Ebook and Paperback Available on Amazon

Do you want ALL the Sophia Henry news?
Sophia Henry's mailing list is the place to be if you like steamy romance novels that tug at your heart strings. Stay notified of new releases, sales, exclusive content with newsletters twice a month. Sign up HERE.

REVIEWS ROCK!

THANK YOU so much for taking the time to read OPEN YOUR HEART I truly appreciate every single one of you. If you enjoyed reading OPEN YOUR HEART as much as I enjoyed writing it, it would mean the world to me if you would consider leaving a review on Amazon.

(If you really loved the book, copy and paste the same review to Bookbub & Goodreads!)

Sophia x

PLAYLIST

Material Girl – Madonna
Open Your Heart – Madonna
Darling (feat. Missio) – Said the Sky, Missio
Say It – Illenium Remix – Flume, Tove Lo, Illenium
Aristocrat – New Politics
Badlands – The Born Love
Last Nite – The Strokes
In Your Room – Depeche Mode
Say You Won't Let Go – James Arthur
Tonight You're Perfect – New Politics
Bills – Grandson
So Close – Andrew McMahon in the Wilderness
Talk Too Much – COIN
Ringer – The Unlikely Candidates
Out of My Head – The Griswolds
Echo – Foreign Air
Vowels - Hunny
Breaking Free – Night Riots
Hell, Yeah – Nothing But Thieves
7 – Catfish and the Bottlemen
Cocoon – Catfish and the Bottlemen
White Dove – Koda
Nothing Wrong With Me – Unlike Pluto
Waves – Krrum
Next To Me – Imagine Dragons
Ride or Die (feat. Foster the People) – The Knocks
Temptation – New Order
Simplify – Young the Giant

ALSO BY SOPHIA HENRY

ACKNOWLEDGMENTS

First, I want to acknowledge YOU! Thank you for picking my books, reading them, recommending them to others, and for all of your kind messages. It means the world to me. Thank you! Thank you! YOU ROCK!!

My boys, Boo Boo and Chachi: You two are my heart. Even though I write for a living, I don't have words to express how much I love you. I appreciate every second of every single day with you. You continue to inspire me and show me how to be a better person. Thank you for being proud of me.

Rhonda Helms, Kathy Bosman, and Tandy Boese: Thank you all for your kindness, enthusiasm, and guidance in helping to make *Open Your Heart* the fun and fabulous story it is today. I truly appreciate how each of you helped me polish this book to make me look like an English pro. I'm so grateful your keen eyes catch the areas where I trip up.

Elizabeth, Amber, Kristen: Thank you for beta-reading and critiquing *Open Your Heart*. I value your opinions and honesty, and appreciate how wonderful you are at kicking my butt into shape, while still being kind. Thank you for all of your encouragement and support. It means the world to me.

Sunni: Thank you for your encouragement, positivity, and kindness. And for coming up with the awesome new name for my readers group. I'm so grateful our love of Missio, and other amazing bands, brought us together.

Missio. (Matthew and David): I first heard your music in January 2017, when I was going through an extremely difficult time in my life. Your music, along with your genuine kindness and openness, helped me on my path to discover who I am and who I want to be. Thank you for being a light for me and countless others. I appreciate you more than you'll ever know.

#Loners. #MissiFam. #MissioMafia: 2017 was an amazing year of self-discovery for me. Those discoveries brought me to Missio, and in turn, to each of you. I'm grateful for your encouragement, support, and friendships. You lift me up and make life richer. I'm so glad I got to connect personally with many of you in my travels. I look forward to doing it again and again and...

The phenomenal staff at Amélie's French Bakery and Free Range Brewing on North Davidson in Charlotte, NC: Not sure if anyone in either place realized that I wrote this entire book within that bakery and brewery, but I did—edits and all. I was drawn in by the delicious food and tasty drinks, but I return for the wonderful people and eclectic, all-encompassing, positive vibe. Thanks to everyone at both places for creating a space where anyone can come in, sit down, and feel comfortable.

I'm extremely grateful and humbled to have phenomenal friends: I will always take a moment to thank my #TZWNDUBC peeps and original RT ladies because I couldn't imagine my life without your encouragement and support. I'm proud to call each one of you my friend, and appreciate that you've always accepted me as I am, no matter what stage of my life.

Every author, reader, blogger, and friend I've connected with in the writing world: This truly is an amazing community of people who build up their peers to help each other succeed. I'm so fortunate to be part of such a supportive environment.

ABOUT THE AUTHOR

USA Today Bestselling Author Sophia Henry is a proud Detroit native who fell in love with reading, writing, and hockey all before she became a teenager. After graduating with a Creative Writing degree from Central Michigan University, she moved to warm and sunny North Carolina where she spent twenty glorious years before heading back to her roots and settling in Michigan.

She spends her days writing steamy, heartfelt contemporary romance and posting personal stories on social media hoping they resonate with and encourage others. When she's not writing, she's chasing her two high-energy sons and an equally high-energy Plott Hound, watching her beloved Detroit Red Wings, or rocking out at as many concerts as she can possibly attend.

For all the latest releases and updates exclusively for readers, check out SophiaHenry.com to SUBSCRIBE to Sophia's newsletter today!

Printed in Great Britain
by Amazon

79439240R00148